THE
WILLOW
WREN

THE
WILLOW
WREN

A NOVEL

PHILIPP
SCHOTT

Published by ECW Press
665 Gerrard Street East
Toronto, Ontario, Canada M4M 1Y2
416-694-3348 / info@ecwpress.com

Cover design: Ingrid Paulson
Cover photograph © Stephen Mulcahey /
Trevillion Images
Author photo: Michael Koch-Schulte

LIBRARY AND ARCHIVES CANADA CATALOGUING
IN PUBLICATION

Title: The willow wren / Philipp Schott.

Names: Schott, Philipp, author.

Identifiers: Canadiana (print) 20200381997
Canadiana (ebook) 2020038208X

ISBN 978-1-77041-573-7 (SOFTCOVER)
ISBN 978-1-77305-700-2 (PDF)
ISBN 978-1-77305-699-9 (EPUB)
ISBN 978-1-77305-701-9 (KINDLE)

Classification: LCC PS8637.C5645 W55 2021
DDC C813/.6—dc23

The publication of *The Willow Wren* has been generously supported by the Canada Council for the Arts
and is funded in part by the Government of Canada. *Nous remercions le Conseil des arts du Canada de
son soutien. Ce livre est financé en partie par le gouvernement du Canada.* We acknowledge the support of
the Ontario Arts Council (OAC), an agency of the Government of Ontario, which last year funded 1,965
individual artists and 1,152 organizations in 197 communities across Ontario for a total of $51.9 million.
We also acknowledge the support of the Government of Ontario through Ontario Creates for the marketing
of this book.

PRINTED AND BOUND IN CANADA

PRINTING: MARQUIS   5   4   3   2   1

For my father,
Ludwig Schott (1934–1994)

Willow wren (*Troglodytes troglodytes*) —
Very small, solitary, nondescript bird. Scarce.
Found in cool, dense undergrowth of conifers in summer. Quirky. Moves mouse-like
on the forest floor. Nests in snug burrows.
Proud, very vocal, active, but furtive. Also
known as the Eurasian wren, winter wren,
northern wren and der Zaunkönig (the
Fence King) in German.

Based on a true story

PART ONE

THE PAST BEATS INSIDE ME LIKE A SECOND HEART.

— John Banville, *The Sea*

CHAPTER

ONE

FEBRUARY 20, 1944

This memory stands out above many others. A glinting nickel in a fistful of pennies. I can feel my mother's hand gripping mine, a thin leather glove squeezing my thick woolen mitten, squeezing it maybe a little too tightly. And I can smell the smoke — sharp and somehow metallic — mixed with the dry smell of powdery cement dust and the tang of brown coal fires and something else that I didn't recognize at that age, something charred. I did not like the smells.

But this is principally a visual memory. The picture is detailed and clear in my mind's eye, like a large format photograph taken by an expensive camera. The front of our three-storey building had been neatly peeled off, as if by an enormous can opener wielded by a fairy-tale giant. The only evidence that there had ever been an outside wall was the still lightly smoking pile of debris on the street out front. But then debris was everywhere in the city, so it was difficult to connect this particular debris to the wall that had once defined the outer limit of our domestic life. It was more as if the wall had magically vanished or had been excised and carried off.

We stood and stared, wordlessly, just staring. Bomb damage was not surprising given the air raid the night before — we'd seen plenty enough of it as we hurried from the train station — but what was surprising was the precision. The wall was gone, but just a metre beyond it the interior was absolutely intact. Nothing was out of place. No chairs had been knocked over. The paintings on the walls still hung straight. We were looking into our living room as if into a life-sized doll's house.

This doll's house impression was so strong that it distorted my sense of perspective. I remember suddenly feeling very small, as if my mother and I had been shrunk to doll size. I longed to grow to my full ten-year-old boy size again so that I could reach into the living room and delicately pick up a wooden chair between my thumb and forefinger. I even made the pinching motion inside my mitten with my free hand.

"Where is Papa going to sleep now?" I asked, when I finally found a way to make words.

"Don't worry. The Party will find something for him."

I nodded solemnly in response, trying to visualize Papa sleeping on top of his desk, papers pushed aside, a blanket and pillow brought by an aide. He had one rigid leg, the result of tuberculosis in his knee when he was a child, so my mental picture showed that leg sticking out from the end of the desk while the other one was tucked up.

"He's an important man, your papa." She said this flatly.

"Shall we go to his office now, Mama? Is that where he is?"

"Yes, I suppose that makes sense. I'm sure he's very busy dealing with this, but since we've come all this way, and you got special permission to leave the camp." The whole family, except Papa, had been evacuated from the city. I was in a Hitler Youth camp, very much against my liking, and Mama was with her sister in Mellingen, also somewhat against her liking.

Just then an older teenager came rapidly peddling up the street on a bicycle, weaving amongst the piles of rubble. He was tall and very pale, with black hair slicked back above a high acne pockmarked forehead. His dark grey uniform was slightly too small for his long thin arms and legs. I recognized him from Papa's Ortsgruppe office, although I did not have reason to know his name yet. Later I would find out it was Erich. I remember being envious of his bicycle, as it was a relatively new dark red Kalkhoff. But honestly I would have been happy with any bicycle.

Erich waved to us frantically when he spotted us.

"Heil Hitler, Frau Schott!" Erich's right arm shot up as he rolled to a stop.

"Yes?" Mama's arms remained at her side. My mother was a solid and serious-looking woman. She was not large, but with her strong voice and her ability to wield an unblinking stare she certainly could be intimidating. That day she wore a very businesslike tan-coloured suit and had her hair pulled back severely in a tight bun.

Erich swallowed and blinked several times before continuing. "Ortsgruppenleiter Schott sends his regards and he also sends his regrets that he was unable to meet you at the train station or here at your home." He paused for a response, but as there was none he went on, "As you can see the enemy attacked again with many bombers. It began at 3:15 this morning. Leipzig Connewitz was especially heavily hit. There are hundreds dead. Killed where they slept." He stopped again, perhaps realizing that he was striking the wrong note. "But of course our Luftwaffe shot most of them down before they could do even more damage. So I am sure they have learned their lesson."

"I'm sure they have," Mama said dryly. "I suppose this means that Herr Ortsgruppenleiter will not be available to see his wife and son at any point today?"

"You are correct, Frau Schott. I'm afraid that will not be possible. He has arranged train tickets for you on the 13:20. He is concerned there will be another attack. Please stay away from the city until you hear from him." Erich reached into his satchel and pulled out two brown cardboard tickets that had red swastika priority stamps on them.

This was of course a disappointment. This visit was to be a special treat to mark my tenth birthday a few weeks prior. For the first time I was travelling without my irritating siblings. And for the first time Papa was going to spend time with me alone and show me some interesting things. I had obtained special leave from camp to do this. I was still going to have a day with Mama in Mellingen, but that was more afterthought than main event. Feeling only disappointment and not horror or sadness in the midst of all this destruction and apparent death may seem odd, but that is honestly all that I felt then. Sometimes small boys have small concerns.

And as it happened, Papa was right. The train was only a few minutes out of the station when the air raid sirens began to scream. I put my hands over my ears and began to rock as I could not tolerate loud noises. I squeezed my eyes shut as well. When I opened them again, I saw that Mama looked very upset. She was looking down at her lap, frowning, and her eyes were moist. She clutched an elaborately embroidered white handkerchief. The transformation to this from the tough woman who had spoken to Erich was unsettling. I remember wishing I could comfort her, but I had no idea how to go about it.

She noticed me looking at her. "I'm sorry, Ludwig."

"No, it's okay, Mama. I am scared of the bombs too." I felt brave and grown-up admitting this.

"It's not that. But I shouldn't make you worry. We'll be fine." She wiped her eyes and nose and turned to the window. I had some inkling as to why she spoke that way but pushed it out of my mind. I was just happy that she looked a little less upset now.

The train began to accelerate. I wondered whether the speed of the train affected the chance that it would be hit by a bomb. I surmised that it probably would and willed the train to go even faster, but then I saw smoke rising far in the northeast. We were heading in the exact opposite direction, so I felt better and smiled at Mama, but she did not seem to notice.

How could I know I would never see our beautiful doll's house again?

CHAPTER

TWO

1934-1936

That may be the specific memory that is currently sharpest and uppermost in my mind as I embark on telling this story, but it is not the most important one, not nearly, nor is it the first one. I should begin with the first memory, or even just a little before it.

I was born on a Sunday in our house at 21 Mozartstrasse in Leipzig, Germany. It was the 21st of January in 1934. Shortly after that I was baptized at the Thomaskirche, which was less than a kilometre from our house and was where Johann Sebastian Bach worked as choir director from 1723 to 1750. I have heard that his bones are interred there now, although they were not at that time. I like the fact that Mozart and Bach were there at the very beginning of my life.

My mother said that I was a delicate, sensitive and nervous baby — that this was especially true of my stomach and that I would spit up constantly, so I was thin and weak for a long time. She also said that a particularly good children's doctor helped resolve this, and that thanks to his expertise I eventually became a much happier and chubbier baby. This is, in any case, what she has written in her own memoirs. But I beg to differ. Of course in fairness I do not remember this doctor, but I am sure that it was my grandmother who made the difference.

My mother's mother, Sara Flintzer (born Sara Hörschelmann), moved in with us in January of 1935. She would have been sixty-nine years old then. She had been a widow since 1917 when her husband, Hugo, died of typhoid fever. A well-known painter and art professor in Weimar, he had also volunteered to work as a medical assistant in a prisoner of war camp during the First World War. That is where he contracted typhoid. My mother worshipped his memory. Oma Flintzer was my favourite grandmother, and I like to think that I was her favourite grandchild. The experts say that very few children can form a long-term memory before the age of three, and none before the age of two. I do not know why this is, but I am an exception. My first clear memory is from right around the age of one and a half. I know the age because it happened while Oma Flintzer was living with us and while I was just learning to walk.

Oma had a large antique wardrobe in a corner of her room. I can picture that particular corner clearly as it was the furthest one from the door, and I can picture the wardrobe clearly as it was very fancy with carved flowers in the corners and darker wood inlayed in a pattern on the doors. One of the doors did not close properly. At some point I found out that Oma kept sweets in there. I was just beginning to learn to walk then by holding onto the walls and furniture and shuffling along. I think people now call it cruising. With this mobility I would make my way to the wardrobe, open the door that was slightly ajar, climb in and help myself to the sweets. I so vividly remember sitting on the wooden floor of the wardrobe with Oma's dresses above me. It was dark and warm and had a pleasant comforting smell. Oma found out right away, but she did not mind, and it became a secret between her and me that we kept from my parents and from Theodor, my older brother. It was regular visits to the wardrobe that made me fat and happy, not that doctor. I became so round that I could not stand up to walk anymore and I actually regressed to a few more months of crawling before my legs became strong enough to support my new bulk.

I have heard it said that your earliest memory tells you something about who you are. I am really not sure what to think of this or what this memory would say about me.

After that, I cannot recall anything clearly for at least a year, and Mama's memoirs do not mention me again for a long while. If I concentrate, I can conjure a few gauzy images but am unsure of their date and exact nature. There are a few fragments of sound, perhaps music? A piano, I think. And shouting from the radio, certainly shouting from the radio. I can also bring to mind some abstract feelings such as a feeling of warm enveloping security, which I think is normal in very small children. But also a contradictory sense that everything was somehow delicate, tenuous. Like holding a soap bubble. This is perhaps less normal.

Clara was born on May 15, 1936. I have no memory of the day itself, but I do remember Mama telling everyone later what a difficult birth it was: a story she told many times, always pausing to smile and say, "But oh what a strong and beautiful baby Clara was." She did not say so directly, but the contrast to me was implied. But no matter, I loved Clara. To this day she is my favourite. Maybe it is because Theodor is older and serious and increasingly took on an irritating man-of-the-house swagger when Papa was away, and maybe because the other three to come seemed so childish and uninteresting to me. Maybe that is why I was always closest to Clara. That is not to say that I did not throw my weight around as big brother with her. Of course I did. I am told that even when she was a very young baby, I would instruct her in a stern and learned voice about the right way and the wrong way to be a baby. I did this at two and three years of age! I really do not remember that, but I suppose I can believe it.

I gave you the wrong impression before regarding the apartment on Mozartstrasse. It does not actually matter, but I want this record to be as accurate as possible. You see, by the time Oma Flintzer moved in with us we must have already been in the new apartment, a half-hour walk south in the more prestigious city quarter of Leipzig Connewitz. So although I was born on Mozartstrasse, I have no memories that I can legitimately connect to it. Unfortunately, the new apartment was at Kaiser Wilhelm Strasse 72. This is unfortunate because I am much less interested in the Kaiser than in Mozart. After the war it was renamed for August Bebel, an early social democrat, who is also considerably less interesting than Mozart.

The reason we moved is that the Mozartstrasse apartment was too small, especially with Oma coming and with what appeared to be a never-ending series of babies coming as well. Papa was now making quite a good salary in his new job as an attorney for a large bookseller, Koehler und Volckmar, so we could afford something larger and better.

The old place had been divided by an entryway and a big stairwell. Its front door was wide like a barn door. It may even be that horses came in there once long ago. When you walked through it into the large entryway you could go one of three directions. You could go straight across to the stairs that led to other people's apartments, or you could go through a door to the right that led to our kitchen and bathroom, or through a door to the left that led to our living room and bedrooms. So, Mama was constantly criss-crossing what was essentially a public space. She said that during the really hard economic times in the 1920s there were as many as twenty beggars a day at the door. She said that this was when inflation was so bad that you would have to take a wheelbarrow full of money to buy a loaf of bread and a dozen eggs. In any case, it was good to leave that apartment, although the name of its street was better.

The new place on Kaiser Wilhelm Strasse was much grander. It was a multifloor apartment in a large building and it had seven rooms! I should clarify that when you count rooms in Germany you include only bedrooms and living rooms and lounges and such, not kitchens, bathrooms, laundry rooms or any other functional spaces. Oma Flintzer had two of these rooms, including her bedroom that had the beautiful wardrobe with the sweets I mentioned before. The other room was her own sitting room with very fancy antique furniture that we had to be careful with. Now that I think back, I am not sure where her servant slept. Perhaps this was not in the room count. Yes, Oma had a servant. This woman was what the English would call a lady's maid and would help dress her and fix her hair and all of that. After this was done Oma would come and supervise Theodor and me getting dressed. It was all very proper.

Mama was glad for this help because Papa was busy with his job and on top of that he had become much more involved in the Party. I am of course talking about the Nazi Party. For a time he was away almost every night and every weekend at meetings. I do not know when he joined, but I have no memory of a time when he was not a member, and I do know that he had originally joined the SA, the Sturmabteilung, which translates as "storm detachment." They were better known as the Brownshirts and were the Nazi Party's street fighting goons before Adolf Hitler became chancellor in 1933. I had no particular reaction to his Party membership in the early years. It was simply part of who he was, no different than his profession or his taste in suits. Moreover, it all seemed profoundly boring to me. The real-world implications of a political affiliation only became clear to me when that real world forced itself into my life during the coming war.

Incidentally, the Brownshirts had brown uniforms because these were cheaply available after the First World War, having been ordered in mass quantities for Germany's former African colonial troops. The colour brown then became the colour of the Nazi movement, much as red is associated with communism. It is impossible to imagine Papa as a street fighting goon, but his membership in the SA speaks to the passion he must have felt, and it dates his membership to before my birth because the SA was thoroughly purged in 1934 by Hitler in the so-called Night of the Long Knives, after which the SS superseded them.

Papa's Nazi membership was not exceptional. Many people were Nazis. Remember Hitler was democratically elected. Mind you, he did not get a majority of the votes, but he did receive a solid 44 percent of them and then used some tricks to leverage that to obtain full power. Papa was a lawyer and many of the professional class and the middle class supported the Nazis. The upper class saw them as grubby upstarts and looked down their noses at them, and the opposing socialists and communists were strong among the working class, but the great bulge in the middle saw Hitler as the best path away from having twenty beggars at your door every day. Mama did not agree, however.

This argument comes back to me now. Maybe I have the exact words wrong — I would have only been about four years old — but my memory astonishes me these days. I was playing in the hallway outside the living room. I can picture the red Persian runner on the dark wooden floor. Its pattern served beautifully as roads for my little wooden cars. The door to the living room was closed. These houses had doors to every room so that they could be individually heated. Through the door I could hear my parents talking, but I could not understand what they were saying, nor did I particularly care to. Then Mama's voice became louder, and I could not avoid hearing anymore.

"Do you really need to be doing Party work all weekend, Wilhelm?"

"You know I do." Papa used a very sharp tone. I pictured him answering from behind his newspaper.

"Don't snap at me. It's a reasonable question. You are hardly ever home on the weekend anymore. You are becoming even more of a stranger to your children." Mama was trying to sound calm, but her voice crackled with the electricity of barely restrained fury.

"You know very well why I am doing this. Why I must do this."

I heard a newspaper rustle. I was right!

"Must?" Mama laughed, but it was a sardonic laugh. Even at that age I knew that people could laugh when something was not funny.

"Yes, must!" Papa was shouting now.

"Okay, you feel you 'must' be in this Party. You have told me many times. I don't agree, but I accept. Accepting is what I 'must' do. But all weekend, every weekend? Really, Wilhelm?"

"Don't exaggerate. It's not all weekend, every weekend. But this weekend is especially important. Reich's Minister Göbbels is coming on Saturday, and it is my privilege to help show him what we are doing here in Leipzig for the people!" My father used the expression "das Volk," which meant something more than just "the people."

"Ha! That idiot!"

I crept closer to the door. Then there was the sudden slam of what sounded like Papa's fist hitting the table and I jumped, almost giving myself away with a little yelp.

"Show respect! Göbbels is a great man! And ours is a great cause! You have your job here and I have my job there. I do not question how you run this house and you will not question how I help to run this country! This is the best I can do. You know that with my stiff leg if war comes I will . . ."

"*If?*" Mama interrupted, shouting now too. "*If* war comes?! Are you mad Wilhelm? It's *when* war comes! When! Those friends of yours — Göbbels and the rest — will not stop pushing until somebody pushes back. And that means war. When, not if."

"I don't agree. The Führer is showing the world our commitment and our power. They don't dare challenge Germany. They become more degenerate by the day, while we become stronger. And if you are somehow right and there is war, it will be quick because we will win. We lost in 1918 because we were stabbed in the back by our own people! Socialists, communists, bums, ne'er-do-wells! The Führer is ensuring that will never happen again."

"Wilhelm, listen to yourself." Mama was quieter again, but I could still hear her well enough. "You have read Tacitus and Cicero, Goethe and Schiller, Shakespeare and Milton. These clowns can barely read the side of a soup can. These are not your people. These are not your thoughts."

"You are wrong, Luise. You don't know what you're talking about." I think he said something else too, but his voice was quieter and then there was the scrape of a chair and I was just barely able to scramble out of the way in time for the door to open and Papa to walk out. His face was red. He might have noticed me, but he did not acknowledge me.

"War," I thought. "There will be a war." The idea seemed both terrifying and exciting to me. Theodor and I had a few toy soldiers. They were made of tin and had once been brightly painted but were now chipped and worn. I think they might have originally belonged to an older cousin. I always lost to Theodor when we played, but I still sought him out for battles whenever he would stoop to play with his little brother.

I described my earliest memory before, the one with the sweets in Oma's wardrobe. One of the few times Papa spoke to me directly about his past he described his own earliest memory. He was born in 1904, so this might have been in 1907 or '08. He recalled seeing the old veterans from the 1870–71 Franco-Prussian War marching through the streets of Bamberg. He was particularly impressed by the highly polished steel helmets and bayonet tips shining in the sun. That was the last war that Germany had won. That was the war that led to Prussia being able to persuade the mess of smaller German principalities to unite with it as one country for the first time. His own father was less keen on watching the march. He died long before I was born, so I never met him, but from the stories I heard he was an austere intellectual with an elaborate Edwardian moustache and beard. Perhaps this is just the cliché that grew around his memory because he was a professor. People also said that he was very disdainful of the military and suspicious of nationalism. But Papa was a typical little boy who found marching soldiers very impressive and he insisted on staying. Papa remembered that.

I am connecting these thoughts now — my parents' talk of war, my toy soldiers and Papa's story of the marching veterans — and I suppose the lesson is that most little boys are excited by soldiers, and most of them grow out of it one way or another, even if it takes a very long time.

I am astonished that I remember that conversation. Nothing for over fifty years and then suddenly now it springs to life in my mind. It is as if my brain is an antenna that has been retuned, perhaps slightly swivelled or lengthened, allowing all of this to come back so clearly. Pin-sharp voices now where for decades there had been only static. Moving pictures now where before there had been only murk and vapour. Even smells. Papa smelled of sweet port wine–scented tobacco and of bright aftershave or cologne. In fact, not only can I bring back their voices, but if I concentrate, I can hear the cars rattling by on the wet cobblestones in the street outside our grand Connewitz apartment, and I can hear the maid humming quietly downstairs and I can hear the wind above, scraping a single tree branch against the clay shingles on our roof. I hear all of this so clearly.

CHAPTER

THREE

1937-1938

Early autumn in Leipzig before the war. It's hard to tell you about it because you really cannot imagine now how beautiful this place was. It was beautiful in every season, but especially so in the autumn because of all the hardwood trees. Those were real autumns with the full paintbox of colours, not the initially pale yellow then quickly dead autumn of Saskatchewan I would later come to know. Just as you cannot really imagine how beautiful it was, none of us then could imagine how that beauty would be transformed to an ugly horror in just a few years. Who could picture the elegant mansions as smoking piles of broken plaster and brick? Who could picture the happy cafés as impromptu relief stations filled with people crying or staring vacantly, sitting on broken chairs? Who could picture the tree-filled parks as wastelands of charred stumps?

I am saddest about the parks. Connewitz had such wonderful parks. The neighbourhood was teardrop shaped, about a kilometre wide, east to west, and about two kilometres long, north to south. It was studded with little squares and tiny corner parks, but the best parks were the large ones along the western edge, towards the rivers Pleisse and Elster. These parks had proper forests. There I would disappear for as long as I could. Imagine! A four-and-a-half-year-old boy playing in the forest on his own. It was a different time. Most boys went with friends, but I did not have any.

My brother Johann had been born a few months prior and there was much drama around his birth. I do not recall the details, but I do know that it all became too chaotic for Oma, who left to live with my aunt in Weimar. I was very sad to see her go of course. No more whispered conspiracies about the sweets. No more compliments on my plump legs or my wit. The house was different. Mama was so busy and under so much stress with Clara and Johann. Theodor was in school now and bossier and more pompous than ever. And Papa was as busy as always with his job and with his Party work. I was left on my own a lot, but I loved that. I especially loved that I could tell Mama that I was going out to play for a couple hours and she never said no or asked exactly where I was going or what I was doing.

As I wrote at the very beginning, I was born on a Sunday. Mama told me that a Sunday's child is special. She told me that a Sunday's child might have the gift of understanding the language of birds. The parks were full of birds. As soon as I left the house I would turn right at the corner and run down to the Pleisse. It was maybe three blocks. There the trees were very large and there was not much undergrowth. I learned the names of the trees early. I might not have known them at four and a half years of age, but certainly by six or seven. There were elms and oaks, and there were beeches and chestnuts, but my favourites were the linden trees with their wide trunks and pleasing shape. There was a particularly large and handsome linden on the riverbank that I called Old Greybark. I sat under him and listened very carefully to the birdsong around me. I could make the city go away in my mind and place myself in a bubble that included only the river, the trees, the birds and me. I know that traffic noise was still there, but I could just tune it out. I could not yet distinguish the types of birds by their song nor, to my immense disappointment, could I understand what they were singing about, despite being a Sunday's child.

I went back again and again that autumn, playing various games by myself but always stopping at least once to listen intently and to try to understand those birds. One day as I sat under Old Greybark, watching starlings squabble over a fallen apple, I realized something. Maybe being able to understand the language of birds did not mean to literally hear them as words. "Back off, Augustus! I saw this apple first!" Perhaps instead it meant to understand their intent in your mind, with the help of observation and a little imagination. This realization felt like the flipping of a switch. Suddenly everything looked and sounded quite different. Suddenly my forest on the Pleisse was full of characters living lives of drama and adventure. Little feathered heroes and villains, workers and philosophers, soldiers and kings. With this perspective I felt that I increasingly understood the meaning and intent of their songs. It was very much like the opera Papa listened to on his Grundig gramophone. You could not understand all the words, even when it was in German, but you roughly knew what was going on and what the singers felt. It was the language of emotion. The rest of that autumn I sat under Old Greybark as often as I could and watched and listened to my little opera stars.

This ended with the first snow, which came unusually early and heavy that year. Many birds left to migrate south and those birds who stayed for the winter were quieter. They seemed to draw more into themselves and away from interacting with others. I admired the ones who stayed, like the crows and the sparrows and the wrens. It was the first of several snowy and hard winters that would continue through the war.

~

"When circumstances forced me to part from Winnetou so that I could pursue the murderer Santer, I had no idea that it would be months before I would see my red friend and blood-brother again."

So begins the great children's novel *Winnetou* by Karl May.

To be honest, I cannot be certain about when I first read it. What I know is that it was after I discovered the language of the birds and that it was before the war started. I was a precocious child and reading such a novel before the age of five was entirely possible. Probable even. So the summer of 1938 feels about right. In any case, it had a strong effect on me. Possibly it changed the course of my life. Those first books without pictures that we read when we are children have a way of weaving themselves deep into the fabric of our subconscious.

I know now that Karl May's melodramatic depiction of the American West is as far removed from reality as those cheap comic books my sons would later read. His great heroes are Old Shatterhand, a German living on the wild frontier, who became the blood brother of Winnetou, a Native American chief. They had all sorts of exciting if, admittedly, highly improbable adventures together. May is not at all fashionable, or even acceptable, to modern readers, but in his time he created a miracle of imagination and inspiration in a strange and often lonely boy. For this I am grateful. So many years later, I often still picture myself lying with my head towards the foot of my bed, propped up on my elbows, reading my *Winnetou* by stolen light leaking through the crack in my bedroom door, thankfully unaware that outside that door, war, like a dark growing stain as yet unseen, was swallowing our future.

I read *Winnetou* often enough that I knew long passages by heart and that my deepest and most desperate desire became to read the second, third and fourth volumes. We had many books in the house, but mostly the classics and hardly anything of interest to children, even precocious ones like me, except for the Brothers Grimm and Wilhelm Busch and the terrifying Struwwelpeter in which boys have their thumbs scissored off for sucking them and girls are turned into piles of ash for the grievous error of playing with matches. Karl May's lessons were far less graphic and far subtler.

"Papa, may I speak to you please?" If I wanted any sort of answer other than a rebuke for my rudeness and impertinence it was important to begin correctly. I picked what I judged to be the perfect moment. From all appearances he had had a good morning at work and Mama was making one of his favourite lunches, pork cutlets in a wine sauce with boiled potatoes and steamed green beans. And as far as I could tell the headlines in his newspaper were mostly positive, from his point of view at least.

"Yes, son, you may." He didn't lower his newspaper.

"I have the first volume of *Winnetou*. I have read it twelve times. May I have the second volume? There are four in total."

"Yes, you may."

It is probably difficult for the modern person reading this to understand the impact of that answer. To get a book now is a simple thing. My sons had scores of books, possibly even hundreds. And it is not that we were poor then — we were easily in the upper middle class — it is more that proper parenting was believed to rest on a foundation of discipline, consistency and the extremely sparing distribution of praise and gifts.

I am sure that my mouth fell open with delight and surprise.

"Thank you, Papa! Thank you!"

"You are welcome."

"Mama and I went by the bookshop yesterday and I saw that it was four Reichsmarks."

Papa made a "mm hmm" noise from behind his newspaper and then turned the page.

"And she said we can go and look again tomorrow."

Another "mm hmm."

I waited, my legs trembling slightly. Feeling unusually brave, I plunged ahead. "So, Papa, could I possibly please have the four Reichsmarks now in case you leave for work early tomorrow and I don't see you then?"

Papa slowly lowered his newspaper and looked me in the eye over his silver rimmed glasses, which sat low on his nose. He was wearing one of the pale grey suits he favoured, accented with a yellow tie and pocket square. He always considered himself a snappy dresser. The stylish effect was somewhat spoiled though by the fact that his hair was thinning and he insisted on cultivating a comb-over. I always found it hard not to stare at this. But this was a serious conversation, so I tried to hold his gaze.

"Ludwig, I said that you were permitted to have this book. I did not say that I would pay for it."

This sort of disappointment is a physical sensation, like your soul acquiring the weight of a lead cannon ball and dropping out of you right down through the floor. I did not have four Reichsmarks. I did not even have one. We did not get pocket money and I was too young and inept to earn anything with chores. I tried very hard not to cry, but I am sure my lip was trembling.

"Oh."

"But I do approve." Papa had raised his newspaper again. "Karl May is a fine influence on young people. Even the Führer admires him. Winnetou is very much like our ancient Germanic heroes. You can learn from him about courage and loyalty and toughness."

Eventually I would get the next in the series as a Christmas gift. The others I read when I was a university student in Kiel. I did so secretly then because it seemed childish, but the attraction was still there for me. May created a world I could submerge myself in that felt as complete and real as the damp grey streets of Kiel and the chalk-dust-smelling lecture halls. Perhaps more complete and more real.

I do want to clarify for you though something regarding my father's comments. I did not know better when I was a little boy, nor did any political angle seem remotely interesting or relevant, but after the war I found out that Hitler's admiration of May was misplaced. In some of May's other works, he wrote very sympathetically about Jewish people and racial minorities generally, and despite the presence of violence in his *Winnetou* stories, Karl May was a confirmed pacifist.

CHAPTER

FOUR

SEPTEMBER 1, 1939

Two important things happened at the beginning of September 1939. I started Kindergarten and Germany invaded Poland. I could actually have gone to Kindergarten the previous year at age four, but as I was already reading and doing simple sums and, perhaps more importantly, as I was amusing myself well and staying out of trouble at home, my parents did not see the need. The Kindergarten was on the way to Theodor's school, so he took me, both of us with our hair slicked down, wearing our fresh school clothes and our leather backpacks. Theodor was going into grade four, and thus seemed impossibly mature to me. I was so proud to go to school now as well.

We knew precisely when the war began because columns of tanks and armoured personnel carriers started rattling over the cobblestones of the main streets. It started at night and went on day and night for the better part of a week. As we lived on a smaller street and the way to school was not on a main street either, we only heard them in the distance, a couple blocks away. They were that loud! Theodor asked Mama if we could make a detour on the way to school to see them, but she said no. She told us that when she was a little girl, at the start of the First World War in 1914, it was very different. Then everyone turned out to watch the soldiers march off to the front. People shouted, "Hurrah! We'll see you boys at Christmas when you have brought peace to the world again with your bravery!" She recalled women running up to the soldiers to kiss them and put flowers in their helmets. Others stood and cheered and threw flowers. The sidewalks were crowded with well-wishers of all ages and social classes. In contrast, she said, nobody was excited this time. No kissing. No flowers. No cheering. The tanks and trucks just rumbled past quiet people who looked away. The mood was tense and sombre. It was not worthwhile for us to see that. She said that the First World War taught people what war really was all about. I did not understand what she meant by that, but it nonetheless made an impression on me.

I also noticed that Papa was even quieter than usual and did not seem excited. We could have slipped off on our own to see the tanks without telling them, just as I sometimes did when I went to the forest, but I was secretly relieved that she forbade us as I was not fond of noise and large numbers of strange people, even if Theodor was with me.

But soon the excitement came back. It might not have been on the very first day of walking to school, but it was within the first week that we saw the planes go by overhead. There were dozens of them flying eastwards in formation, their engines thrumming. Warplanes! Now this was really thrilling to Theodor, and I was quite curious about them.

"Ludwig, look!" Theodor pointed up at them. "Messerschmidts, Junkers, Heinkels, Dorniers!"

I had no idea what these names meant, but the airplanes were very impressive in their grey-green tones with the iron crosses painted under their wings.

"Where are they going?" I had not thought to ask this about the tanks.

"Poland," Theodor said smugly. He always liked it when he knew something I did not know.

"Why? Why is the war there?"

"The Poles attacked a border station! Can you imagine a little country like that trying to attack Germany? They are very silly, and they will be taught a lesson. Papa says that they will lose this war." He paused and then unnecessarily added, "And I agree with him."

I continued staring upwards at the airplanes, trying not to trip as we continued walking. I did not know anything about countries or about warplanes. My interests lay much more with trees and birds. Nonetheless, this was very exciting.

Incidentally, I presume the reader knows that the "Polish soldiers" who attacked the border station were actually SS operatives in disguise. I do not think that anyone other than little boys like Theodor and me really swallowed the story, but nonetheless it provided Hitler with the fig leaf he needed to invade Poland.

Kindergarten began every morning with a stirring rendition of the "Deutschlandlied" ("Song of Germany"), our national anthem. It is still the national anthem of Germany, but they have wisely dropped the infamous first stanza:

Germany, Germany above all,
Above all in the world,
When, for protection and defence,
It always stands brotherly together.
From the Meuse to the Neman,
From the Adige to the Belt!

I had no idea about this at the time, but the Meuse River is in Belgium and France, the Neman is in Lithuania, the Adige is in northern Italy and the Belt refers to a stretch of water between Germany and Denmark. In any case, none of this mattered to me in 1939. Nor did it matter to me that the flag at the front of the classroom had a big swastika on it. I did not know or care that it was a Nazi Party symbol and not a traditional German symbol. And nor did I care that a big gold-rimmed portrait of Adolf Hitler had pride of place on the wall beside the blackboard. I knew who he was, sort of, but he was more of an abstract and distant uncle figure than anyone I had to concern myself with. But I did love the music. I learned later that the great composer Joseph Haydn was responsible for the glorious melody of the "Deutschlandlied." He had written it in 1797 for the birthday of the Habsburg Austrian Emperor Franz II. The lyrics came later, in 1841, and are misunderstood. "Germany above all in the world" was meant to inspire quarrelling little duchies and principalities to unite as one Germany and put Germany above their petty local interests. It did not mean that Germany should conquer the world! Mama taught me this. And the ambitious geography described by those rivers in the "Deutschlandlied" is a fairly innocent reference to the old boundaries of the Holy Roman Empire, which was the closest Germany came to resemble a unified country in the Middle Ages, although it was quite multicultural and only very loosely held together. It wasn't meant as an expansionistic blueprint, but as everyone would find out, that is not the way Hitler saw it.

After the singing, the lessons began and these were less stirring. My doltish classmates struggled to write their ABCs on the blackboard while I stared out the window, hoping to catch sight of a bird. Do I feel bad for calling them "doltish"? It is arrogant and unfair, but that is how I felt then. Theodor was smart, my parents were smart, my oma was smart. It was too soon to say about Clara or Johann, but everyone around me at home was smart, so these kids seemed unnaturally slow to me.

The lessons were mercifully brief as there was also play time in Kindergarten and then the whole thing was done at noon. Theodor's school went until one, so I walked home by myself. It was not far. I would have loved to have gone straight to the Pleisse, to the forest, but I was expected home for lunch. Lunch was the biggest meal of the day. Mama shopped and cooked for it all morning. We had to wait for Theodor and Papa to come home. In Germany everything closed for two hours in the middle of the day so that men could go home to eat lunch and have a nap. Many people do not know that. Not only the Spanish have siesta, but the Germans do too! Ours was shorter and, well, at the risk of promoting a stereotype, more efficient.

One day in the first few weeks of the war Mama cooked my favourite for lunch — a noodle casserole baked with a crust of breadcrumbs and cheese on top and served with a tomato sauce. I sat on a stool in the kitchen and watched her make it, waiting for the crispy, half-burnt noodles from the edge of the casserole. Papa did not like to see these, but I thought they were a great treat. In fact, Papa did not like this meal at all. He called it food for poor ordinary people, to which Mama replied that perhaps she was a poor ordinary person at heart and that perhaps she was sometimes too weak and ignorant to suppress that.

I remember this lunch not so much because it was my favourite dish, but because Theodor asked Papa questions about the war. Normally we were discouraged from talking at lunch, but Theodor had learned that if he asked important-seeming questions, rather than prattling idly, Papa would be more likely to tolerate it.

"Papa, we will soon beat Poland, won't we?" he asked.

Papa looked neither pleased nor displeased to be asked this question as he carefully poured the tomato sauce onto his cube of casserole and then adjusted his white linen napkin.

"Of course we will. I told you that already." He speared a few noodles with his fork with a notable absence of enthusiasm.

Theodor tried again. "Why were they so foolish to attack us?"

This question interested Papa more. He set his fork down and looked directly at Theodor when he spoke. "It is clear that there were two reasons. The first reason is that they hate Germans. We know this from how they have treated our compatriots who found themselves suddenly inside Poland after our territory was given away in 1919. The second is that they think that by attacking us they will force England and France to come to their aid because they have a treaty with them. They are confident that this is how they will win."

He paused and Theodor jumped in, "But they are wrong, aren't they, Papa?"

"Yes, they are wrong. England and France are too weak, and they are too cowardly."

"I'm sure they regret attacking us now!"

"Alea iacta est." It was not unusual for Papa to slip into Latin or even Greek.

Theodor nodded solemnly, either having understood or having thought it best to pretend to understand.

I needed to ask, "What does that mean, Papa?"

He turned to me and smiled. "Those, Ludwig, are the words of the great Julius Caesar as he crossed the Rubicon River in the year 49 BC and thus made the decision to defy the Roman Senate and fight Pompey."

I gave a small nod and waited for him to take a sip of

his mineral water and dab the corners of his mouth with his napkin.

He smiled again. "It means 'the die is cast.' An important irreversible decision has been made upon which the lives of many depend. Poland will fall. War is rarely something to wish for, but at least we will get our territory back and perhaps we will get our pride back."

Mama was focused on helping Clara and Johann eat and it did not look like she was listening, but she quietly said, "Ah yes, our pride. That is important of course." Papa flushed red and looked ready to say something to her but obviously thought better of it. He instead told Theodor that that was more than enough talking and that we should focus on our food while he went to his armchair to have a cigarette and wait for dessert to be served. Canned pears that day, I believe.

~

The other boys would usually meet up after school to play games in the street corner parks, but I hated these games. These games were always competitive, and I was always the smallest and the weakest, and as such I was always the designated loser. Sometimes I enjoyed being around boys in high spirits, but it did not take long for me to tire of their mostly inane games. In any case, the forest was much more interesting.

Fall is a busy time in the forest as the squirrels and the birds prepare for winter. You would think the war would distract me from this, but the excitement I felt when it started quickly went away. This was not because I developed an opinion about the war. Even though I was a very precocious child, I will not claim to have had sophisticated thoughts about war and peace. No, the excitement went away because it was not exciting. After the first few weeks there were no more columns of tanks in the city and far fewer warplanes overhead. It was all abstract and distant, while the forest was real and here. I suppose I heard about the Soviet Union joining in to carve up Poland and the fact that, as Papa predicted, England and France did nothing, but I do not remember any of that. What I do remember from the first couple years of the war — before the war came to us — was my growing fascination with small birds, the sparrows and the wrens.

There are certainly more majestic birds, like eagles, and smarter birds, like crows; prettier birds, like buntings, and birds with a more beautiful song, like warblers; but I developed a soft spot for the small, less showy guys. I have heard that birdwatchers here call them LBJs, meaning "little brown jobs." I was especially fascinated by how hard they worked. When I first learned to understand the language of the birds it was the drama that caught my attention. You will recall that I called them my opera stars. I still loved to listen to and watch the more exciting interactions, but one day, perhaps in the fall of 1939 but possibly sometime in 1940 already, I was sitting under Old Greybark when I saw something very small out of the corner of my eye. It was a tiny wren and what caught my attention was that it was creeping along the ground like a little mouse. It was so funny! And then it would take a few quick hops, cock its head to the side and flit up to a fencepost from a long-since-collapsed fence. There it fluffed itself up and sang loudly, much louder than I expected such a small bird to. The other birds appeared to ignore it. Then the wren hopped back down and grabbed something off the forest floor, a bug I suppose, and zipped into a nearby burrow I had not noticed before. It nested in the ground! How curious!

I watched the burrow for a long while and when the

wren did not come out again, I ran home to tell Mama what I had seen. Papa would have been at work or fulfilling his Party duties and Theodor was not that interested, but Mama had a keen eye for nature too.

"Mama, do you know what I saw in the forest by the Pleisse?"

"First wash your hands, Ludwig, and then you can tell me what you saw." She smiled when she said this.

I did as I was told and then in a firehose torrent of words described the wren and his funny behaviour.

"Ah yes, the Fence King. I love him too."

"Fence King?"

"If you wait until I am done with Johann, I will read you a story." My little brother was being washed, very much against his will.

When she was done Mama sat with me on her lap in our drawing room and read the Grimm's fairy tale about the Fence King to me. I had read it before myself but had not paid close attention. It was late afternoon and strong light came slanting in through the west windows. She smelled of soap and her skin was very soft. My brothers and sister might have been in the room too. I do not remember. I do remember the old brass clock on the mantel chiming just before she began to read.

The story opens with a meeting of all the birds where it is determined that they need a king. They then decide that the bird who flies the highest will be their king. The eagle flies the highest and is proclaimed king until a small voice from the smallest bird, a willow wren, squeaks that he had been even higher — by riding on the eagle's back! The other birds are incensed and shout that the wren could not become king through deceit and cunning. They declare a new contest and state that the king should also be one who gets closest to the ground. The wren then zips into his mousehole and calls out, "See, I am still king!" The birds become even angrier and post an owl by the entrance of the mousehole to imprison the wren. During the night the wren suggests that the owl could rest from this boring job but still keep watch by closing first one eye and then switching to the other. Amazingly this works and the owl falls asleep, allowing the wren to slip out. Ever since that day the wren keeps to himself and avoids the other birds, but every now and again he hops up onto a log or a fence post and calls out, "I am king, I am king," and then flies away before anyone can catch him. And this is why we call the willow wren the Fence King.

This became my favourite fairy tale, and it still is. I suspect the lesson the Grimms meant for us to learn involved the perils of arrogance, but that is not the lesson I learned.

CHAPTER

FIVE

JUNE 15, 1940

Church bells rang uninterrupted for fifteen minutes. It was not a Sunday or a religious holiday. It was an ordinary Saturday, so I was surprised. Although we were not a churchgoing family, I was familiar with the Christian calendar and knew when to expect the bells. I was not generally fond of loud noises, but church bells were an exception. Something special must be happening. Something good I hoped. Papa happened to be home, which was increasingly unusual, so I asked him if he knew what was going on. He was sitting in his favourite chair, reading his newspaper and looking especially pleased. Normally his facial expressions ranged from contemplative to stern, with smiles a welcome rarity.

"I'm glad you asked, Ludwig. It is a very important day for the German Reich! Please find your brothers and your sister. I would like to explain this to them too." Johann was barely three, so I doubted he would be interested, but then I was not too sure about that as I no longer had any sense of the workings of the three-year-old mind. Given that it was a rainy Saturday everyone was easy to find, distributed

35

in various rooms, playing or reading. Mama was in the kitchen and was not interested in joining us. She had not been explicitly invited, but this seemed an oversight, so I asked her, but she shook her head no and said that she knew the story already and did not need to hear it again.

Once the four of us were assembled in a rough semi-circle at Papa's feet, he began. "Children, today is a very important day. You have all heard those church bells. The Führer himself decreed that they ring for fifteen minutes from every church tower in the Reich today and that is because today our forces captured Paris." He waited for a reaction, but none was forthcoming, so he went on. "We entered Paris without a shot being fired. The French have given up and the English are rapidly falling back to the sea. I'm sure that they now regret not taking the Führer up on his offer of peace. Their stubborn support of defeated Poland and their blindness to our common cause against the true threats to the Western world are their undoing. Germany can and will defend the world alone if need be."

"With Italy!" Theodor piped up. "We learned this in school."

"Yes, with Italy, I suppose." A flicker of annoyance at the unscripted interruption passed over Papa's face, but then he smiled again. "A special piece of music has been composed for this occasion. It is called 'The March into Paris.' We will go to the park this evening and listen to the band play it. Isn't that a treat?"

With a subdued murmur we allowed that it was, each of us I am sure secretly hoping that ice cream would be involved as well.

~

The following week Theodor came home from school visibly crestfallen. On Monday, after the fall of France, his class had been asked to write an essay outlining why Germany had decided to invade France. Theodor had gotten a bare pass, which was shocking and humiliating to someone who was otherwise a straight A student. He had outlined the basic rationale for the invasion the way the teacher wanted: Germany had offered peace to France and England after the successful conclusion of the troubles with Poland, but they had refused. This then raised the suspicion that they were secretly preparing to attack Germany, as revenge for the fall of their Polish ally and to remove Germany as a competitor before it became too strong. The French and English deeply desired to cement their victory in 1918 for all time, but the Führer knew that it was his sacred duty to prevent the German people from remaining on their knees forever. Theodor also deftly excused the invasion of neutral Holland and Belgium, reasoning that a less well-defended side door into France actually saved lives. Then he made the statement that took his mark from an A to a D: "While we can justify the invasion of Netherlands and Belgium from a military perspective, why did we also have to invade poor little Luxembourg?"

Theodor was generally much more attuned to the way most people thought than I was, and he was four years older after all, but when I found out what he had written, even I could see that this was an unwise question to ask. Sometimes we Schotts feel the need to argue even just a little bit so that we can assert our intellectual pride and independence. Even ten-year-old Schotts.

The teacher was furious and instructed Theodor to show what he had written to Papa and bear whatever consequences that drew. Papa was by then well known in the district as the Ortsgruppenleiter ("local group leader"). Imagine the Ortsgruppenleiter's son questioning the Führer's wisdom! How embarrassing for Herr Schott.

Herr Schott was somewhat more than embarrassed. I was perversely curious to hear how this conversation would unfold, but Papa told me to leave the room and close the door behind me while Theodor stood before him, head bowed, trembling as he held the paper that Papa had just handed back to him. Naturally I listened at the door. However, I could not hear much as Theodor was mostly silent and Papa used his exceptionally steely quiet voice, the one we all found more terrifying than when he shouted at us. Because shouting was connected to passion it was instinctively understood as irrational and likely to dissipate, whereas the cold tone he adopted when he was even angrier seemed to imply a permanent reassessment of our character and quality. Theodor was pale when he left the room. Through the briefly open door I could see that Papa had picked up the newspaper and that his hands were shaking very lightly.

CHAPTER

SIX

SPRING 1941

A year later, in the spring of 1941, the war was still remote for us, although not as abstract as it had been in the beginning. Rationing had started, and Papa was now constantly at the Ortsgruppe, even for supper almost every night. The news was all of victories, however, so the general mood felt like a mixture of quiet resignation to the present and quiet optimism for the future. Yes, there was a war and it was becoming a nuisance in many ways, but the whole unpleasant business would soon be done with. It would be several years yet before I learned what a horrifying understatement "unpleasant business" was, especially with respect to the victims of the malevolent machine the Nazis had set in motion, howling just out of my earshot.

The Party was insinuating itself more and more into every aspect of life and I am sure that nobody believed this would be reversed when the war ended. This happened gradually, incrementally, like a slowly rising tide. When people are focused on their own lives, as people tend to be, they sometimes do not notice what disappears under that tide unless they happen to look over to a certain spot and then think to themselves, "Hmm, didn't there used to be X over there . . . ?"

Little boys certainly did not notice much of this, but one example of an obvious change that we did notice was that the Nazis insisted that all normal radios be turned in lest the people be bewitched by foreign lies. So the only news we got was from the Volksempfänger, which translates as the "people's receiver." They even inspected the homes of people suspected of not having followed this edict. The Volksempfänger was constructed so that it could only be tuned to official German state radio, although some of the older boys at school claimed to know other boys, not at our school of course, who had figured out how to modify them. This was most assuredly not to listen to enemy news but rather to get better music.

Swing jazz was very popular among the teenagers. State radio played a lot of Wagner and it told us that the Luftwaffe was on the verge of bringing Britain to its knees. There had been no mention of how the Battle of Britain had turned out the previous fall. Why, on March 8 we had even bombed Buckingham Palace! King George must have soiled his pantaloons with fright. In retaliation the RAF had apparently launched a bombing raid on Bremen in northern Germany, but this was presented as the feeble act of a pesky bug that our mighty forces effortlessly swatted away, while no doubt stifling a yawn. That enemy aircraft could fly over Germany at all and even drop bombs struck us as bizarre. An aberration no doubt.

Because Papa was at the Ortsgruppe every night and because Mama appeared to have resigned herself to the situation, she decided to bring him his supper there. As I mentioned before, the big meal of the day was lunch, so bringing him his supper was nothing more complicated than Mama having to make two brown bread sandwiches, one with cheese and one with smoked ham, wrapping them in wax paper and then bundling the four of us up for the walk to the Ortsgruppe office. I loved these walks. They were very special because Leipzig was considered a possible RAF target and was under blackout orders. This seemed laughable because of what we were hearing on the news, but Papa explained that although the British government had abandoned Poland, individual Britons could be quite fierce and brave. Perhaps such a bomber pilot could sneak through. The government was just being extra careful so that little German boys and girls like Theodor, Johann, Clara and me would be as safe as possible.

When I say blackout, I mean it literally. The city was blackest black at night. There was not a single light visible anywhere in the city. The street lights were out, people only had dim lights on in their houses behind blackout curtains, the few cars on the streets did not use headlights and, most impressively of all, when we got to Zwickauer Strasse, the streetcars thundered by without a single light on them — black trains careening through a black night. You might think that the effect would be spooky, but to us it was quite thrilling. Very little that could be considered exciting happened in our house, so being out in the city in the dark felt remarkably adventurous. And with the five of us moving along in a little huddle, it felt cozy as well. Some people must have conjured terrors out of such darkness, but we only conjured wonder.

Mama took advantage of these dark walks to show us the night sky. As big-city kids we had never really seen the stars. My parents were not the camping type — in fact the very thought of it was as absurd as suggesting that they might have converted to Islam and become Bedouins — so we never left the city. Nonetheless, Mama knew quite a few constellations and took care to teach them to us. She also taught us how to tell whether the moon was waning or waxing. The German word for waning is "abnehmend," starting with A, and for waxing is "zunehmend," starting with Z. When you write your ABCs, you write them from left to right. Therefore, when the moon is bright on the left it is abnehmend, waning, and when there is more light on the right, pointing to the end of the alphabet so to speak, it is zunehmend, waxing. This might seem a cumbersome way to remember this, but I use it to this day.

One particularly quiet and clear night we stopped in a small square along the way and Mama pointed out the thinnest fingernail paring sliver of the new moon rising in the east. "Children, see there? Every night it will rise fifty minutes later, so tomorrow we'll see it on our way back from Papa's office and then for many nights it will rise after you are in bed, but in twenty-eight days we will see it here again at this time. No matter what happens in the war, no matter what Hitler does, no matter whether bombers come or not, no matter what your marks are at school, no matter about anything we humans do here on the face of the earth, like ignorant ants scurrying about, the heavens, the moon, the stars, the sun, they will continue undisturbed in their rhythms."

We all looked to the east, eyes wide, but did not say anything.

"So, when you are scared or sad," she continued, "look to the sky and find some peace in the knowledge that there are things eternal, that always continue, that you can always count on."

Papa's office was a marked counterpoint to this discussion of lunar rhythms and things eternal. Here dozens of men and women in grey uniforms were working at desks under very low light, hammering on typewriters, walking very briskly to other desks to whisper to colleagues, rifling through filing cabinets, pinning notices to notice boards, sticking pins in wall maps, talking, sometimes shouting, into telephones. The whole place had an intensity and compressed energy about it, like a box of windup toys being lightly jostled. Mama's comment about ants scurrying came vividly to mind, but it was all very impressive nonetheless, just in an entirely different way than the night sky. It was interesting because although at a casual glance it was the same scene there every night, on more careful observation there were subtle changes too. The mood certainly varied, perhaps due to news from the front but more likely due to local conditions, and the specific things specific people were doing varied as well. We were sternly cautioned not to disturb anyone, so we stood silent as little mice by the door while Mama sought out Papa to deliver his sandwiches. The four of us were all very observant children, so we must have made an interesting sight, lined up from biggest to smallest, our coats still buttoned up, our eyes as wide as silver Reichsmark coins.

Sometimes a young woman who worked for Papa came up to us. I suppose she was an aide or a secretary. She would crouch down to say hello and then give each of us a boiled sweet or sometimes even a small piece of chocolate. Chocolate was becoming scarce, so this was an especially welcome treat. She had very white teeth and very red lipstick and smelled strongly of perfume, but otherwise I do not remember what she looked like, nor do I remember her name. Greta maybe? That is probably wrong. I do remember that Mama did not like her. She became very stiff and thin-lipped every time "Greta" was nearby. Afterwards, on the walk home, she would mimic her high voice and how she would say Herr Ortsgruppenleiter a half dozen times in every sentence in reference to Papa and all the great things he was apparently doing. I always forgot what exactly he did.

"Sorry, Mama, please explain again what Papa does there," I asked on more than one occasion as we walked home.

And the answer was usually a variation on "When he is not combing his hair or smiling at pretty young women, he and his colleagues in the local Party oversee the ration system, make sure that the blackout rules are followed and generally make sure that Leipzig and its people are doing what they can to support the Party and, I suppose, the war effort."

While Mama's tone was unmistakable, I could not suppress a certain sense of wonder regarding my father. He did look very important in his spotless grey uniform with the gold-rimmed red insignia on the collar, as well as a red armband with a swastika on it. Standing quietly but imposingly in the midst of his swirling staff, he gave off the aura of a wizard orchestrating some sort of magic, making things happen, perhaps great things, with the merest nods and hand waves. Papa, as Ortsgruppenleiter, was the head Party official in the Connewitz and Leipzig South neighbourhoods. Before the war this was just one rank below the senior Party official for the city, the Kreisleiter, and two below the regional boss, the Gauleiter. This may sound like a simple hierarchy, but the Nazis were bureaucrats extraordinaire and created another system of parallel but more finely graded ranks for wartime. In this system Papa was also an Oberabschnittsleiter ("senior section leader") and reported to a Hauptabschnittsleiter ("head section leader") in the Kreisleiter's office. But this Hauptabschnittsleiter was a notorious bungler and alcoholic who happened to have important Party connections, so Papa was effectively the Kreisleiter's deputy. Even Mama proclaimed this proudly to neighbours and relatives.

Papa was always at the office until very late in the evening and consequently I was always in bed well before he came home. Mama usually sat by herself during the evenings, mending old clothing or sewing new things. She did not like to have the Volksempfänger on, so the house was very quiet. One evening I was having trouble sleeping, so I got out of bed and walked into the sitting room where I knew Mama would be. I wanted to ask her for a small glass of milk. I found her sitting in an armchair by the window, with her sewing folded on her lap and her head bent down. As I came closer, I saw that her shoulders were shaking and that she was crying. I had never seen her cry before. I did not know what to do. I was about to turn around to sneak out of the room when she noticed me.

"Oh, little mouse, I'm sorry." She wiped her eyes and smiled at me.

"Mama, what's wrong?"

"Nothing, I just . . ." She paused. "I just felt sad. Adults feel sad sometimes for no reason."

I found this curious as Papa never seemed sad at all, not even a little bit, but then I did not see him very much, so perhaps he was sad sometimes at work. A mental image of that whole group of Nazi officials sitting around the office, weeping freely and passing each other tissues came to mind. But I dismissed the picture right away. I reasoned that they probably excused themselves to the washroom when they suddenly felt sad for no reason. Possibly even the Führer cried sometimes for no reason. Mostly he sounded angry on the radio though.

~

I was seven years old in the spring of 1941. It must have been around this time that I got beat up for the first time. The boys I played with who made me the loser of their games were not the problem. They were at least theoretically my friends and I think they liked me. In any case, they never showed any inclination to hurt me physically. No, it was another group of boys, the boys who sat in the back rows of the classroom. I think this is a universal phenomenon. Part of the problem was that I had been put ahead a grade, so I was a year younger than my classmates. I was already a small boy for my age, so this only compounded the size differential. It was probably unwise for my parents to allow me to skip a grade, but Papa, who seemed to otherwise view me as a somewhat aberrant and even slightly defective Schott, was proud of my budding academic stardom and did not consider refusing the offer. The other part of the problem was that I was a poor judge of social situations. It took me many years to understand this about myself, but now that I do, many aspects of the past look very different. It is a little bit like suddenly seeing the old woman in that famous optical illusion where it is either an old woman looking to the left or a young woman looking to the right, depending on how you view it.

On the day in question, the teacher, Frau Krämer, was demonstrating a simple addition problem on the black-board. I had taught myself addition already and had devised a different method for adding numbers with multiple digits. I put my hand up. The teacher was indulgent and invited me to come to the front and demonstrate my method. Twenty heads turned in unison to watch the little Schott pipsqueak march proudly to the front of the class, pick up a long piece of white chalk and in his high voice explain how he preferred to add numbers. Frau Krämer smiled at me and explained that that was very interesting, but that my method would not always work. I disagreed with her, to which she gently countered that whether that was the case or not did not ultimately matter anyway as the method she taught was the approved method. This seemed irrational and arbitrary to me, and I was about to say so, but Frau Krämer asked me to sit down as the lesson had to proceed on schedule. On the way back to my desk I caught the glances of the boys in the back row. They were not friendly glances, but I did not think too much of it.

On the way home that day, at the corner of Mathilden- strasse and Brandstrasse, they caught up to me. There were three of them and I was by myself. Theodor was going to a friend's house, so he had gone a different way.

"Hey! Schott!" one of them shouted.

I ignored him and kept walking, staring straight ahead. This was a mistake, but then I suppose that there really was no right way to address this situation.

"Hey, Schott!" Closer now. "Do you think you're better than us? First you show off in class and now you ignore us?"

I felt a sharp tug on my backpack. Before I knew it, I was on the ground like a beetle flipped on his back, and three faces were looking down at me, laughing.

"Fall down, Schott? Clumsy? Here, let us help you." One of the boys — one with close-cropped hair and pudgy cheeks, Ulrich, I think his name was — reached down and pulled me up. They made a big show of dusting me off with really hard slaps that had me reeling from side to side and then the other two yanked my backpack off my shoulders.

"Since you're so smart you won't be needing any of your schoolwork, will you, Schott? It just makes your backpack heavy and that seems to make you fall down." They began dumping the notebooks out of my pack and kicking them onto the street.

"No! Stop! Please!" I must have sounded pathetic. They finished with a flourish by tossing my now empty backpack into a tree. It took a couple tries, but they managed to get it snagged on a branch about two and a half metres up.

"This is to encourage you to grow, you dwarf! The army will need men, not dwarves!" They laughed and laughed and then sprinted off when a couple of adults approached from around the corner. The man got my backpack down for me while the lady gathered up my soiled notebooks. I was so embarrassed. I could not look these people in the eye when they asked me how I was. I just mumbled thank you for their help and that I was fine. The mix of shame and rage inside me felt like that child's volcano experiment where you mix vinegar and baking soda. The pressure inside me felt physical, but I was determined to exercise self-control and suppress it. But I knew I could not go home the way I looked and the way I felt. I did not want my parents or siblings to know what had happened. Instead, I turned left at the next street and went down to the forest, to the banks of the Pleisse where I washed my hands and face.

I watched the little wren zip back and forth over the river to some inscrutable purpose and I watched a pair of sparrows flit about in the high branches above me in what appeared to be an entirely pointless manner. Somewhere a crow cawed twice and somewhere else a warbler briefly trilled. Then the forest was quiet, and the sounds of the city began to seep in from behind me. The birds were not speaking to me today. They were just wild things going about their wild business and I was just a young boy trembling beneath an old linden tree.

Eventually I began to calm down a little, but I still did not feel right. I stood up and left. The forest would still be there when I felt better, which I knew I would. Emotion is like the weather, whereas personality is like the climate. My climate was mostly sunny and calm, but storms can occur anywhere.

When I got home, Mama looked at me with concern. "Theodor told me some boys roughed you up. Are you okay?"

"How did he know?" I felt the shame and rage bubbling together inside me again.

"The boys who were mean to you happened to run into him as he was going to Uwe's house. They said you were clumsy but the way they laughed Theodor had a pretty good idea what happened."

"Yes, Mama, I am okay." I am sure I was beet red in the face.

She looked at me closely. "They ripped part of your backpack! That's not a cheap backpack!"

Worse was to come. Theodor told Papa too. Whether Theodor was genuinely trying to help or just trying to make my life difficult seemed clear to me at the time — definitely the latter — but now, all these years later, I am not as sure.

"Ludwig, Theodor told me you were attacked." Papa was sitting in his favourite dark brown leather chair and had just stubbed out a cigarette. He motioned me to sit across the coffee table from him on the couch.

"'Attacked' is an exaggeration, Papa. They pushed me over."

"And threw your backpack into a tree."

"Yes." I was looking at the floor.

"Ego amissus pugna sed vici bellum."

I stared at him blankly. He stared back at me, brow furrowed. Then after a long moment he said, "I lost the battle, but I won the war. Or I should say 'et vincere bello,' '*will* win the war.'"

"Yes, Papa." I was not sure what else to say as this did not make much sense to me.

"It's unfortunate that you are still too young for the DJV. Theodor is learning how to defend himself there."

The DJV was short for the Deutsches Jungvolk in der Hitler Jugend. I suppose this translates as the German Youngsters in the Hitler Youth. You could join the DJV at the age of ten, whereas the full Hitler Youth was from fourteen until whenever the army wanted you, which was still eighteen in 1941. The idea was horrifying to me. The DJV. The Hitler Youth. God forbid, the army. All of it — absolutely horrifying. The crowds of boys and men, marching, shouting, waving guns, wearing uniforms, following orders. It was impossible for me to picture myself as part of any of that.

Perhaps he read my look because he continued, "But whether you can fight them or not, you will win the war anyway. Such boys will eventually be in jail or drunk and unemployed or dead on the front. Not you. You are a Schott."

~

A Schott. Family pride was a cornerstone of Papa's life. He was not a fighter either. In fact, the idea is laugh-out-loud funny when you consider his stiff leg, thin frame and painfully formal mannerisms. A fighter with words, I suppose, but not with fists. At the time I thought he meant that a Schott wins with cleverness, that that was the root of his pride. And I am sure that is part of what he meant, but it later became clear to me that he also meant that a Schott wins by being intrinsically superior. What nonsense. I cannot tolerate arrogance.

Opa Flintzer, Mama's father, had been a well-known artist in Weimar at the turn of the century. We owned many of his paintings, as well as painted portraits of many of my Schott forefathers. These paintings hung throughout the apartment, with the best ones, in ornate gilded frames, in the sitting room. Several others hung in the hallway and a few in Papa's office. The oldest ancestral portrait is of a Johann Schott, one of several ancestors with that name, born in 1715 and died in 1791. He was a miller, and before him were five further generations of Schotts, for whom we did not have portraits. All those early Schotts before Johann were also millers, beginning with a Nicol Schott who suddenly appeared in the annals in 1593, listed as owner of the water mill in Ziegenburg, a hamlet in the dark forested hills of Franconia, maybe 200 kilometres south of Leipzig. After Johann there was just one more miller and then a pastor — a very severe-looking man with tight high collars and facial expression that says, "No dancing, no laughing, no living." Perhaps I am being unfair to him. Probably I am being unfair to him. After the pastor was a theology professor and then another professor and then Papa, who was a lawyer.

At the age of seven I had no idea about any of this, but as I grew older, I developed more and more pride in those millers, who did honest, useful work in the villages. Papa, on the other hand, took his pride from the noble branch of the family. His paternal grandmother was the Baroness Frederike Clara von Scheurl. How she married into this family of millers and pastors and professors is a story for another time. But from her we could trace back fifteen generations to a Baron Konrad Tucher von Simmelsdorf who was born in 1260! Can you imagine! Fifteen generations of useless noblemen, probably heavily inbred.

CHAPTER

SEVEN

JUNE 22, 1941

*T*oday something like 160 Russian divisions are standing at our frontiers. For weeks constant violations of this frontier have taken place, not only affecting us but from the far north down to Rumania. Russian airmen consider it sport nonchalantly to overlook these frontiers, presumably to prove to us that they already feel themselves masters of these territories. During the night of June 17 to June 18 Russian patrols again penetrated into the Reich's territory and could only be driven back after prolonged firing. This has brought us to the hour when it is necessary for us to take steps against this plot devised by the Jewish Anglo-Saxon warmongers and equally the Jewish rulers of the Bolshevist centre in Moscow.

German people! At this moment a march is taking place that, as regards extent, compares with the greatest the world hitherto has seen.

*Formations of the German eastern front
extend from East Prussia to the Carpathians.
German and Rumanian soldiers are united
under Chief of State Antonescu from the banks
of the Pruth along the lower reaches of the
Danube to the shores of the Black Sea. The task
of this front, therefore, no longer is the protection of single countries, but the safeguarding of
Europe and thereby the salvation of all.*

*I therefore decided today again to lay the
fate and future of the German Reich and our
people in the hands of our soldiers. May God
help us especially in this fight!*

With those words, screamed at us from the Volksempfänger
by our Führer, we learned that Germany had invaded our
erstwhile ally, the Soviet Union. Actually, those words were
preceded by many, many other words as Hitler was notori-
ously incapable of making a short and simple statement, but
it was approximately at that point that I came into the room
and began to listen.

Mama sighed heavily and said, "That's it then. Like
Napoleon before him, our Herr Hitler will break his army
and destroy his country in Russia. What foolishness."

Theodor and I waited for Papa's explosion in response,
but it did not come. His expression was unreadable. He
just sat there silently. Then he abruptly stood up, turned off
the Volksempfänger and walked out of the room without
saying a word. A minute later we heard him slam the door
and leave the house.

Much as during the invasion of Poland almost two
years prior there was visible military activity in the skies
and on the roads, but children normalize extraordinary

situations so quickly that we did not really take much notice of it this time. The war was simply the way things were. It was difficult to remember the time before or to imagine the time after. Not that it really mattered to us as it had so little impact on our lives, with the exception that Papa was in uniform and at the office all the time, rationing was steadily increasing and both the Volksempfänger and our teachers reminded us constantly that we were at war, beating back the encircling Bolsheviks, Free Masons, Jews and Anglo-Saxon warmongers. They did sound like a scary bunch, but in the abstract manner of the witches and ogres in fairy tales.

~

It was a glorious summer. Really glorious. The Volksempfänger appeared intent on vigorously and repeatedly proving Mama's gloomy prediction wrong and the bullies had vanished for the school holidays. I presumed that their parents sent them to some sort of junior SS camp where they were being taught how to catch knives with their teeth, but I would not have to worry about that until the fall. Most importantly of all, the forest was especially wonderful that summer. There is nothing like light and air filtered through a million leaves to put your soul at ease. I know now that the Japanese call this "forest bathing" and believe that the compounds released into the air by leaves have health-giving properties. Their doctors even prescribe walks in the woods. But at that time I just knew that no matter what, I felt better when I was deep among the trees, in that world of fragrant green. Of course more than the trees there were the birds. My special favourites remained the sparrows and the wrens. Most especially the energetic, diligent little wrens. They were proud and they had reason to be proud.

You might ask yourself, Who remembers a specific summer from that age if he did not do much more than hang around in a forest? Who can distinguish the summer of age seven from that of age six or eight? The invasion of Russia is of course a memory anchor, but the summer of 1941 is mostly one I remember vividly because it was the last peaceful and happy time in my life for at least a decade.

By the end of the summer we knew that Mama was pregnant again. With Johann she had already qualified for the bronze "Cross of Honour of the German Mother," or simply "Mutterkreuz" for short. This was one of Hitler's schemes to encourage Germans to have as many children as possible. The unstated aim was to man the armies and populate conquered lands, but it was all dressed up as a cheery celebration of the joy of large families, with the posters showing a beaming Adolf presiding over swarms of blond children like a peculiar uncle. You received the Mutterkreuz if you had four children. Five was still just bronze level. You needed six for silver, but by the time Paul was born in 1945 nobody was handing out Mutterkreuzes anymore. Incidentally, for a gold Mutterkreuz you needed to bear eight children or more. I never saw Mama wear the medal, which is not a surprise, but from Papa I know it existed.

Papa was proud of his large family and on our Sunday family walks, one of the rare times we were all together, he would strut out in the front like a father goose. It was, however, never clear that he was notably proud of any of the individuals who made up this family. The story went around that he was upset when Clara was born because there was some sort of extra special award for having an unbroken series of sons, but I do not know if this is true.

In any case, the winter that followed was one of the hardest and snowiest in memory. As Mama predicted, Hitler's panzer divisions stalled thirty kilometres outside of

Moscow. To prevent a catastrophic loss of men and materials, General Guderian stopped the offensive on December 5. Two days later the Japanese attacked Pearl Harbor. Germany's treaty with Japan obliged Germany to declare war on America too. Hitler did not care much for treaties and under other circumstances might have ignored this one, but he gladly obliged because he assumed the Japanese would follow through with their promise to then attack the Soviet Union from the east, taking pressure off Guderian's forces. They did not do so. Everyone in Germany outside of Hitler's inner circle knew that declaring war on America was a serious mistake. Everyone knew this, but very few said so.

My third brother, Oskar, was born on an especially foul February day. Mama developed a serious infection and lay in bed with a high fever after the birth. Coal had been rationed to the point that it was difficult to heat water properly, and medicines were in very short supply. Everything was needed for the Russian front. She became so ill that a deaconess came from the church and stood at her bedroom door singing, "Prepare yourself for the journey into eternity." Imagine how terrified we children were to hear this! Even Johann was old enough to at least roughly understand that something terrible was happening to Mama.

But Mama had no intention of journeying into eternity.

PART
TWO

FORTUNATELY, PEOPLE CAN COMPREHEND ONLY A CERTAIN
DEGREE OF MISFORTUNE; ANYTHING BEYOND THAT EITHER
DESTROYS THEM OR LEAVES THEM INDIFFERENT.

— Johann Wolfgang von Goethe,
Die Wahlverwandtschaften (Elective Affinities)

CHAPTER EIGHT

MARCH 27, 1943

This is the night the war came to us. There had already been several false alarms. The thick silence of night would be abruptly torn open by the screaming of sirens. Papa would race off to the Ortsgruppe and Mama would hurry the five of us, dazed and blinking, out of bed and down the steep wooden stairs into the basement of our building to join the other families assembling there. Nobody would speak to anybody else though; each family inhabiting a private bubble of fear. Mama would guide us down there with a flashlight, but then, after struggling into our gas masks, even the flashlight would be extinguished, and we would sit in the absolute dark and wait. As we waited, we would listen for the sound of aircraft engines. Five times before, we strained to hear something between the siren pulses, but there was nothing, just our own breathing in the masks and the usual small sounds an old house makes in the middle of the night.

But then, on the night of March 27, we heard the distinctive drone of the quadruple Rolls-Royce engines of a Lancaster bomber. First distant and faint, and first just one, then closer and then several blending together into a reverberating hum that penetrated my chest and bones. I froze in place, crouched on the floor, my arms hugging my knees and my eyes squeezed as tightly shut as I could manage. Oskar began to cry, and Theodor became angry with him, shushing him with loud whispers, as if the bombers could hear us in the basement and target us in particular as a result.

Mama appeared to remain calm, however, and, after lifting her mask, in a normal voice said, "It's okay. The sound is coming from slightly to the north and listen now . . ." She was quiet for a moment and we all strained to hear something different. "Do you hear that? It's actually beginning to move away. If they had planned to drop bombs on our heads, they would have done so already. They are probably looking for a target. The city is so dark that they might not even realize they are over it. But we'll stay down here until the sirens stop because there could be more coming. You can take your gas masks off though."

This was a relief. Those masks were very uncomfortable and wearing them compounded the terror. We waited and we listened. The engine drone steadily became a little quieter and then after a few minutes I heard two or three percussive thumps coming from my left, which I knew to be the north.

"Are those the bombs, Mama?" I asked. They sounded different than I expected — like the whump of sacks of potatoes being dropped on the floor rather than an intense sharp sound, like a giant firecracker, which is what I imagined a bomb would sound like.

"Yes, those are the bombs. Maybe on Eutritzsch or Gohlis? When you see lightning you can calculate how far away it is by counting the seconds until you hear the thunderclap. One kilometre for every three seconds. But down here we can't even see our fingers!" This was probably an attempt to lighten the mood, but it did not work. As long as the sirens were going off, we sat in a tight silent huddle, fully absorbed in wishing it to end.

It occurs to me now that I did not worry about Papa. We were somewhat safe down there in the basement, but he was exposed out in the streets and at the Ortsgruppe. Mama said that they had a basement shelter too, but his job was to help manage the civil defence and firefighting efforts, so he and his colleagues often needed to go out into the city. I suppose I was still at an age where I considered my parents to be immortal and harm to them was an abstraction that was no more contemplated than the colonization of the dark side of the moon.

~

The next morning was a Sunday, so there was no school and we were home when Papa finally returned from the Ortsgruppe. The raid had been at two in the morning, so he had dark purple bags under his eyes and his comb-over was fully astray.

"They hit Gohlis," he said after he had a long sip of coffee, or what I suppose must already have been Muckefuck (I know, this is an unfortunate-sounding word in English), a chicory root-based substitute.

"I thought so," Mama replied. "How bad was it?"

"Not very bad. There were four or five aircraft and they dropped only a few bombs. They were probably looking for a better, more obvious target, and they were at the limit of their range, so they had to be quick. Maybe they were saving bombs for something on the way back. I haven't heard. In any case, it caused a large fire in Gohlis, but it's out now. There are some injured but no fatalities."

"They'll come back though. It will get worse, won't it, Wilhelm?"

My parents seemed to have forgotten that Theodor and I were sitting right there. Normally, whenever their conversation became serious, they would hustle us out of the room. It had begun in what for Mama and Papa was a reasonably friendly tone, but now I could see that Papa was gripping his cup tightly and that his face was hardening. Mama, for her part, stopped setting out Papa's breakfast and looked at him directly with that unblinking stare we all feared. It was like watching an accident about to happen in slow motion where you cannot do anything to stop it, nor can you stop yourself from looking at it — like the time I watched Uwe ride his bicycle at high speed down the hill to the Elsterfluttbett, a nearby canal, with his eyes closed.

"Maybe. I cannot guarantee that that will not happen. Maybe they'll come back, but the Luftwaffe is bombing all their airfields. The English are becoming desperate. They think America will come, but just like the Poles who thought the English would come, the English in return are just as wrong. The Americans are soft, and they will not allow their boys to die on the old continent again like they did in 1917 and '18." Papa's voice was even and not loud, but it had a hard edge to it.

"Aren't American soldiers fighting us in North Africa already?"

Papa's eyebrows shot up. "It's just a small group, for show. And last month General Rommel destroyed them in Tunisia. Kasserine Pass."

"And last month our 6th Army was destroyed in Stalingrad." Mama maintained an equally even and equally hard tone. "A small victory in Tunisia does not outweigh a massive defeat in Russia."

I knew about Stalingrad. It was the first defeat that had been announced by the government. So many men had been lost that they could not hide the fact. A quarter million soldiers killed, injured or captured. Papa must have been forewarned that the news would be publicly announced so that day he took the Volksempfänger into his study, the holy inner sanctum that none of us were ever permitted to enter. But I soon found out anyway.

Papa's face flushed scarlet. He set his cup down with exaggerated precision and then stood up. I braced myself for what I knew was coming, and I could see Theodor doing so as well.

"Stalingrad means nothing," he shouted, the veins on his neck bulging. "The Russians were lucky. Nothing more. Reich's Minister Göbbels has now declared total war in response. We will no longer hold anything back. If the enemy fights with no restraint, then they will see what we can do when we fight with no restraint! We will push back against the Russians and at the same time we will bomb England into submission. They will sue for peace. Churchill will fall and his successor will understand that they must make common interest with us against the Bolsheviks!"

For a moment Mama looked like she was ready to say something in response, but she did not. She just stared hard at him and let him start shouting again.

"We must stay united! We must back the Führer in deed, word and thought! It cannot be like last time again! If your negativity triumphs, Luise, the Russians will overrun us, and they will have no mercy! None! Every woman will be raped and . . ."

"Wilhelm! The boys!" So, she did know we were there.

"They need to hear this too! Every woman will be raped, and every man, woman and child will be enslaved! There will be no more Germany."

I had no idea what "raped" meant, but it did not sound good.

"You know that I don't want Germany to lose either, but these morons are making it more likely, not less likely."

"Luise!" He slammed his fist on the table, making the cup and saucer jump and clatter. Theodor and I winced but stayed absolutely still, looking straight ahead.

"No, Wilhelm, I'm going to speak now! Yes, they are making it more likely that we will lose the war because their ideology is getting in the way. It's distracting them and making them focus on the wrong things. Their Aryan shit is going to be the undoing of them and this country. What garbage! Aryan purity! Look at us for example! You might have blue eyes, Wilhelm, but you are hardly Siegfried of the Nibelungen, and the kids and I, with our short legs, our brown eyes, our brown hair, our darker skin . . . Only Johann has blue eyes. Nobody is blond. Nobody is tall. Nobody is fair. For all I know we could be part Mongol or even —"

"Luise!" He shouted even louder now, his face redder than I had ever seen it before and his comb-over flying about like stalks of wheat in a gale.

"— even part Jew. Those inconvenient Hörschelmanns, if you go back far enough —"

Right then three things happened in rapid succession. Papa made a motion as if to strike Mama but then pulled his hand back, Oskar began to cry in the next room and the air raid siren went off again. It only sounded for a minute — probably the work of an understandably jumpy radar technician — but it was enough to tip the scene into absolute chaos. I could no longer sort out the screaming, crying and shouting. It became an indistinguishable vortex of sound circling my head at high velocity, squeezing me and compressing me as it spiralled inwards into me. I put

64

my head down on the table, closed my eyes, covered my ears and began to rock. I might have started crying too, it was hard to tell.

When it felt safe to open my eyes and uncover my ears the house was weirdly quiet. Only Theodor was left in the room. He was looking at me with his head cocked.

"Are you okay, Ludwig?"

"Yes, I think so. It was too much. Much too much." At times it felt as if each of my senses was a funnel, gathering inconceivably large amounts of light, sound and smell and then pushing them into my brain, causing it to overflow with sensation. That other people could master and sort this kind of excessive input was a wonder to me. I had long known that I was different, but it was only at times like these that this difference felt like a disadvantage.

I paused and looked around. "Where is everyone? What about the bombs?"

"There were no bombs. It was a false alarm. Papa went to the Ortsgruppe anyway and Mama is with Oskar."

"They were really angry with each other." I said this quietly, not wanting Mama to overhear.

"Yes." Theodor got up and left the room.

CHAPTER
NINE

There were many more false alarms that spring and summer. If we had seen little of Papa before, we saw even less of him now. We still went to school when it was in session, but it became difficult for me to visit the forest as Mama had become very anxious about any of us being too far away from a bomb shelter. Life became worse in almost every way.

Our relative prosperity and Papa's position had protected us to some extent from the worst aspects of the rationing system, but this was no longer the case. As the situation deteriorated Papa felt that it was even more important that we did our part and were model citizens of the Third Reich. This meant Mama now often cooked with ersatz Fleisch, meaning fake meat made from cooked rice mashed and fried in mutton fat, or ersatz Fisch, which was also mashed rice but mixed with onions and the oil from tinned fish. Baking bread became challenging as wheat supplies were mostly diverted to the army, but housewives swapped ideas for substituting ground horse chestnuts or pea meal or potato starch. Ration cards did permit the purchase of some normal bread, as well as meat, eggs, butter and so on, but the amounts were steadily cut back and luxuries such as cream and chocolate were only available on the black market. I must confess though that I loved the ration cards. They were large rectangles of cardboard with neat little squares marked out for each month's allotment of the rationed foodstuffs. Something in the symmetry and in the abstract small-scale representation of real-world goods appealed to me. The squares were steadily cut out as you used up the card. Even restaurants would snip out the appropriate square if, for example, they used some butter to cook your meal with!

Mama may have grumbled about the restrictions, but she was very clever in making the best of what was available. In fact, she was particularly good at figuring out what the neighbours most lacked or most desired. Then she would hoard enough of whatever that was in order to make a good trade. For example, Frau Klempner three doors over had a sister in the country who regularly sent her fresh eggs, but somehow she always ran out of butter before month's end. Mama was able to save enough of our butter to swap for the eggs. Or there was Frau Mendel who kept Balkonschweine — literally "balcony pigs," which is what we called rabbits. Livestock was not permitted in the city, but rabbits were because in the strict and inflexible Nazi way of accounting for all things, some bureaucrat deep in a cavernous ministry in Berlin had deemed rabbits to be pets and not livestock. And they remained classified as such long past the point where anyone looked at them with anything other than a ravening eye. At least once a month Mama would find something from our rations that we could do without so that she could barter for one of these delicious balcony pigs. Any squeamishness we children might have had about eating something cute had long since been abandoned.

These stories seem almost charming now — plucky burghers doing their best in hard times — but please believe me that it was in no way charming to live through. What happened to Frau Scheffler made that very clear. She was a friend of Mama's and a core member of the regular trading circle in this part of Connewitz. She was a tall, thin, bird-like woman with a large nose. I remember that she always wore a black kerchief on her head. Although this made her look somewhat imposing, perhaps like a witch, I remember her particularly because she became the occasional source of chocolate when even Greta at the Ortsgruppe did not have any more for us. Frau Scheffler was always very kind to us and had a shy smile when she handed over a little choco-late. The story was that she had a son who was an officer in occupied France. Somehow, he was able to obtain desir-able foods, including the chocolate, and he regularly mailed parcels of these to her. Everyone assumed that he had looted the delicacies. That there was anything left to loot by that point in the war seemed strange, but nobody in the trading circle questioned this story. The Gestapo, however, were keen to question everything about it. One day in October Frau Scheffler disappeared, arrested on a charge of black-market trading and profiteering.

"Wilhelm, can't you do something for Heike?" Mama asked as soon as Papa appeared that evening. "She didn't do anything very wrong, or at least nothing that everyone else isn't doing anyway."

"I cannot and I will not. Eggs for butter and milk for bread is one thing, but a luxury goods smuggling and trading enterprise is quite another."

"But it's Heike. You know her. The children know her."

"The law is the law, Luise. It's all I could do to prevent you from being brought in for questioning as well. I like fine food as much as anyone, but this all has to stop."

That night there was no shouting. Both of them seemed tired and resigned, which in some ways worried me more than when they were angry.

Frau Scheffler was executed the next day. She was hung at the gallows on Markgraffenstrasse. She was a widow and her only child was her son in France, so her sister had to come from out of town to claim the body. If there was a funeral, I did not hear about it.

It was a "Goldener Oktober," which is a common expression in German, as in, "I hope this will be a golden October" or "Last year we had such a wonderful golden October." I suppose "Indian summer" is similar in English, but it implies that there was a cold period first, whereas golden October does not imply this. In any case, the October of 1943 was golden. Obviously this refers to the colour of the leaves, especially when lit by the low slanting late afternoon or early morning light, but there is more to it. I think fine dust particles are stirred up by the harvest which lend the air itself a subtle golden glow in the sun. This was certainly the case in my forest by the Pleisse.

Mama was so distraught by Frau Scheffler's death that she did not leave her bedroom at all the following day, so I saw this as my opportunity to slip out and visit my trees and my birds. I suppose I was sad about Frau Scheffler as well, but it was more the idea of sadness in my mind than the actual feeling of it. I do not know why that is. Regardless it was so wonderful to be in the forest again after such a long absence. I did not know that it would be my last time.

The bombing had not damaged the forest yet and Old Greybark was as magnificent as always. Lindens make an excellent contribution to the goldenness of October as their foliage is an exceptionally deep yellow that verges on orange and is thus, in the correct light, truly golden. I sat under Old Greybark and looked west to the Pleisse. It was late in the afternoon as I had waited most of the day to get up the courage to defy Mama's orders, but this meant that the sun was at the ideal angle to light the forest like one hundred thousand shards of stained glass, all variants of yellow and gold, but no less the beautiful for their relative uniformity. I loved staring directly at the leaf-filtered sun, with my eyes squinted. Around me the birds were busy as they always were in the autumn. Less squabbling, more business. The wren — or possibly *a* wren but I had convinced myself that I always saw the same specific individual — was zipping about as well. He came very close to me at times on his inscrutable missions. I fervently hoped that he would land on my hand if I held it out very still, which I did for as long as I could stand to, but he did not. He did stop one time on a low branch, about a metre away, and look directly at me for a long while, dipping his tail from time to time. I tried to imagine what he was thinking, or possibly trying to tell me, but I was not sure. My best guess was that he viewed me as a benign curiosity and was waiting to see what I would do, but I did nothing and eventually he darted off.

I loved these birds. I loved these trees.

CHAPTER

TEN

DECEMBER 4, 1943

This is the way the world ends. T.S. Eliot claimed that it ends with a whimper rather than a bang, but he was wrong. At least he was wrong about how the world ends when it is at war. And "bang" is wrong too. It is much closer to the truth than "whimper," but it is still a completely inadequate understatement. But then there is no actual word in English or German for the sound. I remember it as the roar of the universe being wrenched apart and shredded. The roar of atoms being flung away from each other and all order being rendered into primordial chaos. An instantaneous violent return to the world before the world, like in the Hindu cycles of the universe's creation and destruction. It was only by chance, no different than the rolling of a handful of dice and seeing only sixes, that my world did not end at that moment the way it was clearly intended to end. Sometimes the gods make a mistake.

At 3:39 a.m. on the morning of Saturday, December 4, 1943, 442 RAF bombers dropped 1,400 tons of explosive ordinance, including many firebombs, on the centre of Leipzig. They had managed to find a route that largely evaded the air defence systems and therefore caught the city by absolute surprise. The sirens went off only moments before the bombs began to explode all around us. We were still stumbling down the stairs to the cellar when the house shook and we all fell down on top of one another, covered in light plaster dust. Clara and Oskar were crying, and Mama looked like she was on the edge of panic. Johann, Theodor and I were too shocked to show any reaction yet. Papa had apparently run outside, which seemed insane, but that was not at the top of our minds at that moment.

Once in the cellar we crouched together in a far corner, as if increased distance from the steps somehow improved our safety. We crouched and we listened to that monstrous unnameable sound press in from all sides as we felt the house around us and the earth beneath us shake. This went on for far longer than any previous air raid, although exactly how long I cannot say. Then all of a sudden it stopped. The sirens still screamed and there were various other chaotic sounds, but the hellish explosions stopped. They stopped for one maybe two minutes and then there was a tremendous crack, like a whip being wielded by a titan, followed by the sound of a thousand wine glasses being shattered at once. Have you ever fantasized about what it would sound like to smash an entire cabinet of crystal? Perhaps take a stick to it or throw a ball at it? You know you will never ever actually do it — it is a terrifying fantasy — yet you wonder. Many little boys have this secret fantasy. This was the exact sound I had imagined, only amplified to a vast scale.

"What was that?" Theodor whispered.

Mama was quiet for a moment. "The windows, I think."

She was right. The sirens continued for quite a while longer and we could still hear explosions, although more distant now, so we stayed in the cellar until Mama was absolutely confident the danger had passed. When we came upstairs, just as the sun was rising, we could see that every single window had been broken. Often not just broken but shattered into thousands of tiny fragments coating every surface, glinting like diamonds or ice crystals when the sun hit them. The house had twenty-five windows — I'd counted them — and each one was broken. There were also a few cracks in the walls and indeed some crystal wine glasses and china had been smashed as well.

Mama herded us into a corner of the living room that had been somewhat spared from the blast of glass and told us to wait there while she swept the room clear. It was only then that we noticed how cold it had become. It was early December after all and a frigid wind was blowing in through the open windows. A few snowflakes began to mingle with the glass shards as little clouds scudded by, resulting in alternating sunshine and light snow showers. It was perversely beautiful, and the five of us stood quietly, now wearing our winter things, mesmerized by the sparkling scene while Mama swept. Nobody was crying anymore.

"This is impossible, children," she finally said when she was done removing all the visible glass from the room. "It's winter. We cannot stay here. The telephone is not working, so we will have to go find your papa and tell him to send a cable to Tante Karoline and Onkel Peter in Mellingen that we're coming."

I did not like Tante Karoline, nor did my brothers and sister. And it was clear that she did not like us either. Onkel was fine, but he was a doctor and was always busy, so we did not see much of him, but the prospect of living with Tante Karoline was actually more unappealing than staying in this bomb-damaged house. Moreover, it was the First Advent. In Germany this is an important day as it is the official start of the Christmas season. Mama had already decorated the house with fir boughs in vases from which straw stars and angels were hung. The Advent candle holder was also out, taking pride of place on top of the wide low antique wooden cupboard that dominated the north side of the room. This candle holder was made of pewter and had places for four candles. The candles were lit one at a time starting with the First Advent until all four were lit on the Fourth Advent, which is the last Sunday before Christmas Eve. Mama had already baked the traditional Advent cookies, which was a particular treat as we did not get cookies and sweets on a regular basis otherwise. That Advent seemed unlikely to happen now made me more upset than any other aspect of this terrible day.

Mama sensed this and said, "But don't worry. Tante Karoline will make sure we have a nice Advent when we arrive."

I was not convinced.

Mama had weighed all the options before we left the house to find Papa. She quickly dismissed the idea of leaving us behind by ourselves. Theodor thought it would be fine, but the little ones wailed at the prospect as the house felt so different now. She also considered taking us to the next-door neighbour, Frau Doctor Burkhard, but Mama did not like her and she reasoned that the Frau Doctor would be at the hospital anyway dealing with the wounded. Her husband was on the front and they had no children. No, the only solution was to take us with her through the broken city.

Other than smashed windows in almost every house and a few cracked façades, our street was in surprisingly good condition. It was unclear where the bomb had gone off, but it did not appear to have been right in front of the house, which is what it had felt like. Towards the centre of the city was an entirely different story. We could see columns of smoke rising into the morning sky and we heard sirens everywhere. These were not the air raid sirens but those of the fire department and ambulances. We walked slowly in single file. I noted that we were making footprints in a mixture of the light snow that had fallen earlier and the ash that was falling now. There were very few people out in our neighbourhood, but when we got to Zwickauer Strasse it was a lot busier.

To my astonishment I saw a large building — I do not know which one — on fire just up the street. Men swarmed about it, fighting the fire with what looked like not nearly enough water. I expected to hear screaming and shouting, but it was oddly quiet, other than the sirens and the crackle of the massive flames. The Ortsgruppe office was in the opposite direction, so Mama herded us like ducklings away from this scene. Out of the corner of my eye I caught sight of three long humps under blankets. The humps were the size and shape of people, but they were completely covered. These were dead bodies. In spite of the war, I had never seen a dead body before.

Whereas the firefighting was eerily quiet and calm, the Ortsgruppe was complete chaos. Here there was screaming and shouting. We could not see Papa anywhere in the mob of uniformed people rushing from desk to desk and bellowing into telephones.

Mama got the attention of one of the people who recognized her. "Konrad, where is Wilhelm?"

"I don't know where exactly, but in the city centre I assume."

Mama digested this information for a moment. We had seen nothing but smoke in the direction of the city centre.

"What is he doing there?"

Konrad, who I did not know but appeared to be a communications officer of some sort, said, "Luise, they used incendiary bombs. The entire city centre is on fire. Every person we can spare is there trying to help. Our own elite fire brigades are in Berlin because of the raids there. Here we are just trying to call in help from surrounding communities, but the hose diameters are not standardized, so when the Halle boys arrived, we couldn't use their equipment! Germany is supposed to be so efficient! This is a nightmare." Konrad paused, glanced around and then lowered his voice. "Anton didn't even come in and Marcus has shut himself away in his office. Wilhelm was the only one above Arbeitsleiter rank who actually risked his life. He went into cellars and told people to get out, that they were going to be roasted alive. He was right. Those who got out into open spaces mostly survived, but those who stayed inside burned."

It occurred to me that we had stayed inside, in our cellar. I suppose only the city centre was considered a worthy target for firebombs, or perhaps we were just lucky. Probably the latter.

When Papa eventually showed up, he was almost unrecognizable. He had lost his glasses and his face was streaked with soot. He was clearly exhausted and seemed irritated to see us waiting for him at the office. I am sure that he was pleased that we were all right, but he did not make that obvious.

"Yes, go to Karoline. That is a good idea. It's no longer sensible to stay in the city" was all he said. That he would stay behind in Leipzig was unspoken and unquestioned. I waited for one of the pithy Latin quotes he usually proffered at times like these, but none was forthcoming.

It turned out that there would be no way to cable Tante Karoline, so we would just have to show up there. A train was leaving in half an hour, so an aide bundled the smaller kids into a three-wheeled cargo bicycle, while I rode sidesaddle with Mama on another bicycle and Theodor took up the rear on a third bike. A taxi was out of the question as almost all cars had been requisitioned by the Party for civil defence purposes. We were unable to take the direct route to the train station because the bombing had caused buildings to collapse into some streets. Also, as mentioned before, active firefighting and rescue operations were still underway, and this blocked several other streets. The city was essentially unrecognizable. Yes, the streets still ran at their customary angles, but there were so many gaps in the buildings that lined them that I was unable to locate my usual landmarks and quickly became disoriented. Fortunately, the aide and Mama navigated using some deeper sense of the geography that did not depend on where a particular bookstore or bakery was located.

The train station was a scene of bedlam, with pockets of outright panic, and the train ride, first to Weimar and then on to Mellingen on the Jena line, was horrible. Normally going on the train was a rare and exciting treat, but not on this day. There was nowhere to sit as every car was crammed with people doing exactly what we were doing — fleeing the big city for the country or smaller towns that would not be bombing targets. We all stood there, shoulder to shoulder, swaying as the train bumped over provisionally repaired sections of track. A young woman near me had half her face covered with a blood-stained bandage. She was carrying a baby that would not stop howling. A boy my age was slumped in one of the seats, apparently unconscious rather than sleeping and was attended to by a nun. An old man behind me groaned continuously. But other than the baby and the old man, people were quiet. There was no conversation. I suppose that there was so much to say that it seemed pointless to begin. Also nobody had slept enough, nobody had washed, and few had eaten much. Exhaustion hung like a thick fog over the entire train.

~

Tante Karoline was not pleased to see us. This was not a surprise, but at this point in what felt like the longest day of my life, I had hoped for some sort of a break. Mama accurately described her attitude as sweet and sour, like a piquant Gypsy sauce. The superficial sweetness, the smile, could not disguise the sourness that had great depth beneath it and played on all her other facial features, aside from the upturned corners of her mouth. To be fair, to suddenly have your little sister appear with five dishevelled, dirty children would be a strain on just about anyone. Her husband, Onkel Peter, who was at home as it was a Sunday evening, was much friendlier. Tante Karoline shot him a dark look as he distributed Advent cookies to us and asked us whether we would like some water or milk.

"They all cannot stay here. It is simply impossible, Luise," she said once we had all squeezed into their foyer. We were pointedly not invited further into the house. It did not immediately register with me that by saying "they all" Tante Karoline was implying that we would have to be split up, with some of us children sent away.

"I understand, Karoline. This is an unpleasant shock for all of us. Let us all stay tonight. The older boys can sleep here and then I just need one bed for Oskar, Clara and me. We'll make the necessary arrangements in the morning."

And again I maintained a blissful ignorance as to what "necessary arrangements" might entail. We were eventually ushered into the house itself, which was really quite grand and spacious. Our cousins, whom I barely knew, stared at us from a safe distance while we were fed dinner. Afterwards, Johann, Theodor and I were shown to a side room which seemed to be some sort of extra sitting room and piles of blankets and pillows were provided for us. So, not the foyer after all. In fact, this accommodation was quite cozy, and we would have played "Indian Frontier Camp" if we had not been so exhausted. As it was, we had barely made it through dinner without our faces splashing into our soups.

CHAPTER

ELEVEN

DECEMBER 5, 1943

I t happened so quickly. There were phone calls made the next morning and then Mama went to the local Ortsgruppe and came back a couple of hours later with bundles of documents. We were still oblivious to what was happening, but I do recall a dull feeling of unfocused dread, deep inside of me, that I kept pushing down by distracting myself with everything new there was to see in Tante Karoline and Onkel Peter's house, or at least in the parts we were permitted to be in.

Mama sat us down. She took a deep breath and then pushed some strands of loose hair from her face before spreading out the bundles on the dining table.

KLV-Lager.

That's where Theodor and I were being sent.

Specifically, we were being sent to a KLV-Lager near the hamlet of Schönbach, not far from Colditz, a quite famous small town about fifty kilometres southeast of Leipzig. KLV was the abbreviation for Kinderlandverschickung, which directly translates as "children's rural evacuation," and Lager means "camp." "Camp" may sound promising, but I knew these camps were very strictly run, and I knew that this would mean separation from Mama for the first time in my life.

Then Mama turned her attention to little Johann and Clara. They were being sent to live with a family all the way over in Aue, very near to what is now the Czech Republic. I remember Clara crying and asking softly, "Are they nice people, Mama?" to which Mama replied, "Of course," even though I am sure that all of us understood that there was no way she could know that. These were absolute strangers. But Theodor and I were sent to the KLV-Lager based on what grades we were in, as the camps were run in association with the schools. Because I was in the lowest grade being sent and had skipped a grade, I would likely be the youngest and smallest boy at camp.

By that same afternoon we were at the train station. Mama sat on the bench between us with her hands folded tightly on her lap while we waited for the train. Nobody said anything for a long while. Then Mama spoke.

"Do you remember the Brothers Grimm story of the 'Willow Wren and the Bear'?"

"Is that where he gets the nickname of the Fence King?" I asked.

"No, it's the other one. The less well-known one. In the 'Willow Wren and the Bear,' a bear insults the wren and his family. He says that the wrens are disreputable. He is joking perhaps, thinking that it would be funny to see what a little creature like a wren will do when it is angry. The wren asks for an apology, but none is given, and the bear starts to walk away, laughing loudly. What do you think the wren does next?"

I had been staring straight ahead while she spoke, so I turned and looked at her and shook my head to indicate that I did not know. I could see that Theodor, who probably considered himself too old for fairy tales, was carefully listening too.

"Well, the wren shouts after the bear that this means war. The bear shouts back that it won't be an even match, but so be it. The bear laughs even more as he leaves. The wren then gathers all his flying friends — mostly insects and little beasts even smaller than him — and tells them that they must join with him against the larger animals or they will forever be the butt of jokes and subject to the tyranny of those with fur and paws. The small creatures all readily agree to help him. The wren then tells the gnat to secretly follow the bear to discover his plans. This the gnat does. Later he returns to report that the bear met with a wolf, a fox and a few other big furry animals. At that meeting they decided that the fox would be their leader and that he would raise his big red bushy tail to signal the attack and lower it only to signal retreat if they were losing. This news really pleased the wren, who then instructed the hornet to sting the fox under the tail just as the battle was beginning. This worked perfectly! The fox cried out very loudly and instinctively pulled his tail down tightly, momentarily forgetting that this was a signal. This caused the bear and wolf and others to flee in panic, thinking all was lost. But that was not enough. The wren insisted that the bear come and apologize for his behaviour, or he would fight him again. The bear agreed and the war in the forest was over. The small had won and the large were evermore wary."

Theodor and I both nodded and then returned to glumly watching for the train. Nobody said anything further, and nobody cried when the train arrived. As we said goodbye and climbed aboard, I am sure all of us believed that we would be gone for a few weeks at the most. Moreover, Tante Karoline told us that it would be fun, like a summer holiday camp except in the winter. I did not entirely believe her, but this did give me a little nugget of hope to hold on to during the train ride. This hope was snatched away the moment we stepped off the train at the unpromising-sounding Grimma train station (Colditz was closer to Schönbach but had worse connections to Leipzig) and were met by a thin-lipped, bony, very pale, blond young man in a dark grey military uniform.

"Schott and Schott? Come with me." There was no hand-shake or enquiry as to the comfort of our journey. Apparently, we hesitated a second too long for his liking as he then said, in an even sharper tone, "Come on, I said! We are walking. It is far to Schönbach and it will be dark soon. You don't look like very athletic specimens, so we can't waste time."

Theodor and I glanced at each other. It was true I suppose. We were both thin, small, wore glasses and had that indefinable but unmistakable aura of "bookish wimp" that immediately attracts the ire of the non-bookish the world over. The young man, who had not introduced himself, was quickly a dozen paces ahead of us on the road leading away from the station, and he did not bother to look back at any time.

"Wehrmacht uniform? Why is he wearing that?" I whis-pered to Theodor as we struggled along behind, adjusting our backpacks.

"Otto said that some KLV camps are run by the mili-tary, and some even by the SS." Otto was a friend of Theodor's and the source of all manner of interesting and occasionally alarming information.

The SS. Some KLV camps were run by the SS? I did not know much about the SS, but what I had heard made me suddenly feel ill. If the regular military already threatened too much shouting and marching and manly athleticism for my liking, then the SS, by reputation, threatened tenfold more! I glanced at the farmyards and small woodlots alongside the road and contemplated escape, but it was of course a ridiculous idea as it was December and I was not quite ten years old yet. Also, despite my terror at what awaited, I had too much pride to let it show quite so obviously. It was startlingly cold, and nightfall came quickly. For the last half of the two-hour march we only had faint moonlight to guide us, which was eventually supplemented by the growing lights of the camp in the distance straight ahead.

As it happened our camp was indeed operated by the military, but not by the SS. We learned later that it had been an SS-run camp, but the situation in Russia had deteriorated to the extent that all SS personnel were required on the front, so the running of KLV camps was left to a second string of very young or very old or somehow disabled regular Wehrmacht personnel, assisted by a civilian corps of teachers, cooks, cleaners and so on. The camp appeared to be a repurposed tourist resort, possibly having served hikers in the Mulde valley in happier times. Theodor and I were assigned to a makeshift dormitory in an old dancehall with about twenty other boys and were told that we were too late for dinner but could get a bread roll and a small ration of milk before turning in. We were to be in bed by 21:00 and lights would be out at 21:30. As it was winter, the wake-up call would come at 06:30 sharp. In summer it was earlier.

I slept terribly that first night. The so-called mattresses were lumpy sacks of straw, there were too many strange noises and it was cold. Also it was the first time I had ever slept away from my mother. As I lay there, I wondered who among these boys would be the bears, wolves and foxes and who would be the wrens, gnats and hornets.

~

As promised, at precisely 06:30 the next morning the lights were turned on to the shout of "Wake up, boys! The day begins!" The tone was not harsh or unfriendly, but it was certainly firm and did not invite debate. This was okay, as I was always an early riser anyway and, despite my deep misgivings, was at least a little bit curious about the camp and its routines. Theodor and I shared a bunk, with him above and me below. The two boys in the next bunk, also brothers, explained that we would now have an hour to wash and get ourselves ready before the flag raising and breakfast. This was the first problem. I was very self-conscious about taking all my clothes off in the communal bathroom and washing in front of all these strange boys. I just took my nightshirt off and dabbed some of the icy water in my armpits. The head boy, a short round dark-complexioned boy with a bristly crewcut, spotted this and shouted at me, "You, new boy, what is your name?"

"Ludwig, Ludwig Schott." I stared at the floor, fully aware that twenty pairs of eyes were on me now.

"What you are doing is not washing, Schott! You must take everything off and wash all of yourself! To be a good German you must have good hygiene! Hygiene is the foundation of good health!"

I nodded but did not look up. I waited for the sniggering and guffaws that I felt certain were coming from the others, but there was just silence. Theodor was either braver or more astute as he had reluctantly already followed the lead of the others. When the head boy walked away to address a minor infraction of some sort elsewhere in the bathroom, Theodor whispered, "It's not so bad, Ludwig. We're all the same here. Nobody will laugh or tease." And he was right. At least in our dormitory there appeared to be a kind of solidarity borne out of shared trauma. Even so, stripping right down in front of everyone was humiliating and then scrubbing myself with a rough washcloth and cold water was unpleasant, to say the least. I was, however, relieved not to feel any eyes on me as the other boys were all intent on their own ablutions and even the head boy did not seem interested in me anymore.

Once the washing was done but before we could get dressed, there was an additional indignity. The head boy, whose name turned out to be Reinhard, ordered us to line up in front of him, which we did with our hands folded in front of our private parts.

"As per KLV-Lager protocol, you must now declare any health issues such as parasites, rashes, loose bowels or anything else that might present a threat to your fellows!"

There was silence for a moment and then a small blond boy stepped forward to say in very quiet voice that he had a rash on his arm. Reinhard directed him to see the camp nurse immediately after breakfast. I had a blister on the side of my left big toe, but I reasoned that it was due to the long walk yesterday and was not contagious. Moreover, I was keen to avoid a visit to the nurse. I adjusted my stance slightly so that that side of my toe was out of Reinhard's view. Thankfully, no close inspection followed the health question and Reinhard left the bathroom immediately after.

While at camp we were required to be in uniform, which consisted of black pants, tan shirts and narrow black ties. We were also issued wide black belts with big steel buckles and shiny black shoes. Light brown woolen overcoats and black woolen gloves were provided for the winter and short pants for the summer. All of this was ill-fitting and uncomfortable, but the shoes were especially terrible. I considered myself to be reasonably brave, tough even, but with my blister and sore feet, these stiff overly large shoes almost made me cry. While many of the other boys might have sympathized, I intuited that Reinhard and his ilk would not have. In fact, as it happened, a few days later another boy complained about his coat, as the sleeves were much too long. Reinhard barked at him that he should be grateful to have any coat at all given how our soldiers were freezing and suffering on the Russian front. Perhaps he would like his coat sent there instead? The fact that this boy had a perfectly well-fitting coat from home that he was not allowed to wear did not enter into the equation. That the camp, the war effort and the country in general did not run on pure logic was becoming increasingly clear to me.

The shoes presented a special problem for me. In addition to being ill-fitting and uncomfortable, they exposed an embarrassing secret — I did not know how to tie my shoelaces. I was almost ten years old and I did not know how. Mama always tied them for me. I did not have to take them off or change them at school, so there had been no prior occasion when Mama was not available to do this for me. This was not a matter of her spoiling me, Lord knows she did try to teach me, but with the little ones constantly hanging on her apron strings, she did not have that much time. It was quicker and easier for her just to do it herself and hope that I would eventually figure it out. And this was also not a matter of me being stupid. I hope this does not sound arrogant of me, but not only was I not stupid, I was one of the smartest people I knew. This is not a boast but just an objectively measurable fact. To be honest, I do not know why it was so difficult for me. I know what reasons do not apply, but I do not know for sure what reasons do apply. It may be that I simply did not think it important before. Well, it was important now. Theodor was aghast. He had forgotten this about me. When he noticed me struggling and beginning to grumble and curse about it, he made some shushing noises and came over and helped me, crouching so that he would block the view of the others.

"Ludwig, you still can't tie your shoes?!" he hissed under his breath.

"No." I must have sounded pathetic as I was close to tears.

"God in heaven, brother, this is not going to be okay here in camp."

I sniffled and nodded. Theodor had a particular shortcut for tying shoelaces that I had not seen before. Mama's technique was convoluted and this way seemed more achievable. Ultimately it took a week of my brother's fraying patience, but eventually I did it on my own. I was not proud. I was only relieved.

One of the boys had noticed this miniature drama of the shoelaces and, being unusually polite and discrete, asked Theodor whether there was something wrong with me rather than making fun of me as most of the boys would have. He tried to whisper so that I would not hear, but I understood the gist of the question. Theodor, on the other hand, made no attempt to keep his answer quiet. Casting a quick sideways glance towards me he said, "Ludwig? Who knows what the issue is. He's just not of this world."

After putting on our uniforms we were required to make our beds with military precision and to clean up the dormitory. Each boy was assigned a specific cleaning task, and these were more or less rotated. I say "more or less" because Reinhard played favourites and the rotations were skewed to frequently give the more onerous tasks to the boys on his bad list. I was often on this list, not because of any disciplinary infractions but for the same reasons that Ulrich and his gang had picked on me and for the same reasons that our guide from the railway station looked at me with disdain. I was small and skinny and wore glasses and evidently had "victim" tattooed on my forehead in invisible ink that only bullies could read.

The most onerous of these onerous tasks was the emptying of the chamber pot. The camp was served by privies in separate huts, but we were not permitted to leave the dormitories at night, whether for reasons of safety or discipline was never made entirely clear. Neither explanation made sense anyway, but, as with every aspect of camp life, this was not a point that could be debated or negotiated. Consequently, in order to deal with our needs at night a large chamber pot in the form of a tin bucket was set up in the far corner of the room. The unfortunate to whom this chore had been delegated had to take the bucket in the morning when it was often still dark and walk down the icy slippery path to the privy and empty it into what we referred to as the "pit of doom." The bucket then needed to be rinsed and returned to its corner. That this whole procedure was highly noxious goes without saying. It was not only noxious but hazardous as well, because a weak boy like me was easily unbalanced on the icy path by a full and heavy bucket sloshing as I strained to hold it steady. It became a kind of perverse sport for the boys to make a special effort to fill the bucket as full as their excretory systems permitted when I was on chamber pot duty the next morning. As I said, we were actually a fairly harmonious bunch by camp standards, but the English expression "boys will be boys" applies in this situation with vigour. It was apparently just too hilarious to resist when Schott would return from the privy cursing and having to change his pants and wash his shoes.

Flag raising followed at 07:30. For this we had to stand in a shivering circle with the teachers and other camp personnel while the camp director, Herr Tischendorf, stood in the centre beside the flagpole. One of the dormitory head boys would stride up to the pole and raise the swastika flag of the Third Reich while we gave the Nazi salute and all sang the "Deutschlandlied." If it was especially cold, we sometimes sang faster and then Herr Tischendorf would make us sing again. Despite his foolish-looking little Hitler moustache and military bearing, he was actually a fairly reasonable man. He had been a biology teacher in Leipzig and was too old to serve in combat but wanted to do something to help, so this is what he was offered. He seemed to genuinely like children, which we were told was not the case with the previous director when the camp was still run by the SS. That director, a Herr Eckhorn, apparently saw children as no more than unripe adults. This annoyed him as fully ripened adults were needed for the war effort. His methods for accelerating the ripening process were apparently as futile as abusing a green banana and making it suffer in the hopes that it would turn yellow faster. Such bananas go directly from green to brown.

A hurried, invariably grim breakfast followed and by 08:00 we were in the classroom. This was without contest my favourite part of camp life. Although the teachers in camp seemed to assume that we were all dullards and moved through the lessons at an agonizingly slow pace, at least the occasional fragment of interesting information would be imparted and at least it was quiet and it was something I could excel at. I was careful not to excel too flamboyantly, lest a repeat of the Ulrich scenario occur. But sometimes it was hard to entirely avoid this.

Lessons continued until noon at which point a hot lunch was served. It was of a similarly dismal quality to the breakfast. Oh, how I missed Mama's cooking, even with the strict rationing. If we ate quickly enough, we would have some time to rest before the horrors of the afternoon, which began at 13:00. These horrors were the outdoor activities led by the Hitler Youth commanders. Most of the boys aged fourteen and over were members. It was technically a voluntary organization, but those who declined to join were forced to write essays on awkward subjects such as "Why am I not in the Hitler Youth?" and were bullied even more vigorously than I was. The DJV junior Hitler Youth organization for ten- to fourteen-year-olds was perhaps a little looser, but I was still slightly too young for that. Regardless, Hitler Youth–led activities were compulsory for everyone in camp. These activities ranged from team sports, which I hated, to military-style exercises such as crawling under barbed wire or marching with toy wooden rifles on our shoulders, which I hated even more. Worst of all were the activities that combined military training and team sport, such as the objectively bizarre and pointless games of tug-of-war played while wearing gas masks and oversized steel helmets.

The only part I did not hate was some of the outdoor survival skills that they taught, such as compass reading and fire building. These could be interesting and seemed potentially useful, although even here the atmosphere was oppressive with a lot of orders being screamed and public humiliations being given for the slightest missteps. There was always only one right way to do something. Only one German way. Suffice it to say, the afternoons were exhausting and stressful. The opportunities to publicly fail were abundant. I honestly did not care what the others thought of me in any abstract sense regarding my social standing; I only cared in the practical sense that failure could attract abuse and even more chamber pot duty.

By suppertime I was more than ready to withdraw to my bunk and read (I had brought my Karl May with me), but alas the evenings were usually programmed as well. Sometimes marginally tolerable music was offered and sometimes there were newsreels. There was an obvious incongruity between the rosy picture of the war offered by these films and the inescapable fact that we were forced to be in a camp because our cities had been bombed to rubble, but to the extent that we thought about this paradox we kept those thoughts to ourselves.

~

It took only a few days for the camp routine to begin to feel normal. This is not to say that I hated it any less — in fact the opposite is true — but to say that one's capacity for adaptation is remarkable. I simply adapted to being in a hateful situation and it quickly began to feel like this was all that life ever was, or ever would be. I was frightened by how quickly my previous life at home in Leipzig had taken on an abstract, dreamlike quality of unreality. Sundays we were encouraged to write home, and I took full advantage of that, sending Mama long reports of the week's activities in camp. I was proud of myself that I knew enough to underplay the worst aspects of camp life, lest I make her worry too much. I did not write Papa. It is not that I thought of writing him and then rejected the idea; it is that the idea never occurred to me in the first place. I wrote to Johann and Clara in Aue occasionally as well, although being too young they did not write back. At first, I had felt very bad for them, but now I envied them as I imagined them living an idyllic rural life, running through fields and patting goats. (Later I learned that they had been sent to a baker's family, so no fields or goats, and that they were constantly scolded for being a burden.)

Writing letters on Sundays and reading in the little interval between the end of evening entertainment and lights-out time were two of the three principal highlights of my camp existence. The third highlight was a discovery that I stumbled on: I had a talent for making up funny rhymes. As I mentioned, I was not especially concerned with being popular but there were benefits to not being solely identified as a contemptible weakling. One morning while waiting for the flag raising to begin, I spontaneously whispered, "Tischendorf ist ein Schorf" to Jolf, the boy standing beside me. He giggled and passed it along to the next boy and before you knew it the whole group was cracking up. Herr Tischendorf glared at us and we quickly settled down, but I freely admit that this made me feel good, especially when word spread that I was the poet and when even the older boys clapped me on the shoulder and smiled. The little rhyme translates as "Tischendorf is a scab," which I felt a little bit bad about because he was a decent man, but the thrill of being the bard of transgressive little-boy humour far outweighed any sense of guilt.

My next target, and possibly greatest triumph, was Reinhard. His surname was Protz, so that made it very easy. "Der Kleiner Protz ist voll mit Rotz" rang through the camp for days. "The little Protz is full of snot" is as far removed from Shakespeare and Goethe as one can conceive, but if you do not understand the impact of it, then you have not been around very many little boys.

I still got more than my share of torment, but I felt that I had found my place in the camp hierarchy, slightly off to the side, observing but remaining small and mostly unnoticed until I had something clever to say. I also figured out that if you "accidentally" slopped the bucket contents more than once onto the dormitory floor on the way out, the yelling and threats would ultimately transform into exasperation and you would be deemed too feeble for the job. Washing windows was the second most onerous chore, but the gap in onerousness was significant.

CHAPTER

TWELVE

DECEMBER 24, 1943

When a German says "Christmas" he is usually specifically referring to Christmas Eve. Although the Christmas season runs for more than a month from the First Advent to Epiphany and includes all manner of special days, the warm beating heart of the season is Christmas Eve. Every child looks forward to it with a special kind of fervour, as this is when the gifts are distributed. Keep in mind that even in well-off families, spoiling children was considered a terrible vice, so if there was something special you wanted, such as a bicycle or toy train, you had to somehow earn it or wait for Christmas Eve. For adults Christmas Eve was also very special as it was the most family oriented of all the holidays. If it all possible, the family must be together for Christmas Eve.

For both these reasons Theodor and I viewed the approach of Christmas with mounting anxiety. How could we possibly get gifts? How could the family possibly be together? We had already heard that the camp would remain open for children who were unable to go home for Christmas. Herr Tischendorf would stay, despite having family in Leipzig, as would Reinhard and a skeleton crew of staff. The thought of staying there for Christmas was horrifying, absolutely horrifying.

A week before Christmas a letter arrived from Mama. It was not going to be possible to celebrate Christmas in Leipzig, but Tante Karoline had agreed to allow us to come to Mellingen on Christmas Eve. We would have to return to camp on the 26th. Johann and Clara would not be able to come, nor would Papa. The former because it was too far for little children to travel on their own and the latter because the Party needed him in Leipzig. This should have been received as bittersweet news, but I will confess that I was delighted. I had a glimmer of empathy for my younger siblings, but the joy I felt in not having to spend Christmas Eve in the camp with Tischendorf, Reinhard and the lot overwhelmed any such brotherly sentiment.

We would be spending the better part of Christmas Eve day in transit, as we had to walk to Grimma, take the train to Leipzig, take another train to Weimar and then finally the train to Mellingen. Papa met us at the Leipzig train station to give us our onward tickets. He was in a sharply tailored grey business suit and a jauntily perched fedora rather than his uniform. He looked thin and tense, but then I suppose we all did. He ushered us around the clumps of soldiers and their families to the correct platform and as we stood by the Weimar train, he patted me on the head and said, "Ludwig, you will be turning ten in just over a month. I'll talk to your mother and we'll try to arrange for you to spend the day with me in Leipzig."

In normal times the prospect of spending the day with my father would have at best been viewed with mild concern, as his primary interest in me appeared to be to offer clearly worded criticisms or opaquely worded wisdom, which were often also just criticisms but in a more intellectual-sounding disguise. But these were not normal times, and anything, really anything at all, that got me away from the KLV-Lager was very welcome.

"Thank you, Papa!"

He gave me one of his rare smiles in response to my enthusiasm and tousled my hair. He then shook our hands and wished us a merry Christmas before walking off across the platform to one of the station entrances where a woman appeared to be waiting for him. He must have assumed that we had boarded the train and were not watching, or perhaps he did not care, because he then kissed this woman fully on the lips. She looked familiar, but it was far away, and Papa was partly blocking her from view.

"That's the neighbour. Frau Doctor Burkhard," Theodor whispered, although whispering was unnecessary. What I had seen was confusing and the information Theodor had given me only compounded the confusion, so I just stared. Papa and Dr. Burkhard were now walking away briskly, arm in arm. Papa did not look back.

"Come on Ludwig, we have to board now."

~

When we arrived in Weimar, we discovered that the train to Jena, which passed through Mellingen, had been cancelled. Although Christmas Eve in the Weimar train station would still be an improvement over Christmas Eve at the camp, it would be a crushing disappointment compared to what we were expecting. Fortunately, Theodor had the wherewithal to ask the station master to phone Onkel Peter in Mellingen. He was happy that we called and said that he would send an ambulance to get us! An ambulance! He told us that we should walk to the White Swan restaurant. It was slightly less than two kilometres directly south of the train station. There we could have some tea and cake while we waited. He would give the ambulance driver some money to pay for our tea and cake because he knew we did not have any pocket money.

I had never been in such a beautiful restaurant before. Mama had spoken of it, as she had grown up in Weimar, but her description did not prepare me for the splendour of the arched leaded glass windows, the ancient dark wooden beams on the ceiling and the candles on the white table-cloths. If the waiter was surprised to see two travel-worn boys ask for a table near the door, he did not indicate it. The other thing that was special about the White Swan was that it was right next door to Goethe's old house. Johann Wolfgang von Goethe was Germany's most beloved and renowned writer and was a great favourite of Papa's, so we had been marinated in his poems, quotes and witticisms from a very young age. I did not give this too much thought though, nor did I think about what I had seen at the Leipzig train station, as my attention was fully focused on the cake, the first treat I had seen in a very long time.

The ambulance ride was as exciting as expected. I don't think we fully appreciated how privileged we were to have an uncle who was a respected doctor and could pull strings to arrange such an unusual means of transport. Many other private vehicles, including taxis, had been requisitioned for the war effort. The driver seemed kind but did not say much to us as he had to concentrate very hard on the road, which was icy and obscured with drifting snow. Thankfully, being wartime, there was almost no traffic. Onkel Peter tipped him well and greeted us with warm handshakes. Even Tante Karoline appeared to be in a good mood. Mama had been busy settling Oskar when we arrived, but as soon as she was able to come and greet us, she burst into tears and hugged us both very hard.

The candles on the tree were already lit and all was in

readiness for Christmas Eve. Yes, it was, and still is, common to have lit candles on German Christmas trees. Lighting them is a very special occasion and everyone stays to watch the beautiful sight, so it is never left unsupervised. If you use a fresh green tree, there is very little risk.

We entered the living room and my eyes were immediately drawn to the bundles at the base of the tree. To note that none of them were bicycle sized is probably unnecessary. I continued to hope for a bicycle even though I knew it was impossible (and impractical — I would not be able to take it with me to camp) because the impossibility of this dream made the second choice, a proper woodsman's pocketknife, seem realistic by comparison. I did not have a clear immediate purpose for such a knife, perhaps to carve sticks, but I did have a clear image of myself alone in the forest by the Pleisse with the knife folded in a little leather holster on my belt. Perhaps if the bombing continued until no houses were left standing and no shops were open and nothing man-made functioned anymore, I could use such a knife to help my family and me survive. I could make spears for fishing and shelters of boughs and branches.

These thoughts animated my imagination while I robotically sang the Christmas carols we were required to sing before opening our gifts. Mama, Tante Karoline, Onkel Peter, my cousins, Theodor and I were arrayed in a semicircle in front of the tree, our faces glowing in the candlelight, our voices admittedly a cacophony of tones as we struggled through "Stille Nacht," "Ihr Kinderlein Kommet" and "Oh Du Fröhliche." Finally, the children were released, and we fell upon the gifts like a pack of wolves. At home it had been much more orderly — one at a time sorted by age — but here it was a merry free-for-all.

I did not get a knife. I did not really expect one, given the circumstances, or really much of anything for that matter, but my survivalist reverie had sharpened my hopes, so I admit that I was disappointed. Instead there were thick black woolen hand-knit socks. Mama knew that although we had to wear uniforms in camp, we could choose our own socks, so long as they were not in garish colours. Moreover, she knew that my feet were often cold in the large shoes I had been assigned, so big woolen socks would solve two problems. I also received a handful of walnuts and an orange. The orange was a kind of miracle. Clearly Onkel Peter had connections as I had not seen oranges, or really any fruit other than soft old apples and spotted pears, since the beginning of the war. I ate half the orange that evening, one segment at a time, spaced half an hour apart, and saved the other half for Christmas Day, each segment then also to be eaten at carefully timed intervals. I saved the peel and over the next few days, including back at camp, I would hold it under my nose and pinch it to squeeze out a little orange oil. What a heavenly smell that was. I had only a dim conception of what the lands where oranges grew looked like, but my imagination busily coloured in all the gaps with bright sunny hues. I was certain it was a much better place than KLV-Lager Schoenberg or Mellingen or possibly even Leipzig Connewitz.

I do not recall anything about Christmas Day that year, but a conversation with Theodor on the second day of Christmas, before we had to leave, comes back to me.

"Should we tell Mama about Papa kissing Frau Doctor Burkhard?" I asked my brother when we were sitting alone in the foyer, waiting to be taken to the train station.

"No, she already knows." Theodor did not look at me.

"How do you know that?"

"She told me. Yesterday she took me aside and asked whether anybody was with Papa at the station in Leipzig. I wasn't sure what was the best thing to say, so I said that yes, there was a woman with him, but I didn't say anything about the kissing. Mama nodded and said that she thought so, and then she asked me directly if it was the Frau Doctor. I said yes. She looked upset, but she didn't say anything, she just nodded again, kissed me on the forehead and left the room."

Various confused thoughts, like weasels squirming in a sack, struggled to gain the upper hand in my mind. "Will Frau Doctor Burkhard become our new mother?" was what finally emerged.

Theodor snorted. "No. Mama will always be our mother. Even if Papa marries Frau Doctor Burkhard, she will still be our mother and he will still be our father. They just wouldn't live together anymore, which they aren't doing now anyway. Nothing would change except Mama wouldn't go to Leipzig every week to do his laundry anymore. His new wife would do that."

This made sense, so I nodded.

"But they won't get married anyway," Theodor continued. "Kissing does not automatically lead to marriage, especially for people who are married to other people already." He used his authoritative older brother voice when he said this, and that ended the conversation.

Mama joined us on the train to Weimar and then Leipzig as she was going to do Papa's laundry, make sure he had enough food and check on the house (the windows had been provisionally repaired). I studied her carefully when she was looking out the window or reading, trying to detect any change that might be a clue that she was upset about the Frau Doctor. But she looked the same as always: tired and a little grim with the occasional smile for us. When we were preparing to board our Grimma train in the Leipzig station, she kissed us each on the forehead, told us to be brave and then left to go look after Papa, tightening her kerchief around her head as she walked out of sight.

CHAPTER

THIRTEEN

JANUARY 1944

And then there was a fresh anxiety. About three weeks after we returned from Christmas in Mellingen, the boy in charge of distributing the mail handed a letter to me after breakfast. My mother had written this letter just two days prior; the post was still remarkably efficient despite everything else that was no longer functioning properly.

Dear Theodor, Dear Ludwig,

I am writing to share some very sad news with you. Your oma, my dear mother, passed away in the care home in Weimar early this morning. I visited her the night before. She was so very thin and all of her hair had fallen out, but she was calm and peaceful. She could no longer speak because of the cancer, but we were able to spend several hours together just looking into each other's eyes, so I knew that she was not frightened or in pain. I left her with a heavy heart, but I had to catch the last train back to Mellingen as I had left Oskar with your aunt. When the telephone rang this morning, I knew exactly why.

I loved her very much and I know you boys did too. She was always there for me when I needed her. Now we will have to rely on each other more than ever.

Oma Flintzer had a good and long life, so don't be sad for her. It is our loss, not hers.

Your loving Mama

In hindsight this seems like too much detail and emotional content to share with two young boys. Even at the time I was aware that not everyone's mother was as candid as ours. Theodor was in quarantine with diphtheria in a special camp when this letter arrived, so I was unable to show it to him until he was released. A lot of boys had become ill, but I had not really taken much notice of it. They would be gone for a couple of weeks and then, most of the time, they would be back. I wished that Theodor had not gotten ill so that I could share my grief with someone. I did not want to attract attention to myself by crying in front of the others, so I excused myself to go to the privy where I wept for several minutes. If I was honest with myself, I did not really know her all that well. She had been an important figure in my life when I was very small and was raiding her wardrobe for sweets, but I had not seen much of her in the last few years. She had been sick for quite a while and children were not encouraged to visit her while she was going through treatments and so on. Even so, for some reason, her death made me very sad and it launched me into a long period of dwelling on morbid thoughts in general.

Thus far I had not been exposed to much death, even though I expect more people were dying in Europe at that moment than at any point since the Black Death. There were those three bodies covered with blankets after the big bombing raid on Leipzig, but they did not seem real and were easy to dismiss from my mind. And two or three years before I had stumbled upon a dead dog in the forest, in the tall grass on the riverside not too far from Old Greybark. The dog was a blond cocker spaniel who looked like he was just sleeping on his side but for the fact that his eyes were missing. His body was otherwise uncorrupted and did not even smell, but something had already eaten out his eyes, so I was presented with the horror of the empty black sockets, which looked disturbingly depthless and infinite in an otherwise beautiful soft face. This type of dog was rare in Leipzig and his owners would not have been difficult to locate. No doubt they were in distress about their missing dog and would have been grateful for any information, even if it was sad news. I knew all of this, but I did not tell anyone, not ever. I do not know why. Perhaps it was because I was very shy with strangers, or perhaps I feared I would be blamed for his death, or perhaps it was because I did not want to do anything that would bring that nightmarish image back into my mind's eye. Yet it did not make me think about death, not directly anyway. Yes, the dog was clearly dead, but the terror I felt looking at the dog's eyeless sockets felt separate from any thoughts about the nature of death and dying. It was more a primal fear arising from disgust, akin to the disgust of touching feces. This was an animal after all, and its death, while sad, did not feel like it was in the same realm as a human death.

But Oma Flintzer was human and now she was dead. She had been alive all of my life and now would never be alive again for the rest of my life, not even for one brief moment. She had existed one minute and then had not existed the next. This was incomprehensible to me and I felt something very cold constricting my heart. If Oma could be made to not exist like that, could not Mama? Or me? It was as if each person were a book, steadily accumulating pages until one day suddenly, arbitrarily, the book was completely shredded or burnt to ash or dissolved in lye. It seemed so senseless and wasteful and unjust. All that knowledge and experience extinguished. I tried to imagine not existing and it was as if the floor suddenly opened before my feet, revealing a bottomless void. I never felt so scared before in my life, not even when the bombs were falling. The bombs could easily have killed me, but at that time death was a dim abstraction. Now it was a reality, dimensionless and invisible but at the same time keenly felt. For some people death is a large black bird or a tall hooded figure or a dark formless monster, but for me that day it became a sense of an infinite nullity, like deepest space beyond all the stars and galaxies.

My family was crumbling under the combined forces of death, dislocation and women who were not my mother kissing my father.

This feeling was underlined by the events of February 20. I had been fervently looking forward to being accompanied by my mother to see my father at our home as antidote to the chaos and dread and death. There, at least for one special day, the old world of peace and order and family would be recreated for me. But of course this was not to be. Seeing my childhood home opened like a ripe melon cleaved by an axe confirmed all my worst fears.

CHAPTER

FOURTEEN

FEBRUARY 1944

I had only been back in camp from my failed birthday visit to Papa in Leipzig for a day and was still recovering from the shock of seeing our apartment left gaping like a doll's house when another shocking event occurred. It had snowed heavily for most of the day, so the camp, which normally looked so worn and old (but not in a charming historical way), suddenly looked clean and new in the long slanting late afternoon light that broke through the now-rapidly scattering clouds. It was another exceptionally cold day. I probably should not use the word "exceptionally" because by February of 1944 it was no longer so exceptional. Since the war began the winters had all been hard, as if the gods saw how people were tormenting each other and decided that they must demonstrate that they still had the power to torment us just as effectively. I am of course referring to the old pagan gods, not the allegedly just and forgiving Christian God. He was nowhere in evidence.

In any case, there was fresh snow and it was very cold when Herr Tischendorf called Reinhard over to one side of the yard. This was not unusual and would not have stuck in my memory if this had not been followed by a sudden very loud scream, which was all the more startling for the otherwise muffled silence of the snowy day. We all wheeled around from whatever pointless exercise we were engaged in and looked at the source of the scream. Reinhard had collapsed to his knees in the snow and was making a sound unlike any I have heard from a boy before. It was an animal sound, like I imagined a farm animal would make while being slaughtered. It was not a sound I recognized as human. Nobody said anything. We just stood and watched while Herr Tischendorf tried awkwardly to calm Reinhard down, bending over, putting his hand on the boy's shuddering shoulder. It then became quiet but for some barely audible sobbing, yet we all still stood, our oddly synchronized puffs of breath vapour being the only thing that moved for several long minutes.

That evening at supper we learned that Reinhard's father had been killed fighting in Italy. Here was death again. This troubled me in two ways. First, I had only been vaguely aware that there was fighting in Italy. Italy was much closer than Russia. This did not strike me as good news for Germany, or ultimately for me. The boys sitting around me insisted that it was because our Italian allies had failed, and now that our own army had taken direct control the situation would surely improve. Nonetheless, the fact that Americans and British (and Canadians too, I later learned) were able to shoot Germans dead right on the continent of Europe, less than a day's drive from the southern border of the Reich, was worrisome. My companions were much more versed in military affairs and launched into a detailed explanation of why there was nothing to worry about, but my mind was already drifting off because of the second way this troubled me. I had never seen that kind of grief before.

While they jabbered on about the Tiger II versus Tiger I tanks, I tried to imagine how I would react if Herr Tischendorf pulled me aside to tell me that Papa had been killed, say in another bombing raid on Leipzig. I did not picture myself reacting as Reinhard did. I did picture myself being sad, perhaps privately crying a bit like I did after Oma's passing, but certainly not screaming and wailing. I reasoned that I was just less emotional, but Reinhard had never given any indication of an emotional range beyond that of a common garden slug. Moreover, when I contemplated Mama's theoretical death, I pictured something beyond screaming and wailing. I pictured end-of-the-world hysterics and fathomless lifelong grief, so it seemed that emotion was in me too. I wondered then if the difference was in how we felt towards our fathers. I was sure that I loved Papa, but I was coming to see that love is not just one thing. The love I felt for Mama was different than the love I felt for my siblings, which was different again than the love I felt for Papa. Perhaps, for some reason, Reinhard felt for his father the kind of love I felt for my mother. This analysis made sense, but it bothered me a little bit to know this.

The Allied bullet that ended Herr Protz's life in some smoking ruin of a village in the hills of central Italy was the first domino in a series that led to life becoming even worse for me at KLV-Lager Schoenberg. Reinhard was sent away the next day to be with his mother. We never saw him again. I learned years later that he had been killed in the final battle for Leipzig, although whether he was one of the Volkssturm teen soldiers or just a bystander, I do not know. His replacement as head boy was not an improvement, far from it. Reinhard had been mean and at times arbitrarily cruel, but Felix was an actual sadist. It is ironic in a way, because "felix" is Latin for "happy." Maybe Felix was entirely happy in his sadism, or maybe it was a mask to hide a deeper unhappiness. This I wonder now, but a ten-year-old boy does not wonder these things. A ten-year-old boy only knows that someone is a source of terror and pain and wonders how he can avoid the terror and pain. He does not wonder why it exists in the first place.

~

In February 1944 I was in the DJV of the Hitler Youth. Papa had insisted that I join as soon as I turned ten, the minimum age. Even if he had not insisted, life in camp would have become even more unbearable if I refused to join. I would likely have been the only one. On January 21, which was my tenth birthday, Papa sent me a cheerful letter welcoming me to the "brotherhood of patriotic German men." In the letter Papa reminded me that although I may be small, I was a Schott, ergo by definition I would do well. I was encouraged to make him, the nation and the Führer proud.

The DJV led directly to full Hitler Youth membership at fourteen, which led directly to full Nazi Party membership at eighteen. The distinction between DJV and regular Hitler Youth steadily dissolved over the course of the war as the older Hitler Youth leaders were sent off to the front, and it became more expedient to put mixed-aged groups of boys under the command of sixteen- and seventeen-year-olds. Felix was one of these. He was almost the classic Aryan type one consistently saw on the propaganda posters, but much less consistently in real life. He was tall and muscular with a chiselled chin and high cheekbones and blue eyes, but he had dark brown hair, not the glistening blond of the posters. At seventeen he was one of the oldest boys in camp, and by stint of his leadership in the Hitler Youth he was essentially second in command to Herr Tischendorf. Given that Herr Tischendorf was increasingly only seen at the morning flag raising and in his classroom and spent the rest of the time alone in his office (drinking bootleg plum brandy it was rumoured), Felix had more or less free rein over us. Moreover, I had the additional bad luck of having him in our dormitory. He was dormitory head boy and the camp's Hitler Youth leader all in one.

In later years I read William Golding's justly famed book, *Lord of the Flies*. Although he gained his insight into the true nature of children in the English boarding school system, he could just as easily have learned it at the KLV-Lager. It is perhaps a harsh satire of English boarding schools, but for the KLV-Lager it is simply factual description with only the setting and specific circumstances changed.

I immediately was put on chamber pot duty again. I tried my spilling trick and it did not go well.

"Schott! You swine, what did you do?"

"I am sorry, it was an accident. The bucket is so heavy."

"That's 'I am sorry, Herr Schneider,' you disrespectful little shit!" Even though he was not an adult we were expected to address him as one. I had forgotten. "You are not a baby anymore. Accidents are unacceptable in the Hitler Youth! Weakness is unacceptable in the Hitler Youth! You will clean up this piss and shit while the rest of us are at breakfast. Use your facecloth to do so."

"Sir?" This did not make sense. Nazis were many things, but they were not dirty. Cleanliness was pursued with an especially intense fervour. We may have been short of nutritious food and warm clothing, but we were never short of cleaning supplies.

"You heard me clearly! No breakfast! Facecloth! If it is not clean enough you will scrub further with your toothbrush!" This was almost farcical, like something from a Marx Brothers comedy film, but I did not laugh. I managed to clean it up well enough that it was not necessary to deploy the toothbrush. I was also placed on chamber pot duty for the next two weeks. I slopped some of the contents out once, truly by accident, but fortunately Felix did not notice before I had a chance to quickly wipe it up. I should say, "Felix and his henchmen," as there were three other older boys in our dormitory who acted as his deputies and took delight in reporting infractions to him. I do not remember their names, and their faces are interchangeable in my mind's eye. Perhaps there were even four of them.

My marching also came under scrutiny. For some reason, when we were formed in ranks and ordered to march left, I would sometimes march right. It was not an act of deliberate rebellion, nor was there anything wrong with my hearing; it was just that sometimes the command would enter my ear, sail down the nerve to my brain and then get lost somewhere on the way to the part which sorts left from right. Perhaps my brain has more twists and turns than the average brain. This was especially likely to happen when my brain was busy straining to hear a bird or noticing that a cloud was in the shape of Sweden. This had attracted bellows and corrections from Reinhard and Herr Tischendorf, but they seemed to allow a little more latitude because I was the smallest and youngest and as long as I turned 180 degrees to the correct direction right away, they would sigh, or grumble, and life would go on.

Felix, in contrast, was incensed. He screamed at me the first time I did this and smacked me on the shoulder with the butt of a wooden rifle, threatening dire consequences if I was ever so insolent again. I burst into tears, which did not help my case. I found out later that Theodor, who looked like he had been ignoring this, went on his own to Herr Tischendorf and asked him to speak to Felix about me. This must have been effective because while Felix still screamed at me and while he still tapped me hard with his wooden rifle, it was not as hard and he no longer threatened punishment. I do not think that I ever thanked Theodor for this. I suspect that he protected me in other ways that I was not aware of then.

But all of this was just an advanced level of meanness and cruelty; it was not true sadism. The first act of true sadism was after Felix had been in charge for about a week.

One of the ways being in the DJV and the Hitler Youth differed from just being a student at the camp was that there was less time devoted to sports in the afternoon and more military drills and exercises. As I mentioned before, I certainly did not love the sports, but the change was unwelcome, as the replacement activities were much worse. Also Felix did not seem particularly concerned about wrapping the exercises up in time for supper. Once we did not eat until eight in the evening as he had us out on a twelve-kilometre march across the frozen fields and overestimated how fast we would manage to do it. He was furious, screaming at us for the last two hours, but perhaps some spark of intelligence buried deep in his skull prevented him and his henchmen from beating us bloody, as I am sure he would have loved to. Beating would have slowed us down even more. This was not the sadism though. That came later that night.

Although he was a year older, Ernst was as small as me. He was in the bunk diagonally across from mine. I cannot claim that we were friends. Both being small and quiet we should have found common cause, but his interests were entirely different, and I was not especially social nor, do I think, was he. He had wispy blond hair and very delicate features. Ernst made two mistakes with Felix. The first was that he was the very slowest of all of us on the march that day. The second was that he allowed Felix to see that in the small scraps of free time we were allotted he liked to sketch, and in particular he sketched pretty scenes with flowers and little animals from his imagination. He was rather good at it too. I suppose it was his preferred means of escape, as mine was reading or watching birds, although birds were very scarce around the camp in winter. For Felix the combination of Ernst's size, appearance, flower sketching and slow marching was enough to declare him to be a homosexual. That it is even possible for an eleven-year-old to have a sexual preference is not clear, but in our *Lord of the Flies* boy culture, the word was wielded more as the ultimate insult rather than as any sort of factual observation. I suppose that is probably true in boy culture everywhere — or was. In the KLV-Lager, however, this word, this label, carried significant consequences with it. I think in English children sing, "Sticks and stones may break my bones, but words will never hurt me." Here there were sticks too. Possibly a broomstick in particular.

Felix and one of his henchmen dragged Ernst into the bathroom after lights out. He squirmed and wriggled a bit in a vain effort to get away but did not protest loudly. I saw this as it was a full moon and we did not have proper blinds. Several other boys saw this too. None of us moved or said anything. This was followed by some muffled but harsh-sounding talking from behind the bathroom door, and then silence for a moment before a long period of quiet sobbing. Several minutes later the three of them emerged from the bathroom. Ernst was walking very slowly with his legs stiff and slightly apart and then climbed gingerly into his bunk. He did not cover himself with his blanket and continued to sob quietly for as long as I was still awake, and presumably for long after that.

The next morning it was like the chirping of a flock of sparrows whenever Ernst or Felix and his henchmen were out of earshot. Rumours zipped around, overlapping each other and creating a confusion of theories. The dominant theory involved the broomstick and made my mind go blank. I suppose I had some theoretical understanding of what was being discussed, but I could not begin to properly imagine it.

I know that I should have comforted Ernst that night, but I did not. I know that I should have told Herr Tischendorf the next day, but I did not. I should have written to Papa and asked him to use his status in the Party to discipline Felix, but I did not. I was afraid for my own safety and I was ashamed by what I now understood might have happened, as if acknowledging that I knew such things could exist in the world would somehow taint me.

CHAPTER FIFTEEN

SPRING 1944

Spring is ever the season of hope. Even in the KLV-Lager. Personally I hoped that spring would bring the birds back. There were very few winter birds around the camp, but surely we would see more as the weather warmed and the snow receded. The camp also generally buzzed with renewed hope as the *Völkischer Beobachter* ("People's Observer"), the official newspaper of the government, ran optimistic article after optimistic article. Of course they did this 365 days a year, but in spring there was a greater emphasis on the prospects for victory. The more enthusiastic among the Hitler Youth would read the exciting headlines out loud at breakfast. "The Plutocrats Promise a Trail of Death in Southern Italy!" and "The Kremlin Wants to See English Blood!" These are the more obtuse examples, but it was explained to me that the first article was about how Allied troops were deliberately spreading terrible diseases like typhus in the parts of Italy they now occupied and that, to their surprise, this was greatly stiffening local resistance to them, and the second article was about how Moscow was scornful of its supposed allies and hoped that Germany would invade England.

This was a constant theme — that the Soviets and the British and Americans were not natural allies and would soon go to war against each other. Germany would side with the latter as the Anglo-Saxon Warmongers and Gangsters were generally felt to be our estranged cousins, whereas the Bolshevik Hordes were viewed as barely human. Other headlines were more straightforward: "Göbbels's Speech in Salzburg on Our Chances of Victory!" and "Führer Celebrates Five Years of Bohemia Back in the Reich!" None of it interested me much. I did want Germany to win, for selfish reasons of self-preservation as much as anything, but I treated the details of how that was going to be achieved with a mixture of boredom and bewilderment.

Felix became optimistic as well. With the melting of the ice and the lengthening of the days, much longer marches were deemed feasible. By late March he had been in charge of us for a month and felt that the tougher discipline and extra drills had strengthened us to the point that we could consider twenty-five or even thirty kilometres. I viewed this as the lesser of numerous evils. The mock combat, and the trench digging, and the obstacle courses were much more stressful and difficult. Now that the weather was better, I optimistically viewed a "march" as essentially a hike. It was a very long hike mind you, and one during which we were required to sing patriotic songs, but a hike nonetheless.

Moreover, the first one was planned to be into a reputedly beautiful forest region to the northeast. I was even a little bit excited. I would at least be able to see the trees and the birds, even if I could not stop long enough to properly admire them. Perhaps I would be able to impress everyone with my knowledge of nature. My clever chamber pot spilling trick had backfired, and Theodor had shut down any thought I had of more satirical rhymes, even though I had such a good one: "Herr Felix Schneider traegt gerne Kleider!" ("Mr. Felix Schneider loves to wear dresses.") I suppose my social instincts were poor because I thought I would be able to keep my witticism within a small trusted group. I did not have any true friends at camp, but there were some boys whom I felt I could rely on to be discrete. Theodor wisely urged me not to. He felt that it would somehow get out regardless or be overheard. After some internal debate I decided that naming the trees and birds would be a much safer way to demonstrate that I was more than just a scrawny boy with glasses who had trouble carrying a chamber pot.

Classes were cancelled on the day of the first long march. We had done extra work to make up for this for a couple days prior, but to be honest, very little of consequence was being taught anyway. Felix and Herr Tischendorf assembled us in orderly rows by the flagpole after breakfast. Tischendorf was not coming on the march as this was technically a Hitler Youth outing, not a KLV-Lager outing, and he had, in any case, some unspecified work to take care of in his office, but he was there to see us off. I remember the morning well, as it was clear and bright and there had been a touch of frost overnight, leaving random traces of it here and there. I pictured invisible bubbles of freezing air drifting along in the coldest hour before dawn, settling on this roof, but not that, painting this patch of grass sparkling white, but not that.

Felix stepped forward, his recently polished uniform buttons catching the sun and glinting brilliantly. Puffing his chest out he shouted in his best Hitlerian style, "Boys of the Hitler Youth! Today we march to strengthen our bodies! Today we march to strengthen our resolve! Today we march to strengthen our commitment to the Fatherland! But today we especially march to honour the memory of our fallen comrades! A week ago, when the Amis launched another barbaric attack on the Reich's capital." Ami was our nickname for the Americans. It was not necessarily a slur, but with the right inflection it could be. "They killed not only babies, not only women and not only elderly people, but they also killed eight of our young comrades!"

He paused to allow a quiet murmur to ripple through us. Young comrades? As in other Hitler Youth? "The 11th Hitler Youth Anti-Aircraft Battalion suffered a direct bomb hit! All the heroes in that position were killed in the defence of their beloved Reich's capital! Hitler Youth heroes as young as twelve years old died for their people! They served and honoured their Fatherland with the courage of wolves and today we will serve and honour their memory with the strength of bears!" He paused briefly again and then bellowed, "Hitler Youth! Form ranks and . . . march!"

I immediately had three thoughts. The first was today would not be a good day to march the wrong way, so pay particular attention! The second was bears are indeed strong, but do they use that strength to march for thirty kilometres *for no practical purpose*? I thought it unlikely. And the third was *Hitler Youth are firing anti-aircraft guns?* As we marched out of the camp, I fell in beside Jolf, who was always reasonably friendly to me and who seemed to be generally more tuned in to what was going on in the war.

"Hitler Youth Anti-Aircraft Battalion?" I asked quietly.

"Yes, in the cities they are replacing men sent to the front in any role that doesn't absolutely require an adult. I don't think there's an able-bodied man over the age of eighteen anywhere other than at the front now. They're mostly using full Hitler Youth, but as you see here in camp, we DJV are viewed as merely smaller Hitler Youth and in a pinch, they'll use us too. Be glad you're in camp!"

"Oh" was all I could manage.

"And do you know what else I heard?"

"No, what else?"

"There's a whole Hitler Youth Panzer Division now, the 12th SS, and I've heard they're being sent to France to be the first to greet the Allies if they try to invade!"

"That's crazy!"

"That's what I think too, but Hitler thinks that teenagers are extra-fanatical and will fight harder than adults. More hormones and no memory of a time before this government."

Discussing this openly made me nervous. We were towards the back of the column of marchers and Felix was at the front, but his henchmen were dispersed throughout. I just nodded in order to draw less attention to myself, but this mild transgression was exciting too. We were both quiet for a moment and then Jolf whispered in an even quieter tone, "Do you want to hear a joke?"

I nodded quickly.

"Hitler visits the front and talks to a soldier. Hitler asks, 'Friend, when you are in the front line under artillery fire, what do you wish for?' The soldier replies, 'That you, my Führer, stand next to me!'"

I stifled a shocked laugh, looked around me quickly to see if anyone was watching and then looked back at Jolf with wide eyes. He winked at me. This was no longer a mild transgression. This felt like talking about your grandmother's bottom or peeing in church. Fortunately, other boys were chatting quietly as well, so we did not stand out. All the chatting, transgressive and otherwise, was brought to a stop when Felix began singing the first lines of the "Horst Wessel Song" and we knew we all had to sing along with him. It was the Nazi anthem. It celebrated an early martyr to their cause who had been killed by the communists in 1930.

Raise the flag! The ranks tightly closed!
The stormtroopers march with calm, firm step!
Comrades shot by the Red Front and reactionaries.
March in spirit within our ranks.

And on it went for several stanzas. Thankfully I do not remember the rest, even though I must have sung it a hundred times.

"Forward! Forward! Blare the Bright Fanfares" was another favourite, as was "We Are the Army of the Swastika!"

We sang a few rounds of these grim Party favourites and then, as we crossed the Mulde and started heading into the dense Thuemmlitz woods, a brave lad near the front began to belt out "Hiking Is the Miller's Delight!" I joined in immediately as it was, and still is, my favourite walking song. It is decidedly non-military but also decidedly more fun. Happily, Felix did not object. Perhaps he noticed that our step became livelier with it and decided to put practicality before principle for a change.

After this song the troop was quiet as we entered deeper into the woods, leaving the small farm fields and meadows behind. Now there was a chorus of scattered birdsong with various species intermingling. You could also hear the wind in the treetops and the crunch of boots on the gravel path. Everyone remained silent, enjoying, I presumed, the birds and the vibrancy of nature in the springtime. After ten or fifteen minutes of this I thought the mood was right to begin to point out which species of bird was responsible for which song. I decided to start with a simple one so that they would not think I was showing off.

"Boys!" I called out. "Did you hear that just now? And here it is again! That is the famous robin redbreast! He stays all winter, but only sings like that in the spring and summer!"

There was silence for a moment, and then one of Felix's

henchmen bringing up the rear of the troop shouted, "Schott! Can you eat this bird?" This was followed by snickering, which confused me.

"I suppose, but he would be hard to catch and there would be very little meat . . ."

"So no, you cannot really eat this bird. Then shut your foolish donkey mouth, you little know-it-all! This is a Hitler Youth march, not a BDM stroll or a Wandervogel outing!" The BDM, or Bund Deutscher Mädel (Federation of German Maidens), was the girl's equivalent of the Hitler Youth. The comparison to girlishness made my stomach lurch and tighten. I involuntarily glanced at Ernst, who was ahead of me a little. He was looking at the ground. And the Wandervogel ("wandering birds") was a nature hiking movement in the 1920s and early '30s that the Nazis condemned as elitist and stupidly romantic. The henchman went on, "What good does it do the Hitler Youth to know what bird sings what song unless that bird can be trained to kill Bolsheviks or trained to make itself fat and jump into our pots!" This got almost everyone laughing. One of the boys behind me slapped me on the shoulder in a way that seemed good-natured but at the same time unnecessarily rough.

"You're funny, Schott! A real comedian! Robin's songs indeed." The boy chuckled and slapped me again, making me stumble a little.

Felix did not look back during any of this but just started loudly singing the "Horst Wessel Song" again.

We walked on until midday, having covered perhaps a third of the distance. Our packs were becoming heavy and the pace was flagging. Felix called a halt in a meadow that had a stream running through it. He gave us twenty minutes for lunch, which does not sound like very much, but given that lunch consisted of a piece of smelly cheese and a single, albeit thick, slice of stale potato starch bread, it was enough. We dipped our tin cups in the stream to drink from and to soak the bread in. Some boys put their sore feet in the stream too and were quickly yelled at by the rest of us to move to the downstream end. It was nice to sit in the soft grass and not be walking, even for a few minutes. At this point I noticed that the sky was darkening in the southeast. Blue-black clouds were rapidly piling up, one on top of the other, reaching towards the sun. Other boys glanced at this and looked at each other. Felix did not seem to notice or care. When the twenty minutes were up, he shouted for the troop to reassemble and begin the march onwards, directly into the weather. Nobody, least of all me, dared to suggest turning back or at least taking a shortcut to the nearest village where there would be shelter.

As I had feared, within half an hour of our lunch stop it began to rain. At first the rain was in the form of a series of light showers, but then the clouds lowered themselves onto us and began to empty out in earnest. As the morning had warmed, we stowed our coats in our rucksacks, so now we pulled these out again as quickly as we could. They were wool and not in good condition, so the protection was limited, but it was better than nothing. Felix seemed to be making a point of not putting on his coat. Thinking perhaps that he would inspire us, he also grabbed the flag from the boy behind him who had been in charge of carrying it. Yes, we marched with a flag like a proper little old-fashioned army. The Hitler Youth flag was a decidedly unimaginative derivative of the national flag — a swastika on a red background, but with the minor innovation of a white horizontal stripe across the middle. Felix turned around to face us and walked backwards, waving the flag as he exhorted us to push on and push on hard in the names of the martyred 11th Hitler Youth Anti-Aircraft Battalion, the Führer and the Fatherland. He then turned back to face forwards and began walking very fast indeed, taking comically large strides, flagpole jauntily set at an angle against his right shoulder. I remember wishing he would slip and fall in the mud as the trail was becoming boggy, but this did not happen. His khaki uniform shirt was soaked through to the skin and his arms were pink with a combination of exertion and cold. The rest of us struggled to keep up, often slipping, sometimes falling. Then the rain turned to wet snow.

From that point on the march became a debacle. It was far worse than the time we were late for supper because we were too slow. This time we were as fast as we possibly could be under the circumstances because we all knew what was at stake. We all knew the story from the previous fall when thirty Hitler Youth in the Black Forest ended up in hospital with hypothermia and pneumonia after being caught out in similar weather. Two of them died. There still was the option to leave the trail and seek shelter in a village or farm, but Felix was determined to press on with the plan. He still did not put on his coat. Even the weakest of us kept pace, but this was at least in part because Felix's own pace began to gradually, at first imperceptibly, slacken. He was not a machine after all, but I had the idea firmly implanted in my mind that he would rather die than admit an error or in any way betray the perverse standard he had set for himself. This was the first time I had seen that sort of potentially lethal fanaticism, but it would not be the last.

The only thing that prevented a Black Forest type of disaster, or worse, was another change in the weather. March is notorious for this spinning of the meteorological roulette wheel every few hours. Perhaps that is what the gods actually do. Why not? It is no less plausible than any other explanation once one is willing to accept the idea that all-powerful, but curiously invisible, beings are in control of major events. The sun came out so suddenly and so unexpectedly that we all stopped, even Felix, and some of us audibly gasped. There were several minutes of snow and sun at the same time, which I appreciated was beautiful even though I felt miserable, and then the clouds dissipated entirely. The sun was warm enough that the snow and water began to quickly evaporate off our coats in little tendrils of vapour that glowed in the sunshine. We became a column of boys threading through the forest like a steaming snake.

We arrived late back into camp, but only three boys needed to be taken to see the nurse, and there were no fatalities. Felix looked triumphant. He and his henchmen sang those blasted Nazi marching songs all through dinner, but thankfully did not seem to notice or care that most of us did not join in.

After dinner Jolf sidled up to me and whispered, "Psst, Ludwig, want to hear another one?"

No one was close enough to overhear us, so I nodded.

"One labourer says to another, 'Did you hear what the Führer said in his latest speech? He proclaimed that no one should be allowed to go hungry or suffer from the cold!' His co-worker sighs and replies, 'So now we're not even allowed to do that.'"

~

I could have had the first of my nightmares that night, but I am not sure. To be truthful, I am not even sure it was that year. Perhaps it was earlier. My memory is excellent for the real, but less so for the unreal. I will place it here as it is as good a time as any and it does not really matter. I had this nightmare many times through the latter part of the war and for years afterwards. In it I am crouched in the middle of a vast field. The field is completely flat and featureless and extends to the horizon in all directions. I am unsure of my size because there is nothing to compare against. I look for blades of grass, but there are none. The ground is a solid green-coloured material like an endless slab of painted wood or cement. The sky is cloudless blue. I am nervous, but at first I do not know why. Then I know. I begin to hear a rumbling. It is faint and very far away, but it steadily becomes louder. As it becomes louder the ground begins to shake. Soon it is so loud that I cannot stand it and I put my hands over my ears. I am still crouched in a tight ball on the ground. I squeeze my eyes shut because I know what is coming, even though I cannot put it into words, and I do not want to see it. The sound and the shaking are overwhelming. Against my will, as if torn open by an external force, my eyes open. I am surrounded by stampeding soldiers. Millions of soldiers are running past me, paying me no heed. I am tiny, much tinier than a boy, like a little insect. Their boots land heavily to either side of me, again and again and again. I close my eyes again and the overwhelming sound and the shaking continue, but I am not squashed. Once more I open my eyes and now I am enormous and they are the size of insects, like ants swarming past, parting around me as they would around a tree. Still they make this noise though, just as loud, and still the ground shakes, just as hard. Then I begin to scream. I scream and scream until I am louder than them and at that moment I am suddenly awake, screaming.

I am by far not the only boy to occasionally wake up screaming at the KLV-Lager, so nobody pays any attention.

CHAPTER

SIXTEEN

MAY 31, 1944

Leipzig was heavily bombed again by the Americans on the 29th of May. Apparently the attack had been in the small hours of the morning and by breakfast that day word had reached Herr Tischendorf that his home neighbourhood had been heavily damaged and was on fire. He took one of the two old staff cars kept parked at the KLV-Lager and left immediately.

We didn't learn any of the details until two days later, when another teacher told us the terrible story before class. He said that when Herr Tischendorf arrived, the fire was out, but the entire city block that his house had stood on had been transformed into an enormous heap of smoking rubble. Not a single wall still stood. Apparently Herr Tischendorf then began wildly clawing at the debris, heaving bricks and hunks of plaster aside. He could hear whimpering and moaning from somewhere deep in there. Civil defence workers and neighbours were digging on either side of him too, calling out to anyone who might be trapped and able to hear them.

A young girl, covered in dust and blood, was pulled out alive from what had been the neighbour's place. Herr

Tischendorf's fingers were raw and bleeding by the time he reached where he estimated his family's cellar shelter would be. The three floors had all pancaked in, collapsed and compressed and jumbled. The shelter had been no shelter. He found his disabled son, Max, first. Max's face looked peaceful, as if asleep, but his chest had been crushed. Next, he found his wife, or at least what he knew to be her from her clothing, location and size. Her body had been smashed beyond recognition.

The teacher who told us this, Herr Kraus, did so in a quiet steady voice. He was a very small man with round glasses and unruly black hair. He stood before the classroom with his hands tightly clasped before him. It was obvious that he was making an effort to control his emotion. His eyes were red rimmed. I was shocked. I was shocked by the graphic nature of the information and I was shocked that we were being told any of this at all. There was no requirement to explain Herr Tischendorf's absence. He was the head teacher and he was, in essence, our overlord, so his comings and goings were none of our business. Moreover, to this point no authority figure had told us anything that could even faintly be construed as negative about the war. Whether Herr Kraus was trying to inspire us to anger against Germany's enemies or whether he was trying to sober us with the true horror of war was unclear. Even Felix seemed unsure of how to respond. Herr Tischendorf returned after a few days and did not seem any different at first, but the rumours of his drinking plum brandy in his private office began to gather strength again, although this time with a sympathetic undertone rather than a scornful one.

In all the chaos and destruction the postal service continued to astound, for that day we received a letter from Mama dated the day of the latest bombing raid.

Dear Theodor, Dear Ludwig,

As you will have heard, Leipzig was badly attacked again this morning. They say over 10,000 buildings were damaged and half of those completely flattened. Papa thinks it is impossible for us to return home until after the war. He also understands that it is terrible for the family to be split up in four locations. He has used his connections to find a home for us in Colditz, only three kilometres from your camp. We will be able to get Clara and Johann from Aue. They are so sad and homesick there. It is a very small place though and you boys still need to go to school, so you will have to stay in camp, but you can come to our new temporary home on Sundays and holidays. We are moving immediately, so I will see you this Sunday.

Your Mama

It was a Wednesday, so we would see Mama, Clara and Johann in just four days! To go from the horror of hearing Herr Tischendorf's story to the jubilation of this news in the span of an hour caused a kind of emotional whiplash that led me to being unable to concentrate for the rest of the day.

~

On Sunday, immediately after the mandatory flag raising, anthem singing and "Heil Hitler" saluting but before breakfast, Theodor and I excused ourselves from camp and set off for Colditz. Even though it was so close, we had never been there with the Hitler Youth or for any other purpose. It was an easy forty-minute walk down a road through flat farm country along the Zwickauer Mulde river, southeast of Schönbach. There were many people out in the fields. I did not know very much about farming, but it looked like they were hoeing weeds. I was surprised by the number of them and by the fact that they all wore the same loose-fitting grey clothing. They were absolutely silent as they worked, and none of them looked up at us. When I asked Theodor about them, he said that they were labourers from Poland. I did not think to inquire further, and Theodor would not have known more then anyway, but later I would learn that these were in fact not just labourers but *slave* labourers, who endured inhuman conditions and were often worked to death.

Colditz is important in this story, so I will take a moment to describe it properly. At the time there were probably about 6,000 normal inhabitants, but because it was a desirable place for bomb refugees to escape to, not only from Leipzig but also from Dresden and Chemnitz, I am sure that the population by the time we arrived was easily double this. The reason it was so desirable is very interesting. Dominating the town was the ancient Colditz Castle, first built in the year 1083 by Count Wiprecht of Groitzsch, the Margrave of Meissen and the Saxon Ostmark. The castle that stands now dates from 1506, as the medieval one was badly damaged in a fire that also destroyed most of Colditz. I was told that the fire was accidentally started by a baker in town. At the start of the war the Nazis gave Colditz Castle a new and thoroughly bureaucratic name: Oflag IV-C. Oflag IV-C was established as Germany's most secure prisoner-of-war camp. "Oflag" is short for Offizier's Lager, or "officer's camp," as its prisoners were all Allied officers. And these were not just any Allied officers. These were top-ranked officers, those considered "incorrigible" and especially those who had attempted to escape from other POW camps. This is why Colditz was a desirable destination for refugees and why Papa pulled every string he could to find us a place here — the Allies would never bomb this town.

The castle is set high atop seventy-five-metre cliffs on the east bank of the Zwickauer Mulde. The river draws a lazy backwards S through the western edge of town with a little of it to the west and most to the east, under the castle. Papa had found us two rooms in the 400-year-old Colditzer Brewery, on the east side, right on the market square beside a bakery. Whether that was the notorious bakery from 1506, I do not know, but I liked to imagine so. We were only a hundred metres from the castle wall. I write "we" although Theodor and I did not sleep there and really had no right to feel any sense of belonging other than that was where our mother now lived and so was as close to the definition of home as we were going to get under the circumstances. The town itself was beautiful. Because it was on the riverbank, many streets were steep and winding and all were paved with cobblestones. On some streets the houses were the medieval half-timbered style and on other streets the houses were an ornate baroque style with coloured plaster. The Colditzer Brewery was the latter and the plaster was a mocha coffee colour with darker brown trim. Papa had rented two rooms for us in the back, facing away from the square. There was a small iron stove in the main room for heat and cooking and heating wash water, and Mama and the three little ones slept in two small beds in the adjacent room. The toilet was a privy in the lane. This was a considerable reduction in living circumstances from Tante Karoline's in Mellingen (let alone our beautiful house in Leipzig), but Mama was delighted to be out from under her sister's ever-critical gaze and to be once again mistress of her own domestic realm, no matter how diminished.

"Theodor and I could sleep here." I pointed to the floor

beside the stove after the happy greetings were all done and I had had a good look around.

"No, Ludwig, I'm sorry," Mama said. "You need to stay at the KLV-Lager. There is no school here that you can go to."

"It is very close, Mama. We can walk there every morning and walk home every evening!"

"No, I'm really sorry, truly I am, but I don't think they would permit that. The camp needs to be kept secure and they can't have boys just coming and going. Also there's your father to consider. He will not let you leave the Hitler Youth and they often have activities very early and very late. And the floor here? There would barely be enough space." She did look remorseful as she said all this. Theodor must have realized that she was right as he hated the KLV-Lager as much as I did, but he did not jump in to bolster my arguments. He just sat quietly on the bench against the one wall, absentmindedly rolling a ball back and forth to Oskar, who was sitting on the floor nearby.

"But Mama, with Papa's position there must be a way to bend . . ."

Mama cut me off. "Are you going to be a lawyer like your father with all these arguments? It is just not possible. You know how your father is about the rules. If the Party said do not breathe on Sundays, he would hold his breath until he passed out."

I was about to make a bitter remark about his respect for marriage rules but fortunately thought the better of it. It was especially fortunate because at that moment Papa appeared in the door. He was dressed in one of his fashionable light brown Sunday suits, complete with a wide brimmed hat and a green hatband that matched his tie and pocket square. He had a bundle of spring flowers in one hand for Mama and a small sack of sweets for us children in his other hand. He and Mama gave each other pecks on the cheek and Mama took the flowers without an audible thank you. The five of us stared at the sweets the way a pack of hyenas would stare at a juicy bone.

Papa said, "Children, you will share this in the manner that old Germanic law dictates: the eldest will divide the sweets into five piles and then the youngest will choose first, followed by the second youngest and so on."

This was objectively fair and wise, but subjectively annoying as I would be the last child to pick who did not have the honour of being responsible for the division.

After carefully putting my allotment of sweets into my pocket I asked, "Papa, did you walk from Grimma?" I am sure the tone of wonder was clear in my voice. Not only was Grimma fifteen kilometres away, but with Papa's stiff leg and his attire the mental image was absurd. Nonetheless, I knew that there were no trains from Leipzig to Colditz on Sundays.

He chuckled. "No, my son, I was able to get a car. The driver will wait with it at the café on the market square for as long as I need. I can stay a few hours at least."

There was a long moment of quiet as it seemed nobody knew what to do next. We had not all been together since early December, which seemed like a very long time ago. Interactions with Papa had always been somewhat formal and usually took place in the context of the deeply embedded routine back home in Leipzig. Here in Colditz we were unmoored from these routines and consequently stood there, looking at each other with pasted-on smiles, unsure of what was desirable, permissible or appropriate to do next. Mama snorted quietly and turned her attention to Oskar, who was beginning to fuss. Papa stood just inside the doorway for a few moments longer until, having apparently made up his mind, he declared, "It is Sunday and it is a lovely day, so we shall take a walk."

"All the little ones need baths, but you can take Theodor and Ludwig," Mama said without looking at him.

And so the three of us set off.

"May we go to the castle, Papa?" I asked.

"No, Ludwig, no children are allowed there. That's where they keep the most important enemy prisoners. Even I would need a special pass. We can look at it from below though." He led us out into the main market square, nodding briefly to his driver as we walked past him and offering the Hitler salute to a pair of SS officers walking the other way across the square. "The best view is from the bridge," he explained. This was not far, so within a couple minutes we were standing at the east end of the bridge, looking back across the centre of town and up at the castle, which loomed over everything from its vantage point crowning a high rock outcrop. The castle was a confusion of white buildings of varying sizes and shapes abutting each other at odd angles. Each building had numerous small barred windows, and each was surmounted by a sloped red-tiled roof. Square towers jutted out from some of these buildings and the whole thing was encircled by a windowless white wall about a quarter of the height of the tallest buildings within.

"See how large it is? It has 700 rooms. Currently about 500 enemy officers are kept in there and we have about seventy men guarding and supervising them. The walls are two metres thick; the cliff faces, as you can see, are shear and there is only one way in or out. And even if by some magic trick a prisoner managed to get out, he would find himself in the very middle point of the Reich, 650 kilometres from the nearest border!"

"Has anyone escaped so far?" I asked in a cautious tone. The thought of so many enemies so close by was a little bit frightening, but more in the way of a scary story than a true threat. I wondered whether some of these men were looking out of those windows right now, seeing us on the bridge looking up at them.

Papa hesitated briefly. "No, it is absolutely escape-proof. It is the most secure prison in the Reich and probably in the world."

~

Later, after Papa left and I described our viewing of the castle, Mama told us a story about her encounter with Allied prisoners in the First World War. She explained that some French officers were being held in a prisoner-of-war camp in Weimar, where she grew up. She would have been between ten and twelve years of age at the time.

The German and Allied governments had concluded an agreement in 1916 that permitted each other's officers to leave their prisons to go for walks, so long as they signed a document promising on their honour as officers that they would not take advantage of this privilege to make an escape attempt. Imagine this! Such was the trust in an officer's sense of honour at the time. And imagine such a thing being a priority for negotiation between bitter enemies in the midst of the slaughter of millions! In any case, a preferred walking path for the French officers in Weimar took them past Mama's house. She would make a point of watching for them and going up to greet them across the garden fence using correct and polite French. Mama was very proud of the fact that she learned French as a child. Thuringia, which Weimar was the capital of, had been an ally of Napoleon a hundred years prior, and a cultural connection to France had remained, at least among the intellectual elite, which Mama fancied her family belonged to.

As far as she knew, no officers on either side ever broke their promise. All of them returned to prison after their walks and then in some cases would go back to working on plans to escape from within by tunnelling or hiding in laundry trucks and so forth. This was apparently permitted under the code of honour. It perhaps goes without saying that such a civilized agreement was not in force during the Second World War. More's the pity.

CHAPTER

SEVENTEEN

JUNE 6, 1944

A history enthusiast will recognize this date immediately. On June 6, 1944, the American, British and Canadians landed in great force on the beaches of Normandy, France. I have no specific memory of this day. It was a Tuesday, so it would have been an ordinary day at the KLV-Lager. I mention it here to allow you to place the events in my little life in the greater historical context. I am sure that the news reached us within the next day or two, but again I do not recall this specifically other than some general chatter about the bravery of the SS Panzer Hitlerjugend division in the early days of the invasion. It turns out that Hitler was right about one thing: these young lads reportedly fought with a ferocity that terrified the enemy. They appeared to have no fear of death whatsoever. The thought of this terrified me as well.

As an aside, at some point after the war I found out that Hitler had slept in that morning! He and Göbbels were in the Berghof, Hitler's retreat in the Bavarian Alps, and had been up until three in the morning, reminiscing about the good old days. Hitler knew that an invasion was imminent but felt certain that it would be farther north towards Calais where the English Channel was at its narrowest. Rundstedt and Rommel, his two chief generals in France, had disagreed on the appropriate defensive strategy with respect to the placement of the all-important panzer divisions. Rather than make a decision, or give the authority to decide to one of them, Hitler stated that the panzer divisions were to be left where they were and that they were only to be moved on his direct orders. On the morning of D-Day both generals saw that the panzers needed to be moved to Normandy immediately, but neither dared to ignore Hitler's orders, and his aides at the Berghof did not want to wake him in case it was a false alarm. You see, Hitler had just the day before warned everyone around him not to be fooled because the Allies would make a fake landing before they made the real one. They finally woke him at noon. Apparently, he was pleased by the news as he believed that the German forces were so superior that any invasion would be repelled, and it was time to get it over with and crush the Allies' foolish hopes. Then all those divisions could finally be moved to Russia where they were really needed. Now some historians believe the delay in the arrival of the panzers may have made the difference. The success of D-Day hung in the balance and Hitler's late night with Göbbels tipped it. I have always disliked staying up late.

Be that as it may, one way or another alea iacta est, as Papa would say. The die is cast. A third front had been opened. Enemies were now approaching from the south, the east and the west, pressing in inexorably like massive screws being turned one slow quarter turn at a time. All around me was optimistic talk, but whether it was inborn pessimism on my part, precocious realism or somehow being attuned to deeper currents, I could not internalize this optimism. I wanted to believe, but I could not. This whole enterprise — the Nazis, the KLV-Lager, the Hitler Youth, the Reich — now had a distinct whiff of doom about it. I did not care about any of that though. I cared only what it meant for me and for my family. The propaganda was very effective. If the Russians got to us first, they would kill or enslave everyone, and they would destroy everything. If the Americans and British were first, it would be better but only marginally, as Roosevelt was a gangster and Churchill a murderer and both were in any case Stalin's stooges and would do his bidding. The world had gone from feeling vast and boundless, as I am sure it does for most children, to feeling alarmingly claustrophobic. I could not directly confront these feelings. What ten-year-old could? An obsession with the concept of escape began to take hold of my thoughts.

CHAPTER

EIGHTEEN

SUMMER 1944

Within weeks of the move to Colditz I found an escape of sorts. Sundays with Mama and the family in the brewery rooms were already an escape from the hated KLV-Lager, but they were not an escape from the war and the impending cataclysm.

The town was full of soldiers and our immediate neighbour blared his Volksempfänger through the thin walls whenever he was home, which evidently included most Sundays. Herr Rittmann worked in some capacity up at the castle and would wag his finger at me when he saw me walking by. "Don't let those dirty Tommies or Kanaken get a hold of you. We try to keep them in, but sometimes one slips out." (Tommies were British and Kanaken were Canadians. The French, Dutch and Poles had largely been moved out to other camps and the Americans were yet to arrive.) This contradicted what Papa had told me, and I made a mental note to ask Mama. In the first few months Papa often visited, and while it was good that he came, he was also a direct reminder of the war and a particular focus of worry with respect to how it would all end.

No, the town of Colditz was not the escape I needed. The escape I needed was a kilometre directly west of town in the Colditzer Forst. (No, I did not miss an E in that word. The explanation will come soon enough.) I could see it from the road as we walked to Colditz from Schönbach on Sunday mornings and was immediately curious. Just beyond the fields to my right was an unbroken line of dense green. It seemed to be mostly conifers, probably firs, but with clumps of deciduous trees scattered through as well.

After the first several visits, certainly by early July, it became clear that we did not need to hang around our two small rooms all day. When Papa was visiting from Leipzig, he was satisfied with a greeting, a perfunctory report of the week's activities in the Hitler Youth and perhaps a short family walk. In total this might take up an hour of the day. Afterwards, as soon as it seemed appropriate to do so, Theodor would leave to seek out his friends who were also in town. Mama was often busy with the little ones and would encourage me to go out and see my friends as well. She seemed unaware that my time in the KLV-Lager and the Hitler Youth had not done anything to enhance my social standing and that I did not have any friends to visit, but she also did not seem especially concerned about what I did so long as I returned for our early supper before we had to walk back to the camp.

The Colditzer Forst was quite unlike the forest along the Pleisse in Leipzig. This was a true forest, with no urban noises or smells to mar it. Much as I am told Inuit have multiple words for snow, we Germans have multiple words for forest that each carry a distinct meaning. This forest was technically called a Forst rather than a Wald or an Urwald. (Incidentally, for some reason all nouns are capitalized in German.) A Forst is a forest that has been planted by man recently enough that if you look at the right angle, you will see that the trees are growing in regular rows. These are working forests that provide building lumber and firewood. An Urwald, on the other hand, is an original wild forest that has never ever been logged. These are rare in Germany. More common is a Wald, which was probably logged at some point, perhaps in the Middle Ages, but has regrown in a more or less wild fashion, perhaps with some areas of more recent Forst mixed in. Although the Colditzer forest was called a Forst, I considered it a Wald, as it looked and felt quite wild to me.

Fears about escaped Tommies and Kanaken notwith-standing, I walked past the castle and over the bridge to the west with confidence and excitement. Immediately upon entering the forest the temperature became cooler, the light more diffuse and the smells more of moist earth and pine needles. At first it was silent, as if everything had stopped and held its breath when I entered. Then the birdsong began — first a twitter here, a chirp there, and then the full ensemble. I could have wept. The area immediately around the KLV-Lager had remained an avian desert for some reason, even through spring. And the trees, the glorious trees! As I had expected on viewing the forest from the Schönbach road, it was primarily tall straight firs. In a true Forst these would all be of a uniform age with no under-growth. But as I mentioned, in my opinion this was a Wald, not a Forst. I stood there, breathing in the magnificent air and listening to my friends, or rather to those I knew would soon become my friends. Theodor had his friends to visit and now I would have mine.

The path into the forest divided into three, running roughly west, northwest and southwest. The path to the west was absolutely straight, as if marked on a map with a ruler, and extended as far as I could see between rows of uniform trees like sentries lined at attention. While this symmetry had its own beauty, I was drawn to the northwest path, which was narrower and began to bend and wind right after the intersection. I could see some oaks, birches, beeches and ash trees scattered amongst the taller darker green firs. There were also more shrubs and small bushes along the northwest path. This was much more appealing to me and I reasoned that it would be much more appealing to the birds and animals.

I was right. Soon the main path disappeared from view and I was truly immersed in the woods. As expected, along this winding path the birds were more numerous. They hopped along the branches, flew back and forth over the path and sang to each other from all directions. The path soon split and split again, but I had no fear of becoming lost. Although the sun was not visible through the trees, I still had a strong sense of direction. My mind automatically mapped the twists and turns and forks in the trail, so I was always able to find my way back without having made any particular effort of memorization. I thought that everyone could do this, that it was a basic human trait, but apparently that is not the case. After one right turn and two left turns I came to a small glade. To the left was a stand of very uniform firs, but ahead and to the right it was a lovely mixed hardwood forest. But what got my full attention was a beautiful cluster of five oak trees, alone on a very slight rise in the middle of the glade. These trees were massive. They must have been very old — not as old as the famous Ivenacker Oak in the north which is said to have sprung from an acorn in the late 900s AD — but since the largest was two metres wide at its base, it was at least 200 years old.

This was it. This was the spot. All it took was an easy forty-five-minute walk from Colditz. Considering the direction and distance, I realized that I was likely only about forty-five minutes from the KLV-Lager, with a line south from the camp and a line west from Colditz intersecting at ninety degrees at the oaks. This realization floated up in my mind like a bright red balloon on a grey day. I found a smooth boulder in the shade under the largest oak and sat down on it. The Hitler Youth could not touch me here. The enemy could not touch me here. The war could not touch me here. That this was illogical magical thinking did not occur to my conscious mind. I felt I had stepped through a portal into another, better world. In this world I would be a forest ranger and keep the forest safe. I would know how to build a small house — correction, a small treehouse! — and I would know how to find food and keep myself safe and healthy and happy. *Winnetou* had useful information regarding this and was a good start, but I would assemble a small library to help. No actual people besides me were required in this world.

This extended reverie was interrupted by a quiet staccato chirp from the bushes to my left. It had a squeaky character to it that made my heart leap. Could it be? I listened intently. There was a background hubbub from a score of other birds in the trees all around, but I was able to mentally delete these and listen only for the one sound. Then came the confirmation: a bubbly cascade of cheerful song, rising and falling, but ever the aural essence of joy. It was a wren! Perhaps even my wren! The Fence King!

Leipzig was at least forty kilometres away in a direct line as the wren flies, but some wrens fly much further when they migrate, so it was not out of the question that "my wren" would flee the bombed-out city and coincidentally find the same refuge as I did. Improbable, but not impossible. Given that this forest and this glade and these oaks in particular already felt enchanted and somehow outside of the normal rules that govern the world, I decided that he was indeed the same wren. This was perhaps the best day of my life since the war had begun.

I continued to listen to his song while watching the bushes intently. After a long few minutes there he was, just as he had been back along the Pleisse, flitting along the ground, low and fast, keeping away from the other birds, attending to his own business with characteristic verve. I could have happily watched him for hours and hours while planning my future life in the forest, but I was aware of the consequences of returning late to Colditz. Besides, this would all be here for every Sunday to come. I said a silent goodbye to the Fence King, stood up, dusted myself off and looked around. One path out of the glade went into the stand of firs to the south. My sense of direction told me that this would likely be an alternative path into and out of this place, so it was worthwhile to explore it on my way back home. I knew that if I made a couple left turns to ultimately orient myself eastwards, I would pop out of the forest near the hamlet of Hohnbach, only a few hundred metres south-west of Colditz.

This took me into a very deep part of the forest where the firs still dominated but were very old. They blocked most of the light and their needles made the ground acidic, so not much else grew other than mushrooms. As I made my last turn to point myself towards the eastern edge of the woods, I saw something that made my heart jump into my throat. There, off to the side of this small path, was a rough ring of stones with blackened wood in the middle. The wood was still smouldering slightly. A few tin cans lay nearby and a piece of grey cloth, possibly a towel, hung from a low branch. Somebody had camped here or was still camping here! Perhaps they had heard me coming and run away? Perhaps this was their lunch fire and they were out gathering food and would return in the evening? Or return immediately? Or were watching me right now?

I ran. I ran so fast, the trees blurred, my legs deciding where and when to turn. After maybe fifteen minutes I was out of the forest, right at Hohnbach.

I did not want to tell Mama about any of this, but I felt I had to tell someone. On the walk back to camp I decided to describe the campfire to Theodor. I did not tell him about the glade with the oaks though. I had the irrational feeling that telling someone would disrupt the magic. I asked him whether it was escaped prisoners.

"No, Ludwig. You heard Papa — nobody escapes from the castle. Herr Rittmann was just trying to scare you. And even if they did escape, they would not be so foolish as to camp so close by. If I were an Allied prisoner I would make for the Swiss border as fast as I possibly could, and that's south, not west."

"Oh, okay, that makes sense. Who do you think it was then?"

Theodor lowered his voice, even though there was nobody anywhere close by who could overhear. "Probably deserters."

"Deserters?"

"Yes, men who have been recruited but do not want to serve in the Wehrmacht." He lowered his voice further, glancing around before he spoke again. "Can you blame them? Get killed in Russia or Italy or France — take your pick. Better to lay low and eat mushrooms and rabbits in the forest for a few years."

"Are they dangerous?"

"No. You should be careful if you're in there by yourself, but you don't have to worry about those guys. They do not want to be seen by anyone, not even little boys."

This made me feel better, but I drew a mental wall between the part of the forest with the glade and the other part of the forest with the campfire. I managed to make this wall impermeable so that no worry could get through it, under it or over it. Still, I could not avoid the peripheral awareness that the worry was out there, a small formless dark shape beyond the wall, like something not quite visible out of the furthest corner of your eye.

CHAPTER

NINETEEN

AUTUMN 1944

One Sunday in the autumn of that year stands out. Lunch, such as it was — just a thin potato soup I think — was finished and Mama asked me to take seven-year-old Johann outside to play. I wanted to get to the forest, but I agreed. Playing with young children was tiresome, but I understood my duty. No, at ten I did not consider myself one of the "young children" anymore in that sense. I was not old, but I was not young either. I was much closer to being a teenager than to being in diapers. We went out in the lane to toss a ball back and forth. Johann was already more interested in sports than I was, or ever would be, but ball tossing was really more of a game than a true sport, so I tolerated this. We had only passed it back and forth four or five times when there was the sudden sharp report of a gun behind and above us, from the castle. Johann dropped the ball. This was followed by a couple of seconds of silence, and then several more shots in rapid succession: *bang bang bang bang bang*. I fancied I could hear shouting from up there too, but that seems improbable. I certainly did sometimes hear dogs barking though. That sound carries further than people shouting.

We ran inside to tell Mama.

"Yes, I heard that too," she said.

"What is happening?" I asked.

"Perhaps an escape attempt."

"An escape attempt? But they never succeed, so the prisoner has been shot. That is what the shooting was?"

Mama sighed and put down the sewing she was working on. She looked at me for a moment, as if trying to decide something. "Did your father tell you that they never succeed?"

"Yes."

"That's not true. Several have escaped, but the Party doesn't want people to know that."

"Is this because they do not want the people to be afraid?"

Mama laughed out loud, which startled me. "Ha! No, Ludwig. It's because of pride and because they don't want people to lose confidence in them. They have too much pride to admit that their unescapable very best top security prison has flaws. The truth would undermine confidence in the government. People might think, 'If they are wrong about this, what else could they be wrong about?'"

I digested this information for a minute. I had several questions. "Mama, should I be scared if prisoners are getting out?"

"No, you don't need to be scared. When the war ends and the Allies march in here, I do not know what will happen or how those soldiers will behave." I took note of the definitive "when." "But I do know that these officers who might escape are just interested in getting to the border as fast as possible and aren't interested in attracting attention by hurting anyone, least of all children."

This confirmed Theodor's view and it made sense. I was relieved. "How are they getting out?" I wanted to know.

I knew this would occupy my puzzle-solving mind for a while, because the castle looked so redoubtable.

"Nothing is ever confirmed of course, only rumours. Herr Rittmann works as a bricklayer up there and he has to repair some of the holes the prisoners make in their attempts. When he has had a few drinks, he likes to tell stories. Maybe he exaggerates or is trying to impress people with his stories, but they seem true to me. You have to remember, Ludwig, that these prisoners are the best and smartest from the other side. Many of them are there because they have already escaped from other prisons. The second thing you have to remember is that they have lots and lots of time on their hands. Officers can't be made to work like regular prisoners, so I imagine that they spend all day dreaming up ways of getting out. And the final thing to remember is that Colditz Castle was not built as a prison, it was built as a castle! Castles are designed to keep people out, not in. This still means big thick walls and sitting high up on the cliffs and only one main door, but it also means that there are parts of the design, such as the sewers and laundry system and kitchens and guards' quarters that could represent weak spots from the inside."

"Oh . . ." This was fascinating to me. Even Johann, who had ignored the first part of the conversation, perked up. Clara had also come over to listen. Papa incidentally was not there. His Sunday visits had become increasingly sporadic through the summer. Party duties kept him occupied eighteen hours a day, seven days a week, he wrote.

"So, you can maybe imagine what sorts of schemes they come up with. I have to do laundry now and start thinking about how to feed you guys for supper."

"Oh Mama, tell us one escape story please!"

"No, I said I'm busy now. It's a good puzzle for you to think about how you would do it. Escape skills are important sometimes. I'll ask Herr Rittman if he knows what happened today and I will tell you next week."

It was still a long time until supper and the clothes all looked clean, but I did not argue with Mama. Perhaps she would not ask Herr Rittman if I raised a fuss now. I excused myself and left to visit the forest, but on the way I stopped on the bridge and looked for a long while up at the castle. I reasoned that if I wanted to escape it I would wait until night and then I would climb to the roof of the tallest tower and take a parachute I had secretly made of bedsheets and jump in the direction of the river where the drop was the longest. Then I would swim downstream to confuse the dogs. I would do this if I were not afraid of heights and if I had better climbing ability and if I could swim. I reasoned that if I were old enough to be in prison, I would be old enough to have overcome those three impediments.

~

The following Sunday was rainy and cold. Again Papa did not come to Colditz, which made it four weekends in a row. I understood why though, as at camp we had been hearing a lot of news, both through formal announcements and rumours. It seemed the war was drawing nearer to Germany itself. The Allies had finally bumped up against the Siegfried Line, which was the fortified western border of the Reich. They had tried to jump over it with para-troopers, but we defeated that attempt just last week. They could not cross the Rhine!

More ominously, and this was of course from the rumours, not the news, we heard that most of the civil authorities in Aachen had fled during an intense Allied assault. These were the equivalents of Papa and his colleagues at the Ortsgruppe. Aachen was the westernmost city in Germany and was very important, not so much from a military perspective as from a symbolic one: it would be the first German city to fall and it was the capital of the "First Reich," founded by Charlemagne over a thousand years ago. I heard that the top officials were executed for their cowardice and that everyone else who fled was stripped of their ranks and sent to the Russian front as privates, which was in essence a delayed form of execution. I wondered, "When they get to Leipzig, what will Papa do?"

But although it was inexorably coming closer, the major land war still felt safely distant. Of more immediate interest were the goings-on in the castle. As soon as I had taken my wet coat off and wiped my muddy shoes on the mat, I asked Mama whether she had spoken to Herr Rittman.

"Yes, Ludwig, I did. He told me an interesting story. Apparently a well-known British officer named Lieutenant Sinclair was killed. There have been several dozen escape attempts, but no one had been shot dead before. Our guards are good at shooting to injure or frighten, rather than to kill."

"Why do they not want to kill them?"

"They are too valuable. They can be used to trade for our own officers. Also their good treatment ensures the good treatment of our men. It is said that we even have Prime Minister Churchill's nephew in there and that Hitler has said that anyone who harms him in the slightest way will pay for it with their head!"

"Wow!"

I remember how pleased Mama was that I was enjoying the story so far. In retrospect I realize that she loved to gossip, and this, I suppose, counted as a sort of gossip.

"Sinclair had made five previous escape attempts. Twice from another prison and three times from Colditz. On two occasions he was caught again very near the border. Imagine how frustrating that must have been for him! Herr Rittman told me of one attempt where the lieutenant and his confederates carefully copied Rothenberger's uniform. Rothenberger is one of the top guard's officers. Imagine this: they even melted down bits of lead pipe from the bathroom to pour into handmade clay moulds to make copies of the buttons and eagle insignia! They also recreated his moustache and carefully cut Sinclair's hair in the same style as Rothenberger. Sinclair was the size and shape of Rothenberger, and he spoke fluent German. He then spent months before this attempt carefully observing Rothenberger's mannerisms. I think you can guess what the plan was. When it was dark, Sinclair, disguised as Rothenberger, marched up to one of the sentries at the gate and demanded it be opened. The prisoners had paid attention to the sentry rotation schedule and had picked this one because he was the newest and seemed the least confident. They were mistaken. The sentry replied that he was under strictest orders not to open the gate for any reason at this hour. Only the commander, Oberst Prawitt, could override it. Sinclair was relentless though. He kept demanding and then began shouting, threatening court martial. This attracted the attention of other guards, including the real Stabsfeldwebel Rothenberger!"

I gasped.

Mama chuckled. "That was, as you can imagine, the end of that attempt. Then last week he tried again. The sixth time. He had his friends create a diversion by pretending to try to escape out the far side of the castle while he rushed the wall. There are actually several rings of walls on the side we can't see, away from the big cliffs. He got over the first when they fired the warning shot. He kept running to the second wall. He was killed by the next shots. After all those creative and carefully thought-out plans, this one seemed silly and doomed. It was especially silly since the prisoners have homemade radios in there, according to Herr Rittman. They know what's going on. They know the Allies will come eventually. Perhaps he was going mad with frustration and impatience to get out. Herr Rittman said that they gave him a proper funeral with full military honours. Our guards even sewed a British flag for the coffin."

This level of respect between combatants who would happily kill each other on the battlefield seemed strange to me, but also wonderful and moving. The adult world and how people in it related to each other was complicated and I feared I would have trouble understanding the rules when I got to that age. If I got to that age.

CHAPTER TWENTY

DECEMBER 26, 1944

The second day of Christmas, 1944. This is not a
Christmas story though. I will explain, but to do so I
need to start with what happened in July.

A very serious, almost successful, assassination attempt
had been made on Hitler on July 20. That, combined with
the Allied breakthrough out of Normandy, changed many
things, most of which I did not learn about until later, but
one of which was presented in a proclamation by Hitler
Youth leader Artur Axmann in late September (just after
Sinclair's death as it happens), read out to us by Felix in
front of the flagpole:

> As the sixth year of war begins, Adolf Hitler's
> youth stands prepared to fight resolutely and
> with dedication for the freedom of their lives
> and their future. We say to them: you must
> decide whether you want to be the last of an
> unworthy race despised by future generations,
> or whether you want to be part of a new time,
> marvellous beyond all imagination.

What I did not know then was that after the assassination attempt, Hitler purged the General Staff of over 200 top officers, mostly executing them by firing squad, including the plot leader Claus von Stauffenberg, but apparently also hanging some of them from meat hooks and allowing them to slowly die that way. The executed were not only plot supporters but also officers who were suspected of opposing Hitler's plan for Germany to go down heroically in apocalyptic flames, fighting to the very last man. This was the Götterdämmerung, the "Twilight of the Gods," that had become Hitler's final fantasy. If he could not win the war — which he still did hope to do with some sort of miracle weapon like an atom bomb or by having the Allies turn on the Soviets — then he would lose it in the glorious fashion described in the last part of his favourite opera, *The Ring of the Nibelung*, where the old Germanic/Norse gods are vanquished in an orgy of world-ending destruction.

Even without this background information, Reichsjugendführer Axman's speech was highly alarming. We knew enough of the war's progress to read between the lines. Men were being consumed on the Russian front like wheat through a threshing machine. Now with the success of the D-Day invasions it was a simple math problem: more soldiers were needed, but they were dying faster than they could be replaced by men of military age. Ergo, change the definition of military age. Sixteen was now the age for mandatory enlistment, and much younger children were being accepted as volunteers. A story circulated that the Americans had captured an eight-year-old boy in Aachen who was shooting at them in uniform (presumably much too large). In any case, the sixteen- and seventeen-year-olds steadily left camp through October, including of course Felix, who was absolutely jubilant to get his chance to leave us snot-nosed weaklings behind and directly engage the Bolshevik Hordes or the Anglo-Saxon

Gangsters. I can still hear him singing at the top of his lungs as he and his group of recruits marched out of camp at dawn on a crisp autumn day.

This brings me to the second day of Christmas. Theodor and I were back at camp from two days in Colditz when we heard the news that Felix had been killed. No doubt many of the other Hitler Youth recruits had been killed too, but Felix's younger brother was still at the KLV-Lager with us and had been told by Herr Tischendorf. I thought perhaps a general announcement would be made, but there was none. Most of the boys had been sent to poorly equipped Volkssturm units — literally "people's storm," but the meaning was "people's army" — on the Russian front, but Felix had been relatively fortunate. Those considered to have elite potential, or those with connections, could get assigned to the depleted 12th SS Panzer Hitlerjugend division instead. You may recall that this was the unit that had gained notoriety in Normandy for the savagery of its boy soldiers. So, it was the Gangsters, not the Hordes for Felix. He met his end trying to storm the American position on Elsenborn Ridge in eastern Belgium in the Second Battles of the Ardennes, or what in the English-speaking world is more commonly referred to as the Battle of the Bulge.

The story grew that Felix had rushed the position alone, through machine gun fire, while the others had wavered. His brother speculated that it was a selfless suicide charge with a grenade to protect his comrades. I speculated that he tripped and accidentally pulled the pin out too soon. But with uncharacteristic discretion, I kept that speculation to myself.

The camp had changed. The deployed older teens had been replaced by another wave of younger children from the increasingly uninhabitable cities. The leadership had shifted to the more mature fifteen-year-olds and a handful of elderly veterans who had been assigned to KLV-Lager

Schönbach. If the lower cut-off for service had been reset to sixteen, the upper had been raised to sixty. Herr Tischendorf was just over sixty and so retained his position as titular head, but the "Felix role" was taken up by a short bald man named Hauptmann (Captain) Kohl. He walked with a distinct limp, shouted a lot and was forever telling us about his derring-do in leading various charges out of the trenches in the First World War. I immediately thought, "Der Hauptmann Kohl: sein Kopf ist hohl!" ("Captain Kohl: his head is hollow!"). It was a jaunty little rhyme that had a particularly pleasing rhythm, but I did not share it with anyone and soon stopped humming it to myself.

One of Kohl's first acts was to implement live-fire military exercises for the fourteen- and fifteen-year-olds, which included Theodor. Given the increasingly dire straits the German military industry and supply services found themselves in, this meant that these exercises were conducted with eighty- and ninety-year-old rifles. The widely accepted, albeit whispered, story was that some of them were quite literally museum pieces. Nobody was visiting museums anymore anyway. This was terrifying, so terrifying. There were several injuries from backfiring and other malfunctions, but no fatalities at least. We also had to fortify the camp by digging trenches all around it and constructing tank traps out of three sharpened logs fastened to each other at right angles to create a large six-pointed object. How this would stop tanks, which could presumably just blast them out of the way with their cannons, was unclear to me, but I knew not to ask.

Worst of all, Kohl declared that we were all to be instructed in guerilla warfare tactics. I write "worst of all" because of what this implied. It implied that even if — or was the leadership beginning to accept that it was a "when" not an "if"? — Germany lost the war, we were expected to continue to fight as an underground resistance group. It also implied that the "we" who were expected to continue to fight included all Hitler Youth. In fact the very youngest like myself might even make better guerillas because we would be less suspicious to the occupiers. At first we thought it was just Kohl's kooky idea, but rumours began to spread of the High Command's Werewolf plan, which was exactly that — a guerilla army that would fight on no matter what, sort of in the way that the Yugoslav Partisans and French Resistance had continued to fight us.

Theodor told me that he thought all of this was silly and that I should not worry. They would not make ten- and eleven-year-olds fight. He did not comment on the fact that as a fourteen-year-old he was in much greater danger of being drawn into the fighting, either in the Volkssturm or this Werewolf group, and I did not ask him about it either.

Whatever little bit of fun there had been in camp was gone. The little jokes, the less annoying activities, the bits of useful education, the nicer songs, the occasional edible meal — all gone. It was just stale bread, thin cabbage soup, military and guerilla training, long marches and endless chores and labour. Our class time had become perfunctory and revolved around yet another revised curriculum that featured the worst sort of Nazi drivel. I suppose that I did not know that it was drivel at the time, but I did know that it was boring, profoundly boring. In addition, the weather in the autumn of 1944 was grim. Everything was grim, grim, grim. And it was grim in a uniform way, like a poorly made cold porridge, so no particular memories stand out that I would care to write about. My one solace were Sundays in that stand of oaks in the Colditzer Forst, with the wren and all the other birds. These are still warm memories, but there is nothing interesting enough in that to write about. The closely observed habits of wrens and tits and sparrows do not really belong in a memoir.

~

Christmas was quiet, especially compared to the previous one in Mellingen. It was nice that all five of us kids could be together with Mama, but Papa had to stay in Leipzig again and there was no money for gifts and there was very little food to do anything special with. Mama had hoarded a few ration coupons and traded them for a nice piece of fat pork, so we did have that, which was also the first meat in a little while, but there was nothing else special. We did not have a Christmas tree, but the town put one up in the market square and we admired it. The castle was of course not decorated for Christmas (would that not be funny?), but somehow the way it was lit made it look almost festive with the fresh snow on the roofs of the towers. I suppose it is all up to the brain to interpret what the eye sees. The same object can subjectively appear to be either festive or terrifying without objectively looking any different.

Herr Rittman stopped by to wish us a happy Christmas and to tell us that the Allied officers in the castle were eating much better than we were. This was because the Geneva Convention stipulated that prisoners were entitled to receive parcels from relatives delivered by the Red Cross. Up until last year these had been quite generous with chocolate and real coffee and such, but this year fewer parcels had gotten through and those that did were perhaps not quite as lavish. What he said next was interesting and made a strong impression on me. He said that the prisoners shared all the parcel contents equally so that those who did not get a parcel enjoyed the treats as well, and that they even shared a few little things with the guards, who they could see were increasingly poorly fed.

Papa sent us a letter, which arrived on Christmas Eve.

Dear Luise, Dear children,

I am writing to wish you a happy Christmas. I wish I could be there with you, but important work for the Reich keeps me here in Leipzig. This work will hopefully play some small part in making future Christmases happier when we can all be together again. The situation for our beloved Fatherland may appear to be difficult, but we must trust in the Führer. He has knowledge that we do not have, and he has wisdom that we do not have. Everything will be well in the end, I assure you.

I hope that my big boys are being helpful at home and dutiful in the Hitler Youth and I hope that my smaller children are behaving well.

Your husband and father,

Heil Hitler!

Wilhelm/Papa

CHAPTER TWENTY-ONE

JANUARY 1945

Theodor was gone. It happened so quickly that neither he nor I had time to properly react, not that a reaction, proper or otherwise, would have made any difference whatsoever. Soon after New Year's Day, an unfamiliar officer and several soldiers appeared in camp with three or four old army trucks. We saw him march into Herr Tischendorf's office with Hauptmann Kohl. Shortly after we were all called to assemble in neat age-sorted rows in front of the flagpole.

"Please pay attention, Oberstleutnant Kessel has an announcement to make on behalf of the Wehrmacht and the Reich." Tischendorf then stepped aside to allow this unfamiliar officer, a tall muscular-looking man in a very neatly pressed uniform, to come forward and address us.

"Loyal Hitler Youth! The time has come for you to fulfill your sacred duty to your Fatherland! Your fathers and brothers are fighting bravely against an enemy that is pressing in from all sides. Reich Plenipotentiary for Total War Göbbels has decreed that all fourteen- and fifteen-year-old Hitler Youth are now ready to take up the fight!

You have been waiting for this day and now it has arrived! We will depart for the front in one hour. Heil Hitler!"

Fourteen-year-olds — this meant Theodor. He did not say anything but went immediately with his cohort to the dormitory to pack. I caught his eye as he went past. He looked unspeakably terrified.

I found Jolf in the crowd of boys milling about. Regular activities appeared to have been suspended while the older boys prepared to leave. Tischendorf was nowhere to be seen, but Kohl was strutting about, supervising the departure preparations and generally appearing to be in his element.

"Which front, Jolf, do you know?"

"Eastern. One of the soldiers told Ernst who told me."

"Oh no." I did not know what else to say or how to react.

"It looks like they're going after Russian tanks. See the Panzerfausts in the backs of the trucks?" Panzerfaust translates as "tank fist" and were like bazookas. The thought of these skinny, half-starved, barely trained boys being flung against Red Army tanks was unbelievable. I could not actually picture it. Theodor with a Panzerfaust. Absurd. While I was trying to process these thoughts Theodor came by again, his canvas rucksack over one shoulder, his lips pursed and his eyes distant and unfocused. He noticed me and briefly snapped back into focus. He shook my hand and quietly said, "Look out for Mama and the little ones, Ludwig. When Papa's not there you're the man of the family now."

I did not respond. And then he was gone. He climbed into the back of one of the trucks and then the tailgate was slammed shut and the truck shuddered out of the camp, belching black smoke. I waved, but I know that he did not see me.

CHAPTER
TWENTY-TWO

FEBRUARY 1945

It had been extremely cold through all of January. This cold was made worse by the starvation rations now being issued. Cold damp air penetrated into the poorly heated buildings of the camp and it penetrated through our increasingly thin and ragged uniforms. We had recently gone from three to two to now one meal a day. This naturally made the cold feel even worse. To compound our misery, the news from both fronts of the war was consistently bad. We had lost in the Ardennes (the Bulge) and we were losing in East Prussia. Russian soldiers were on German soil for the first time in history.

Finally a day came that was relatively warm, with the sun showing through for the first time in many weeks. We had been called to assemble by the flagpole, so there were scores of bony faces turned towards the sun, eyes squinting. Normally Hauptmann Kohl would insist on "eyes forwards," but he allowed us this one small comfort. He had assembled us to read another of Göbbels's speeches. Kohl cleared his throat loudly before beginning to read:

The major Soviet winter offensive that began from the Baranow bridgehead and in an unusually short time spread from Poland into the Wartegau and the other German Gaue in the east has radically altered the military situation. In the past the Reich defended itself far from its borders, but now the enemy occupies German territory that is very important to us both militarily and agriculturally. We can no longer use wide-open spaces as a weapon. We are now fighting almost entirely for and on German home territory. Each village and each acre, each city and each factory, that we are forced to give up means a direct reduction in our war potential, entirely aside from the fact that giving them up is a bitter loss to countless Germans, even costing them their lives. It makes no sense to talk around this or to ignore it. It is good that we all know exactly where we are so that each of us knows what has to be done. The long lines of those fleeing from the east flows towards the west through our cities and villages. Even the most inattentive observer cannot miss them. It is hard to describe their misery and privation. Still the people in these wandering columns are fortunate in comparison to those who had to remain at home and fell into the hands of the Bolsheviks.

The ignorant know-it-alls throughout the world are getting a clear answer to their cynical question as to whether the Soviets are really as bad as we always said, or whether perhaps those stories were only the massively exaggerated product of war propaganda. Naturally there are always people who learn only from experience, not from education. We have never flattered ourselves by believing that they could be persuaded with words or warnings. We did make our own people strong in the face of the deadly danger that threatens them and the entire continent from the east. One can only tear out one's hair when a leading politician of the USA plutocracy says that the United States would welcome a shift to the left in Germany and all of Europe as long as it did not end in Bolshevism. Looking at our continent, one does not need to be a particularly sharp observer to see that the radical red wave is rising slowly, but with uncanny consistency, and that if we do not halt and restrain it, it will devour all of Europe. Our wandering columns know what that means. Horror is reflected in the eyes of men, women and children. When a farmer leaves house and farm and land and livestock, walking for many hundreds of kilometres with only what he can carry, thinking, "anything to escape from that terrible prison," it is because hell is behind him. We have reports and pictures of the atrocities committed against men, women and especially children . . .

Here Kohl paused and made a point of looking around at us, catching as many eyes as he could.

. . . by the bestial Bolshevist soldateska. They are too terrible to publish. The cultured world should cry out with anger and horror, if not about the misery that threatens us, at least about the misery that threatens them.

> The Four Horsemen of the Apocalypse are
> racing across the east and southeast of our
> continent.

And on it went in increasingly gruesome detail. I think Kohl read from the speech for close to an hour. Hitler had more flair with the language, but Göbbels knew how to implant fear into your brain and how to encourage it to burrow in deeply.

"Why did Kohl have to read that to us? I will have trouble sleeping tonight," I said to Jolf after. We had heard many speeches before on the radio, or extracts quoted by Kohl or Tischendorf, but this was the first time we had been assembled to have an entire one read out to us like that.

"I think it's obvious, isn't it? The Russians are probably closer to overrunning this area than the Americans and he wants to inspire us to fight them to the death rather than accept occupation."

"Or inspire us to flee."

"Flee where? Will the Americans really be that much better? And how far away are they?"

This bothered me because Jolf was usually more positive. It was a Monday, so it was six whole days until the partial and temporary solace of Colditz. I found a quiet corner where I would not be observed, and I wept.

~

The bad news just kept coming. The first official report from the propaganda ministry was that 200,000 people had died in Dresden during two nights of intensive British and American incendiary bombings in mid-February. Hellfire had melted steel supports in buildings, rendered cars into amorphous blobs and quite literally vaporized people. Dresden was less than a hundred kilometres directly east of us. Children were already arriving in the camp from there, brought by the truckload in rattling old farm trucks. Days later some came on foot, having been rejected by other over-full camps. All were pale and thin and quiet. We were pale and thin and quiet, but these children were more so.

"How can that be? 200,000? Were there even that many people left in Dresden?" I asked Jolf as we stood in the courtyard stamping our feet and rubbing our hands against the cold, watching another group of bomb refugees being sorted and processed.

"Factor of ten, Ludwig. It's a good rule of thumb. Whenever the Party says something where it suits their purposes to exaggerate, divide by ten. This is an example because it shows the enemy to be cruel and barbaric. Or enemy losses in a battle because it shows us to be strong and winning. So probably 20,000 killed."

"But why? Why kill so many people who are not even soldiers? Have they not won the war already?" I asked. This was still dangerous talk, but we were by ourselves and Jolf was safe.

"I don't know. War is crazy. The Führer calls them gangsters, but I wonder what they call us. I'm sure our people have done the same or worse." Oddly, given the way Felix and Hauptmann Kohl behaved, I had not carefully considered this before. It could have been a shocking statement, but even at the age of eleven I had already lost my capacity to be shocked.

(An aside: about three weeks before, on January 27, Soviet forces entered the Auschwitz extermination camp and liberated the 7,000 survivors. Eventually it was determined that 1.1 million had been murdered in that one camp alone. So yes, our people did worse. Far worse.

An entirely different category of worse. I would learn this soon enough.)

"I suppose so, maybe. I just hope it all stops soon."

"It will. Two weeks ago, Zhukov's divisions reached the Oder, just a hop and a skip east of Berlin. They stopped there, but probably just to strengthen their flanks and supply lines. And last week the Canadians took Kleve on the Rhine in the west."

I just nodded and did not say anything in response. I wondered where the front was in relation to where Theodor had been sent. I caught the eye of a newly arrived young boy. He looked like a ghost. His skin was white and his eyes dull. I smiled at him, but he did not smile back.

"But, Ludwig, it will get worse before it gets better." Jolf inclined his head slightly in Hauptmann Kohl's direction. He did not have to explain. Kohl had just finished screaming at a group of refugees to line up properly for dormitory assignments and now he was screaming at a group of our boys to stop staring at the refugees and get busy digging more foxholes. It was one of those grey winter days that are so common in Germany. The old snow on the ground was grey. The sky was grey. All the new arrivals were shades of grey and Kohl's uniform was grey. In my memory of that day the very air was grey. But Kohl's bald screaming head was red. It was like one of those black-and-white photographs where one object, like a balloon or a rose, is picked out in red as an artistic effect. This is a vivid memory.

~

One Sunday in late February was the second last time Papa visited Colditz and I remember it because it was the last time he spoke to me directly.

It was another relentlessly grey February day, distinguished only by a noticeable increase in traffic on the Schönbach to Colditz road. When I write "traffic," I do not mean cars and trucks. There were some, but very few. It was mostly people on foot or with small wagons pulled by donkeys or horses. These wagons were piled high with furniture and household goods. Sometimes a small child was perched on top. One of these children waved to me. He had the happiest face I had seen in a while. They were mostly heading away from Colditz. I supposed that this was because the road eventually led west. Some of these people might even be coming all the way from Silesia, which I had heard had fallen. Rumours were circulating that the Russians killed every German they found there — every German who had not had the good sense to flee. Man, woman or child. These people would rather be under American occupation than Russian, so they were going west, as far west as they could. I kept walking east, unnerved. To settle my anxiety, I thought of my spot in the forest under the oaks. Winter is difficult even there, but in spring we can survive.

Papa was already at home when I got there. He was in uniform rather than his usual Sunday suit. His comb-over was oiled carefully in place, but his face was gaunt, and he had large purple-grey bags under his eyes. He smiled at me and greeted me warmly. He then declared that he would like to speak to each of us children alone for a moment. He indicated that I should go in first. Mama ignored these proceedings, busying herself with preparing lunch, such as it was.

Papa sat down on the edge of the bed. He motioned me to sit beside him.

"How is the KLV-Lager?"

"It is all right, Papa, similar to before, except that the older boys have gone to fight, and we now have many new younger boys from Dresden and elsewhere."

"Are you learning useful things in the Hitler Youth?"

"I suppose." I did not want to encourage this line of questioning as I was worried how he would react if I let slip how much I hated the Hitler Youth and the military training. I suspect he knew, but it had remained unspoken between us.

He smiled and paused for a moment. "Remember what I told you when those boys were bullying you in Leipzig a few years ago. You are a Schott. You might not be one of the best fighters, but you will be one of the best thinkers."

I nodded, looking at the floor.

"I don't know what will happen. I have faith in the Führer and faith in the nation, but I'm not stupid enough to think that a German victory is guaranteed anymore. Virgil said fata viam invenient, meaning 'fate will find a way,' but in my experience, fate is a very mysterious force." He paused again, appearing to wait for a response. I could hear the others outside the door, moving around and talking quietly and I could hear a truck rattle by on the cobblestones outside. When I did not say anything but kept staring at my shoes, he went on. "Ludwig, you are only eleven, but you are growing up quickly, much more quickly than I did at your age. And you are clever. When the time comes you will know what to do. Your mother will need help. I am counting on you."

"Yes, Papa," I said quietly, still not meeting his eyes. This was a strange and awkward conversation, not at all typical of Papa, and it had numerous implications that I knew were going to plague my thoughts like clouds of flies.

He briefly put his hand on my right shoulder. "Thank you, Ludwig. Please send Clara in."

CHAPTER
TWENTY-THREE

APRIL 1, 1945

Easter Sunday was Papa's last visit to Colditz. I saw him but did not speak to him beyond the standard greetings. He was in uniform again and he looked terrible, no longer impressive or wizard-like in any way. All of us children kept our distance, not that we normally clamoured for his attention, but we instinctively understood that he had come specifically to speak to Mama. I expected that we would be sent outside, but they ignored us and withdrew to the bedroom. I could hear them talking, but I could not make out anything that was said. The tone sounded emotional, but there was no shouting. Papa emerged after ten or fifteen minutes, bid us goodbye and left. I could not read anything from his expression. Mama stayed in the bedroom a few minutes longer and then came out, having evidently composed herself. Her eyes were red rimmed, but any tears had been dried away by the handkerchief crumpled in her hand. This created an ambience of emotional discomfort in the small front room that I was keen to escape.

Spring was underway in the forest. Clara and I briefly glanced at each other. I am sure we both wanted to find a way to comfort our mother, but neither of us had any notion of how to go about it. We also had questions about what was going on with Papa, but asking these questions was unthinkable. Mama just stood in the middle of the room for a long minute or two and then, without saying a word, sat down in the corner to attend to some sewing. The four smaller children played or read quietly. I stood around for a few minutes, unsure of what to do, and then went outside.

CHAPTER

TWENTY-FOUR

APRIL 13, 1945

These dates are all easy to remember as they anchor to recorded history. They will come rapidly and thickly now.

On April 13, Hauptmann Kohl strode out of his office with an enormous smile on his face. We had not seen him so happy in months, perhaps ever. A group of us were engaged in some sort of pointless enhancement of the camp's defences, I do not recall specifically what. Kohl motioned to us. "Boys, boys, gather around!" We stopped what we were doing and went over. Others nearby did as well, although there was no formal general call to assemble.

"The tide of the war will turn!" Kohl declared, pumping his fist in the air. "The head gangster has died! You will remember from your history lessons that this is exactly like the miracle that saved Frederick the Great in 1762 when Prussia was on the verge of being destroyed by foes pressing in from all sides! The death of President Roosevelt is the same now as the death of Czarina Elizabeth was then! Fate and history will echo for a just and righteous cause like ours!" Kohl beamed at us. "Heil Hitler!" he concluded.

We responded with a tepid "Heil Hitler" and went back to our chores. Czarina Elizabeth had been succeeded by the pro-Prussian Czar Peter, who concluded a peace deal with Frederick, thus splintering the enemy alliance. Perhaps Kohl and the Nazi leadership had special knowledge about the next American president that made them so happy. I doubted it.

This fantasy lasted exactly two days.

The sound of artillery fire is different than the sound of bombs. It is a harder thudding sound, preceded by a long whistle as the shells travel through the air. It was a Sunday and I was preparing to walk to Colditz, but that was precisely the direction the sound of artillery was coming from. I was immediately panic-stricken by the thought of what might be happening to Mama and my sister and brothers. We had been hearing rumours for days now that both the Americans and Russians were getting close to Colditz. It was a toss-up which army would arrive first. I was standing at the camp gate, undecided about what to do when Hauptmann Kohl began shouting, ordering us to assemble.

"Hitler Youth! You have seen your brothers and friends depart for the front! Now the front has come to us and it is our time to hoist the banner proudly and step forward to defend the Fatherland!"

What?

"We will immediately engage the defensive plan and man the trenches! I have obtained a few additional weapons! These will be distributed to the twelve- and thirteen-year-olds while eleven and younger will act in a logistical support role!"

Most of us were so aghast at what we were hearing that we did not notice Herr Tischendorf emerge from his office and walk forward. He stepped in front of Kohl and in a louder voice than I had heard him use in a long time shouted, "I am commander of KLV-Lager Schönbach and I hereby countermand Hauptmann Kohl's order! Boys, prepare to evacuate the camp."

Kohl was evidently prepared for this turn of events, although he worked his jowls for a couple of seconds before responding. "And I am commander of the Hitler Youth here! This is a military matter, not a school or camp matter! The defence of the Reich is paramount, and under Emergency Decree 1945-17.3a I assume absolute control of KLV-Lager in the name of the High Command!"

"I do not accept this!" Tischendorf responded. "The war is over, so there are no longer any military matters for you to be in control of." Tischendorf took a step towards Kohl. He was the taller man and perhaps hoped to use his height advantage to intimidate.

"The war is not over! There has been no surrender. There will be no surrender. That is treasonous talk, Herr Tischendorf! I hereby place you under arrest." He motioned to two of the more fanatical thirteen-year-olds to seize Tischendorf.

The rest of us could not believe our eyes or ears. As nobody was paying attention to us, the great majority of us dispersed. Let Kohl believe we were following orders to man the trenches, but without saying anything to each other we quickly crammed our few sad belongings into our rucksacks and fled the camp. This might sound dangerous, but staying felt far more dangerous, and in any case the camp was in a chaotic uproar. Kohl did not have enough boy fanatics to exert his will and, as far as the rest of us were concerned, Tischendorf was still in charge and he said we were to evacuate.

I was fortunate in having somewhere nearby to evacuate to, but many others had to somehow make their way back to Leipzig or Dresden or the other cities where Lord knows what was going on. The postal system and the news (or, more rightly, propaganda) service and the trains, which had all continued to function for a remarkably long time in the rapidly shrinking sliver of a Reich, had in the last few days finally faltered. We no longer had any idea what was going on anywhere else. But evacuate and disperse we did, as the camp seemed likely to become a focus of fighting. Anywhere else was better.

I was on the road to Colditz with two other boys when Jolf caught up with us. He had been running.

"They've hung him," he panted.

"Hung who?"

"Tischendorf! Kohl set up a little court with Herr Braun and Manfred." Herr Braun was the most strident Nazi among the teachers and Manfred was the thirteen-year-old head boy of dormitory No. 4. "The three of them declared Tischendorf guilty of the capital crime of treason and with the help of Erwin and Kurt tied a noose around his neck. They hung him from the oak by the gate. He struggled and cried for help, but nobody did anything. Some even laughed. Kohl had his revolver out. I'm sure he would have shot anyone who tried to help. I just stood there." Jolf began sobbing. "It was horrible, so horrible."

We could hear more artillery fire ahead of us in Colditz and now we could hear shots being fired behind us, in or near camp. Jolf kept sobbing and sobbing.

We all began to run, towards the artillery and away from the shots. Artillery seemed more abstract than the shooting and it was also quite intermittent. As we approached the bridge, we could see that an enormous homemade-looking British flag was draped on the castle walls, but the castle was being hit by artillery shells. This was confusing. The town itself was weirdly calm. I invited Jolf to come home with me, but he wanted to go on to Rochlitz, another ten kilometres south, where he had an aunt. Our two other camp comrades also dispersed to places they knew.

Mama must have been watching out the window, as she rushed out to greet me.

"Ludwig! You're safe!" She hugged me and began to cry. I could see that she had been crying a lot.

"Yes, Mama. How are the others?"

"Safe, we are all safe, thank God. Except Theodor and your father. I don't know anything about Theodor. Come in, come in. What is happening at camp?"

I explained, but I left out the part about the confrontation between Kohl and Tischendorf and the latter's summary execution. I was having trouble processing that, and it would be years before I could speak of it.

"But what about here, Mama? Who is shelling the castle and why?"

"The Americans. Herr Rittmann says they are just a kilometre or two west now and the Russians are perhaps ten kilometres east. The Americans are apparently confused and think the castle is a military base. This is why the British prisoners put out that flag. They did that just an hour ago. Herr Rittmann says that the High Command wanted the prisoners to be moved south, deeper into the unoccupied territory so that they could be used as bargaining chips, but the head prisoner, Lieutenant Colonel Tod, refused. Kommandant Oberst Prawitt thought about it and then decided to agree with Tod, not with High Command! Hopefully the Americans figure out what is happening and stop the artillery. Hopefully this ends peacefully tonight or tomorrow."

But I was overwhelmed and exhausted beyond the point of being able to entertain hope or any feeling or thought other than the intense desire to curl up under a blanket and draw comfort from the sounds of Mama going about her evening routine. Later, when the house was quiet, I lay for a long time with my eyes open, because every time I closed my eyes I saw Herr Tischendorf hanging from the oak tree by the gate of the camp, moonlit, all alone. Mercifully when sleep came it was deep and long and dreamless.

CHAPTER

TWENTY-FIVE

APRIL 16, 1945

The Americans entered Colditz at 8:00 in the morning, crossing the bridge, having come down the 176 from Bad Lausick and encountering no resistance to that point. On the bridge, however, they came under fire from an SS squad on the riverbank just north of the castle. We could hear the shooting. It was very intense, but it did not last long. Even after the shooting stopped Mama insisted that we stay indoors. That was fine with me. I was far more afraid than I was curious. I knew that occupation by the Americans (Gangsters) was preferable to occupation by the Russians (Hordes), but there were far too many unknowns to feel anything other than fear.

Mama was washing the little ones, perhaps trying to make them presentable for the occupiers. While she busied herself with that, I went into the bedroom to read my Karl May and take my mind off what had happened, was happening and was going to happen. Despite our squalor, Mama kept everything as neat as she could, so it surprised me to see a piece of paper lying loosely on the bed. Normally all letters and papers were carefully filed in the little antique desk in the corner. I looked at the paper. It was handwritten. Probably a letter. I knew it was almost certainly not meant for my eyes, but Theodor had said that I was "the man" now and I felt it was important to know everything I could about what was going on. I picked it up and sat with my back to the door in case Mama suddenly came in.

It was a short letter from Papa.

> Leipzig, April 14, 1945
>> Dear Luise,
>> I hope this letter reaches you. I have entrusted it to Konrad who will pass through Colditz on his way south for the final stand. Yes, I must write of the final stand. The Americans are very near now, and Leipzig will fall. The Reich will fall. As a decent German I simply cannot bear witness to the destruction of the Fatherland. I must end my life rather than see this happen. You will not hear from me again.
>> Heil Hitler,
>> Wilhelm

I stared at these words for a long minute, willing them to say something else. What he had written was an impossible abstraction, as if he were reporting from the dark side of the moon. I could feel my mind preparing a secure box to put this information in and lock it away from immediate further conscious inspection. I carefully placed the letter in the exact same position on the bed where I had found it and then, feeling dazed but little else, I picked up my Karl May book and left the bedroom.

PART THREE

HELL IS EMPTY AND ALL THE DEVILS ARE HERE.

— William Shakespeare, *The Tempest*

CHAPTER
TWENTY-SIX

APRIL 17, 1945

Colditz had fallen or been liberated, depending on your perspective. Within hours there was nobody who spoke openly of the former. Within hours everyone hailed the liberators, or at least offered no sign of anything other than acceptance of their arrival. Nazi uniforms and regalia were quickly thrown out, hidden or burned. The Colditz Ortsgruppen leadership tried to look as casual as possible in civilian clothing. As the little battle at the bridge was going on, they had managed, somewhat frantically no doubt, to destroy the local records of their identities and actions, but the Gau, which was the next higher organizational level, had intact carbon copies, so this just slightly delayed their identification.

My first direct look at one of the Gangsters was when an officer and two GIs knocked on our door the morning after the fall/liberation. Mama answered the door while the rest of us clustered behind her, staring wide-eyed at the green-clad aliens. Other than the groups of Polish slave labourers in the distance, I am not sure I had seen a foreigner before. Certainly not one from across the sea.

"Good morning. We are here to assess the possibilities for housing our officers." It was one of the GIs who spoke. His German was astonishingly good. "How many rooms do you have?"

"We have just this room and a small bedroom. There are five of us," Mama answered, keeping her tone polite and calm.

"I see." The GI said something to the officer in what I assumed was English. It sounded like ducks quacking. The officer wrote something in a little coil-bound notebook.

"Thank you, madam. We will not be troubling you anymore. Have a good day."

So. These were the Americans. In this admittedly very brief encounter there was no evidence of gangsterish behaviour. The other GI had even offered us a smile. I suspended my judgement though. There was not enough evidence yet. Mama said nothing and withdrew to the bedroom. I had not mentioned to her that I had seen Papa's letter. Now that I allowed myself to think about it, my thoughts were in turmoil. Although death had become a familiar topic, suicide was not. I had never heard of somebody killing themselves, and the idea seemed bizarre to the point of straining credibility. What possibly could be worse than the infinite void of nothingness? How could a rational person voluntarily choose the infinite void of nothingness? I must have misinterpreted what he wrote. I wished I could read it over again, but Mama was in the bedroom. Without Theodor around there was nobody to discuss this with. I certainly would not tell the little ones! I pondered the problem for a while and eventually convinced myself that suicide was not a real thing and that Papa was using an obtuse metaphor.

With this settled I began to become restless and longed to go to the forest. The war was over, was it not? The Americans would not have bothered with an empty forest, so it would be exactly as it was before. That is what I needed — something that was exactly as it was before. I knew that Mama would not permit it though, so I sat and jiggled restlessly. Partial salvation came when Mama opened the bedroom door a crack. Her eyes were red.

"Ludwig, go to the market and see if the Amis are distributing any food. We have nothing left here." Then she closed the door again.

~

Our brewery flat was very close to the market, so in a matter of steps I was there. It was busy with trucks full of American GIs rumbling through and clusters of locals either watching the Americans quietly or talking amongst themselves. Before I could assess the food situation, a boy came running up to me. It was Walther from camp. I did not know him very well, but each of us was relieved to see a familiar face in the midst of all this uncertainty.

"Ludwig . . . ! Did . . . you . . . hear . . . ?" Walther was breathless with excitement, so the words came out one at a time, panted more than spoken.

"About Herr Tischendorf, yes." I was happy to see Walther, but I did not want to encourage this line of conversation.

"Not just him. Kohl. Did you hear about Kohl?"

"No."

"He shot himself! The Amis were approaching the camp and pretty much everyone except Herr Braun and Manfred had left. Even Kohl could see that there was no point in trying to fight. He was probably worried he would be captured. So, he put his pistol in his mouth. It was a horrible mess! Manfred told Erwin who told me. The Amis took Herr Braun prisoner but let Manfred go."

Suicide was a real thing. Hauptmann Kohl was crazy, and Papa was not crazy, at least I did not believe so, but still both were fervent believers in the Nazi cause, which was not a good thing to be now. My mind went blank. I made an excuse to Walther and joined a line of people that was forming behind one American truck where it looked like some sort of food was being distributed. But there was none. It was a false rumour and the crowd was dispersed with shouts from an American sergeant. I went home empty-handed.

CHAPTER TWENTY-SEVEN

APRIL 18, 1945

With a firm "We have to eat," Mama sent me out again the next morning, this time with a small canvas bag in which she put a pair of silver earrings. Being upper middle class for several generations back on both sides, our family owned a lot of valuable things. The bulkier items, such as many of Opa Flintzer's paintings, were in bank vaults in Leipzig, but a lot of the jewellery and some of the silverware had come with us to Colditz. There were rumours of an informal farmers' market at the edge of town. Reichmarks had become toilet paper, so the only recognized currency was real silver and gold. Soon American cigarettes would fill that role too.

The first thing that caught my eye when I entered the market square was that the Americans were building several tiny houses on the far side, near the river. Herr Rittmann was in the square and waved me over.

"See there, Ludwig," he said quietly, indicating the odd construction. "Do you know what the Amis are building?"

I shook my head no.

"Outhouses! The Amis are building pit toilets for themselves!"

I made a quizzical facial expression.

"Exactly! Why, you wonder? Why use pit toilets when all the homes their officers are billeted in have beautiful indoor plumbing! Even the regular GIs have access to proper flush toilets at the school next to their camp."

He paused, waiting for a comment from me I suppose, but I did not say anything. I glanced nervously at the American soldiers, who were not very far away.

"You can't guess, can you? It's so funny! They are afraid of the Werewolves!" Herr Rittmann threw his head back and made a quiet "ah-oo" wolf howl. "That stupid Göbbels's propaganda worked! They really believe that resistance fighters are hiding amongst us, ready to booby-trap toilets and blow their well-upholstered Ami asses high up into the sky!" He laughed loudly at the absurdity of this thought. I became thoroughly alarmed that we would attract unwanted attention, but none was forthcoming. The Americans continued to ignore us. "If there is even one real Werewolf fighter in all of Saxony, I will eat my shoe. However, I might have to eat my shoe anyway. Speaking of which, I imagine you are going to talk to the farmers. There are a few by the sports field, just south. Good luck!" Herr Rittmann continued to watch the Americans while I left the square and headed down to the old sports field.

It was too early in the season for anything fresh, but the farmers, who were incidentally all women, had eggs, meat and bread for sale. I could see this from where I stood at the edge of the field. I watched as people came and went and I tried to analyze the transactions so I would know what to do when I had finally amassed the courage to approach one of the farmers. But I was too far away to hear what was said, nor could I see the smaller objects being handed over in trade. One short round woman with a neat red apron and a white spotted green kerchief on her head smiled a lot and was off to the side a little, with her food spread out on the hood of a burnt-out SS staff car. She seemed like the best choice, being out of the noisier crowded area and looking friendly. But still I could not go. I clutched my canvas bag and began to get upset. Would Mama believe me if I went back and said there was no market, or that they were sold out? But we had so little food left at home, and I had already failed once. This was my responsibility. Going up to a strange woman with the intent to bargain was as terrifying, however, as cowering in our cellar in Leipzig when the bombs were falling. Perhaps worse even. Here it was all up to me and failure was a definite possibility, whereas in the bomb shelter my fate was entirely out of my hands. It was like the difference between being the pawn and being the hand that moves the pawn. Moreover, in this instance, I was meant to be the hand that moves the pawn when I had absolutely no experience playing the game or knowledge of its rules. The woman in the apron and kerchief noticed me standing there and beckoned me over. At the same time a townswoman whom I recognized as living around the corner from us came over.

"You're Luise's son, aren't you?"

I nodded.

"It's okay if you don't know what to do here. Hilda is good and fair. I'll help you."

Before I could protest, the townswoman took me by the hand to the smiling farmer, who was apparently named Hilda. I glanced nervously at the staff car, wondering whether there might be something gory in there, like blood splatters, but it was comprehensively blackened on the inside.

My two silver earrings got me a dozen fresh eggs, two loaves of rough-looking dark bread, a half pound of butter and a pound of fatty pork. I had no idea whether this was a good deal, but Hilda and the townswoman assured me that it was. The latter got a larger quantity of meat but had traded a very fine-looking gold bracelet and a handful of cigarettes for it, so my confidence increased that I had done well. Nonetheless, although I was not too sure how much jewellery we had, I sensed that this arrangement was not going to keep us fed for very long.

~

As I came around the corner onto Nikolaistrasse on the way back to our flat, I almost walked right into a patrol of three American soldiers. They were Black. I had never seen a Black person before in my life. I only knew about them from storybooks and a little bit from history class when the German colonies in Africa were discussed. These were lost after the First World War. Was there discussion of cannibalism? I think there might have been, but I could not instantly recall right then. I gasped and I think I would have peed my pants with terror had my bladder not already been empty. The three of them stopped and laughed. It was a kindly laugh. What a sight I must have been to them — small, thin, terrified. One of them crouched down on his haunches and placed his hand gently on my shoulder.

"Junge, okay, nein, nicht . . . alarm," he said in a broken but understandable mix of German and English. "Gummi?" he then asked and pulled a package of chewing gum out of his jacket pocket. Chewing gum! I had heard of it, and there was surely some around in Leipzig before the war, but I did not know anyone who had it. I knew that the Americans were famous for it. Was it a trick though? The soldier seemed to read my mind. "Okay, wunderbar, yum," he said and popped one piece in his mouth, smiling broadly as he chewed it. He then handed the rest of the package to me, which I accepted with a quiet "Danke schoen."

The other two soldiers seemed a little unhappy with him and one glanced nervously up and down the street while the other said something quite stern to my new friend. Later I would find out that the U.S. Army had strict anti-fraternization rules in place. The soldiers were not allowed to speak to any Germans of any age, again because of fears that a devious Nazi Werewolf resistance might even use children to befriend and then murder Allied personnel. By June the prohibition was lifted for children, but not until September for the general population.

CHAPTER TWENTY-EIGHT

MAY 1, 1945

During the next week and a half, a new routine developed, focused on the wary observation of our occupiers and a daily obsession with finding food. Even though Mama and I didn't speak of it, we knew that Papa was dead and could not help us, and we presumed Theodor was dead and could not help, and the Americans continued to keep their distance and would not help us. We were left entirely to fend for ourselves, but this quickly felt normal.

Then two things happened on the first of May that I will never forget. The first was the news that came over the radio. We did not have a radio in Colditz, but Herr Rittmann did and called us over to say that for the last several minutes there had been the repeated announcement: "The German wireless broadcasts serious, important news for the German people." Herr Rittmann thought it might be the announcement of the formal end of the war. Mama was not interested, but Clara, Johann and I rushed over to listen. After a few dozen more repetitions of "The German wireless broadcasts serious, important news for the German people," there were three loud drumrolls and then there was silence for a moment. Then the announcer again:

> It is reported from Der Führer's headquarters that our Führer Adolf Hitler, fighting to the last breath against Bolshevism, fell for Germany this afternoon in his operational headquarters in the Reich Chancellery.
> On April 30 Der Führer appointed Grand Admiral Dönitz his successor. The grand admiral and successor of Der Führer now speaks to the German people.

Dönitz, who I had never heard of before, came on, his voice faint and scratchy:

> German men and women, soldiers of the armed forces: our Führer, Adolf Hitler, has fallen. In the deepest sorrow and respect, the German people bow.
> At an early date he had recognized the frightful danger of Bolshevism and dedicated his existence to this struggle. At the end of his struggle, of his unswerving straight road of life, stands his hero's death in the capital of the German Reich. His life has been one single service for Germany. His activity in the fight against the Bolshevik storm flood concerned not only Europe but the entire civilized world.
> Der Führer has appointed me to be his successor.
> Fully conscious of the responsibility, I take over the leadership of the German people at this fateful hour.

Dönitz went on to outline that his main thrust would be to continue to fight to save the world from Bolshevism while trying to bring the Anglo-Americans onside in this struggle. It was a familiar refrain, and one that sounded laughable now.

"He should pull all the troops off the western front and try to shore up the eastern. As we can see, the Amis aren't that bad. It would be nice if they gave us food, but it's nothing like the stories coming from the east . . . Well, I shouldn't tell you children," Herr Rittman said.

He was prescient. First of all, Dönitz did encourage his troops to surrender to the Western Allies rather than the Russians, saving close to two million from a one-way trip to Siberia. And secondly, the Russians were coming to Colditz.

~

Later that morning there was only one farmer, a toothless elderly woman, at the market. I did not recognize her. She was sitting by herself under a large oak, with her meagre offerings spread out in front of her on a colourful baby blanket. Hilda was not there.

Greatly worried by the disappearance of the market, I overcame my reluctance to talk to the old woman and asked, "Where is Hilda? Where is everyone?"

"Have you not heard little one? Ivan is coming."

"The Russians? Here?"

"Yes. The Amis and Ivan had agreed before that their armies would meet here, at the Mulde." She jerked her thumb over her shoulder. "But Ivan was slower than expected." She turned her face aside and spat something out of her mouth before continuing. "The Amis are withdrawing to the west bank tomorrow morning and Ivan is moving in. Many people are leaving the east side today."

It was true. I had seen an unusual number of people headed west over the bridge, pushing handcarts, carrying large rucksacks. Colditz proper was entirely on the east bank. There were just a few houses on the west. I thanked the woman and ran home as fast as I could in order to tell Mama so that we could secure a place in one of those houses over the bridge.

But she disagreed.

"No, Ludwig, we have to stay here. There will be no place over there for us to stay. Every house over the bridge is already over-full and I don't know how far west we would have to walk to find somewhere — probably a hundred kilometres or more. We cannot with the little ones." She was calm when she said this and, for the first time since the letter from Papa had arrived, it did not look like she had been crying. I, on the other hand, was becoming frantic.

"But the Russians, Mama! The Russians! Have you not been hearing the stories? They have been raping" — I knew roughly what this was by that time — "and robbing and murdering even!"

Mama sighed and closed her eyes for a moment. Then she opened them and looked at me directly. "Ludwig, I know very well about the Russians. You know Frau Bergen two doors down, yes? Her sister just arrived a few days ago from Cottbus. The Russians took that city on April 22. The fighting was terrible, she said. Thousands killed. Cottbus had been heavily bombed before too, so she said that in the end the whole city was just one giant rubble field surrounded by a ring of mass graves. After they won, the Russians raped every woman they could find, often more than once, including Frau Bergen's sister. Two of her sister's friends killed themselves after, they were so ashamed."

"Mama!" I could not believe that she was telling me this and, moreover, that this was supposed to be part of an argument to stay!

"Wait, Ludwig, I am not finished. I am telling you this to make you understand that I know more than you do how terrible the Red Army can be, yet we will stay. We will stay because I also know that this is how the Red Army behaves after winning a battle. The men are in a frenzy of hate. Here it is the Americans that won the battle and the Russians that are coming have not fought for many days. There will be a peaceful transfer of authority. I trust Colonel Armstrong to make sure his Soviet successor abides by the Geneva Convention. The Americans will be just right across the river after all! I think the Russians will be on their best behaviour when watched like this."

"I am still afraid, Mama."

"I understand, but it will be fine. Also I should tell you another reason why we can't leave."

"What is that?"

"I'm pregnant. I'm due in October."

A brief and entirely horrifying hygiene class at the KLV-Lager had given me the basics. I did the nine-month math and was confused. I suppose Papa had been here in January, but with these two rooms and all the kids, how was that possible? Perhaps he also came once during the week when Theodor and I were not there. Nonetheless it created an unsettling mental image of an extremely rapid . . . transaction. I added this to my growing storehouse of off-limits memories, thoughts and images. I was becoming good at deliberately compartmentalizing my mind.

~

The Red Army marched in early the next morning. Whereas the Americans were healthy and well fed, the Russians were mostly as starved-looking as we were, often just boys in torn and ill-fitting uniforms. But they looked very proud as they paraded into the market square for the brief hand-over ceremony, which consisted of nothing more than a handshake between Colonel Armstrong and Major Kozlov. Several locals had come out to wave red flags to welcome our new masters. If you looked at the flags carefully you would notice that there was a circular hole in the centre. These were Nazi flags with the swastika cut out. Communist or fascist, red or brown, blue, green or purple, nobody cared anymore. Please just end the war and please do not hurt us.

CHAPTER
TWENTY-NINE

MAY 8, 1945

On Tuesday, May 8, Germany finally surrendered. It should have surrendered months earlier, but at least it was clear that there would be no dragged out Werewolf resistance as the Party leadership had wanted. The war was truly over. We heard the news from the Russians shouting. Kozlov issued extra vodka rations and Mama kept us inside. As far as I know the celebrations were limited to singing and vomiting.

Mama had been right.

Later I heard one funny story from the end of the war that is worth sharing. Apparently the supreme commander of the Luftwaffe, Hermann Göring, surrendered to the Americans in southern Austria where he was trying to make a getaway with his daughter. They were in a luxury Mercedes-Benz filled with expensive luggage. Once in custody he chatted happily with the American officers, toasted them with Champagne he had brought along and posed for photos, smiling broadly and generally being charming. When Eisenhower found out about this, he was very angry and immediately ordered Göring to be treated like a high-security-risk prisoner. He was the highest-ranking Nazi left alive, Hitler, Himmler and Göbbels having all died by suicide. Göring followed them a year later in Nuremberg. He had been sentenced to hang for war crimes, but he felt that this fate was dishonourable so he killed himself with a cyanide capsule hidden in a gold fountain pen that he had either managed to bribe his American guard into bringing to him from his confiscated personal effects, or he had tricked him into doing so — history is unclear on this point.

CHAPTER

THIRTY

MAY 15, 1945

The next Tuesday at dawn there was a knock on the door. Mama and I were early risers, so we were both already awake. I am sure we both thought the same thing — Russians, which at this hour was troubling. I motioned for Mama to step out of view and I opened the door. Standing there was an emaciated boy, covered in dirt and sores, wearing a filthy tan-coloured uniform tunic, holding wet boots in one hand and a small bundle of wildflowers in the other.

"Hello, Ludwig," he said weakly.

It was Theodor! I honestly did not recognize him at first, but when he said my name I knew.

"Theodor!" I shouted and hugged him, the first time I had ever done so and, to the best of my recollection, the last. Mama pushed me aside. A frenzy of tears and hugs followed. Theodor was in terrible condition. He explained briefly that he had been walking for days, often with nothing to eat and often sleeping rough. His boots fit so badly that his Achilles tendons were exposed through open sores that were weeping pus. Unsure of where the lines of control were and wanting to evade the Russians, he had looped to the west and arrived on the American side of the Mulde, which he'd swum across. That was all Mama would let him tell us before attending to his wounds, feeding him from the little we had and allowing him to rest.

Before he submitted to Mama's care he said, "These flowers are for Clara. It's her birthday, is it not?" Indeed it was. Our little sister was turning nine. She wept when he handed her the flowers. Theodor slept almost the entire day. While he was asleep Mama gave me a particularly fine silver ladle and asked me to get the best piece of meat I could for it.

By that evening Theodor had perked up considerably. I did manage to trade the ladle for an especially nice cut of pork, as well as for some bread and old potatoes. This was the closest to a feast we had had in a long while. We let Theodor eat as much as he wanted, but he was cautious, knowing that it would be a mistake to overeat after so long a period of starvation. (An aside: there were many stories after the war of men returning from years of imprisonment in Siberia, being fed an enormous welcome home meal and then promptly falling dead. Perhaps this is apocryphal, but it is believable.)

While Mama was busy with the dishes, Theodor asked me quietly about Papa. I told him about the letter. He looked down at his lap for a long moment, and then looked up at me, his lips pursed and his jaw tight, but he did not say anything.

Mama went over to Herr Rittmann's and came back with a half bottle of homemade blackberry wine. It was awful tasting, but it did feel good to celebrate something. After a sip and a grimace Theodor began to tell his story.

"After you last saw me at the camp, Ludwig, we were driven to Grimma where we boarded a train for Olbernhau in the Erzgebirge." These are the Ore Mountains in English, on the Czech border. "Then we were marched up to a high ridge in the mountains near Neuhausen where there was an old camp and where the serious training began. Nobody told us where the front was at that point and nobody asked. I assumed the Russians were close, but as I couldn't hear any artillery fire and there were no aircraft overhead, I decided that there was no immediate danger. Our commanding officer, Hauptfeldwebel Neumeyer, was fortunately a reasonably nice man with a good sense of humour. He had been a hairdresser in civilian life. He had been badly wounded on the eastern front and had no use of his right arm. This is why he had been taken off active service and put in charge of us. His deputy was an idiot though. He reminded me a bit of Kohl, but even dumber. In any case, Neumeyer would do things like get us to assemble and then shout, 'Do you want to win the war?' to which we would dutifully shout back, 'Yes, sir!' and then he would quietly reply with a wry chuckle, 'You go do that then.' It gave me the unsettling feeling that he thought that this was all pointless and he was just going through the motions of his job."

"More wine, Theodor?" Mama offered.

"No, thank you. So, you might be wondering about my strange uniform. It's from the Afrika Korps! That's all they had for us. Desert uniforms in the winter in the mountains! Fortunately we also had some good woolen blankets to wrap around ourselves. And the boots were used Polish army boots!"

He glanced at the hateful footwear, which were set just inside the door to dry.

"They were warm enough and might have been fine if they fit properly, but as you can see, mine did not. After a couple months of building useless tank traps, digging useless ditches and firing useless nineteenth-century rifles we finally got our first taste of fighting about a month ago. I don't recall the exact date. Incidentally they didn't let us practise with the Panzerfausts as the ammunition was too precious. In any case, this happened when I was on kitchen duty. My Achilles were already beginning to seriously trouble me, so I was excused from training and marching for a couple days and was put in charge of making sure the giant soup pot didn't boil over. Suddenly it was *peng peng peng* and bullets came flying through the kitchen! They knocked the soup pot over, but luckily I was not hit. I threw myself to the floor and waited. No more shots followed. Neumeyer said afterwards that it was actually the Americans in the valley below on the Czech side shooting up at us! But they were not interested in properly assaulting the ridge. They soon left and we never saw them again."

"The Americans? Really?" I asked.

"Yes, away from the main battles and the main thrusts of the armies, the so-called front is not what I imagined it to be. Rather than being a clear line between opposing forces, it is a vague zone where groups of soldiers move between and around each other, occupying small areas in a constantly changing patchwork, often only vaguely aware of where the enemy is. In the Erzgebirge through late April and into early May we had numerous German, Russian and American units in this situation. Actually it was not just those three armies — we also had Hungarians and Croatians up there. The Croatians were our allies and occupied the next building over on the ridge. They were from the Handžaru Croatian SS Mountain division, which sounds intimidating, but it was made up of boys even younger than us! They were once an elite unit. Pavelic, Croatia's little Hitler, was so proud that the Handžaru was the first non-German Waffen SS division. If that bastard could see them suffering up there in the Erzgebirge! Those boys were even sadder and even more scared than us, if you can imagine such a thing. After a few days they were sent down the mountain to the northeast to fight the Russians. I would be surprised if any survived.

"Funnier were the Hungarians! These were the crème de la crème of the Hungarian officer corps from the so-called Arrow Cross Movement, which remained loyal to Germany after Horthy, the fascist dictator of Hungary, decided to switch sides and join the Allies. These guys came up here with all kinds of luxuries, as well as with their wives who wore furs and jewels! They attempted to carry on a shadow play of Budapest high society in their mountain hut. They had cases and cases of fine Lake Balaton red wine with them and they had a hand-powered gramophone that they played Bartók, Lehár and Liszt on. It was quite wonderful to hear, although also quite surreal. What was more wonderful though is that they drank so much of that wine that they did not pay attention to their weapons, which they left lying about. So, given that our rifles were terrible, and knowing that the fighting was getting close, we stole as many as we could!

"Around this time something absurd and idiotic happened. Or I should say, something even more absurd and idiotic! A Hitler Youth commander came up to the camp and ordered us all, there were perhaps a hundred of us, to march into Neuhausen and see the barber there."

"The barber?" Mama asked. We were all rapt. Even the little ones were listening to every word. Theodor took a long swallow of water (not blackberry wine!) before going on.

"Yes, the barber! Can you imagine? You see it was April 22, Hitler's birthday, and this idiot, the Hitler Youth commander, deemed it essential that we get our hair cut so that we would look our best for the celebrations. The funny thing was that the Russians had already captured the power plant further down in the valley, so there was no electricity in Neuhausen. The barber had to cut all of our hair with scissors! But he did it. Haircuts for Herr Hitler! The absolute idiocy of it all! But we were still convinced we could win the war. See what happens when you give a bunch of teenage boys weapons and pump them full of propaganda? Most of us missed Neumeyer's hints and thought we could take on anything and turn the war around."

Mama snorted. "Those clowns. You poor boys." The rest of us were wide-eyed. My experiences in camp had given me a taste of the absurdity and cruelty behind the pomp, but this was absurdity and cruelty on a whole other level.

"In any case, this bravado was soon dispelled. Within a couple days the camp came under air attack from the Russians. We were told to move down the road, carrying our rifles, our Panzerfausts, our kit and even our mattresses. Low-flying fighter planes strafed the road. Fortunately we could hear and see them coming, so we were able to jump into the ditch in time. The planes then turned around to take a second run from the other direction. As they were turning it gave us the chance to jump over to the opposite ditch unobserved. This worked well, nobody was killed! Our mattresses, which we had abandoned on the road, suffered tremendously though!

"After this attack we were told to return to the camp, as the Russians did not immediately follow up with the expected ground assault. A short while later an SS officer appeared in our camp, accompanied by an SS doctor and his assistant. The doctor and the assistant seemed nice enough, but the officer was a grim sort. He barked at Neumeyer that he was there to recruit soldiers for the Waffen SS. They were now taking sixteen-year-olds, he said. Neumeyer explained that his Volkssturm boys were fourteen and fifteen years old. The

SS officer didn't skip a beat and countered that they would be sixteen soon enough, so that was fine, they would also take 'future sixteen-year-olds.' However, the SS has a peculiar pride regarding size. They always had the tallest soldiers. The officer himself was at least 195." That's centimetres, which equals about six foot five inches.

"Their minimum had been 175, but they had dropped it to 160 in the latter days of the war. When the officer wasn't looking, the doctor pressed the measuring bar down to make the boy's height even lower. I didn't think he'd have to bother with a dwarf like me, as I was comfortably under 160 regardless, but he was obviously concerned as I was among the tallest of the dwarves, so for good measure he also declared that I had a heart defect. This is not true. He really was trying to pass as few of us as possible. Those who he had to pass were asked to sign a document that stated that they voluntarily joined the SS. One bold comrade of mine looked at that and said that he couldn't sign it because he was not joining voluntarily. He was told to strike out the word 'voluntarily' and sign it anyway!"

Theodor took another drink of water and smiled weakly at us. "Yes, it was a strange time up there, but it became even stranger. Before he took the few unfortunate taller boys back with him down the mountain, he gave us a short lecture. Apparently, the famous tank commander General Heinz Guderian had been put in charge of recruiting and training and had just issued a directive that he was honoured to share with us. The directive was that we were to read Karl May's *Winnetou* and learn from him —"

I interrupted Theodor by laughing out loud, in both astonishment and delight. See, Karl May was important!

"Yes, Karl May. Should we find our weapons inadequate, we were to learn from the tactics of the wild Indians wherein one sneaks up behind an enemy soldier who has a desirable weapon, strikes him on the head with any handy object such as a rock or stout branch and then steals his weapon! Can you imagine? This is being passed on in all seriousness as tactical advice from General Guderian!"

Even I could see that this was perhaps not the smartest application of *Winnetou*. I thought that perhaps forest survival advice would be given.

"Needless to say, to the best of my knowledge nobody followed this directive. And in any case, it was tanks that we faced, not foot soldiers. Shortly after the SS man left, the Russian assault on the mountain began. We could see the tanks moving up the road from the valley on the Saxony side and we tried to hit them with our Panzerfausts, but it was useless. It's a close-range weapon and the tanks were still too far away. Also we honestly didn't know what we were doing. Through field glasses we watched them crush our tank traps as if they were made of toothpicks. At this point Neumeyer told us that the war was effectively over and that we were relieved of our duties and were welcome to do as we pleased. Then he saluted us with his good arm and got into the one functional car with his deputy, who drove the two of them off to the southwest at high speed."

Theodor paused and rubbed his forehead. "I know I slept most of the day, but I'm very tired again now. There's not that much more to tell. I'll finish tomorrow."

~

The next morning, Theodor took up the remainder of the story. We assembled again in a semicircle around him. Even little three-year-old Oskar paid attention.

"So, the officers were gone, and we were under no obligation to fight anymore. It took only a fraction of a second to process this. Before his car was even out of sight, we all began throwing our Panzerfausts away — even the keenest among us — and we were all tearing the insignias off our uniforms. I doubt any of us really believed the Russians would be fooled, but we were going to do whatever we could not to be identified as soldiers. It was easy to outrun the tanks and we were soon in a kind of no man's land further southwest along the border. It was here that we heard the war had ended. The 8th of May, which I suppose is a week and a day ago now. But the danger had not passed because we could still be captured by the Russians and executed or sent to labour camp in Siberia. We were by far not the only ones with the same idea. As we came down from the ridge and got onto larger roads, we found that they were full of German soldiers streaming west. The lucky ones had found civilian clothing, but most were like us, trying to disguise the fact that what we were wearing had once been a uniform.

"This large number of people fleeing also meant that food was impossible to find. We could tell where Russians had already been because the road would be lined with discarded vodka bottles, and we could tell where the Americans had been because the road was lined with their discarded ready-made breakfast packages. The vodka bottles didn't interest us of course, but we examined each of these breakfast packages carefully, hoping that some scrap would remain, but there was never anything edible left.

"Things were getting quite desperate for food by the second day when one of the group of us walking together remembered that a secret military food storage depot was nearby. Predictably it had been mostly plundered, but we did find some food that we were able to put in a wheel-barrow. We did not get very far with that wheelbarrow. Almost immediately a German tank, also headed west, rolled up to us and an officer got out. He pointed his pistol at us and demanded all the food. At that point we decided that we would be better off splitting up. Most of us had different destinations in mind anyway. Fortunately I had memorized the *Atlas of Saxony* when I was younger, so I was able to mentally map out a route back to Colditz that I thought might avoid the Red Army."

"The *Atlas of Saxony*!" I interjected. "I remember when we used to trace all the little roads and paths together like we were explorers!"

"Yes, I remember that too." Theodor smiled at me. Then he continued his story. "I made my way to Schwarzenberg first where I was very lucky to find a family that offered to take me in for the night. They did not have much food, but they shared what they had with me, so I was no longer completely starved, and then the next day I began walking north towards Chemnitz, hoping that the Russians hadn't gotten there yet. In fact it was in American hands, but a typhoid fever epidemic had broken out and the city was under complete quarantine, so I had to make a big detour around it. I slept in the woods, just south of Chemnitz and then again just north. This second time I was lucky again. A man saw me in the woods and offered to let me stay at his place where he had a little bit of food too. In other times this would have been frightening, going with a stranger, but I was desperate, and he was very kind. The war really sorts people into their true types, doesn't it?

"Then one more thing happened, on the last day of my trek, so the day before yesterday. As I passed Burgstaedt, an American recognized that I was wearing a modified uniform and in German shouted 'Halt!' I panicked, not wanting to be captured so close to home, so I ran away across the field as fast as I could. He fired some shots at me but missed — obviously — and he made an attempt to run after me, but he gave up right away. I pushed through forty kilometres that day and night and arrived at the Mulde in the dark early morning. It was then that I figured out that although the Americans were on the west side where I was, the Russians were on the east where you were, and that the bridge was guarded. So, I took all my clothes off and made a bundle of them to put on my head and then I swam across. The guards must have heard something as they took some shots in my direction, but again no bullets came close." Theodor took a deep breath and smiled at us. "The rest you know."

CHAPTER
THIRTY-ONE

JUNE 1945

Theodor stayed out of sight, mostly in the bedroom, for close to a week until we were sure that the Russians were no longer interested in capturing or summarily executing ex-soldiers, and certainly not young teen Volkssturm conscripts.

Fairly quickly their focus had shifted from revenge to reparations. Proclamations were issued stating that the Union of Soviet Socialist Republics was owed an incalculable debt for both the damage caused by the German invasion, but also for the costs associated with our liberation from our "Fascist oppressors." Subsequently teams of Russian soldiers and officers began seizing anything they deemed of value. In particular they appeared to be focusing on art objects and industrial equipment. In addition, larger houses were ransacked for jewellery and silver and antiques, but they did not bother with little hovels like ours. The castle was emptied of any art that looked remotely valuable, and in town anything with an engine and any tools more sophisticated than a hammer or a shovel were confiscated as well. All of this was brought to the train station and loaded onto railcars. Then as the train slowly left the station, headed east ultimately to Russia one presumes, a team of German prisoners of war were ordered to dismantle the track behind the train, loading the rails onto it, one pair at a time. This was a very surreal thing to watch happen. Steel was valuable of course, especially for the post-war reconstruction, but this seemed an unnecessarily extreme measure. I was standing there with a few other grubby children like myself when a Russian officer saw us watching and said in broken German, "Russia move forward to future. Germany move backward to past!" This was perhaps as much the motivation as reparations. Back to revenge.

Now that Theodor was free to move about town, we had another pair of hands to help find food and also to find cigarette stubs, as tobacco had become an important impromptu currency. Full cigarettes were of course best, but we had learned how to make hand-rolled ones from the butt ends discarded by the Allied soldiers. The Americans in particular threw away cigarettes with up to a quarter or even sometimes half remaining! Occasionally they winked at us as they did this.

The informal market had dwindled to one or two farmers who showed up to town intermittently, the others having all fled the Russian advance. Some shops in town did have a few things to sell now, but the supply was still wholly inadequate. I was frustrated because I knew that I could find food in the forest across the bridge. There would be mushrooms for sure and the first berries would be out now too. Also by early June word had begun to spread that conditions were quickly improving on the American side of the river and that food had generally become much more available there. The bridge was still blocked and guarded, and I did not know how to swim, but Theodor did. He would not know where to go in the forest, but he could be sent to the market and to scavenge for cigarette butts on the other side.

Swimming the Mulde between the zones of occupation was strictly forbidden, but neither the Russians nor the Americans seemed especially intent on patrolling the banks, so as long as Theodor swam out of sight of the sentries on the bridge, he was usually fine. Even so, on two occasions he was spotted by a random patrol, once American and once Russian, and was shot at. In both cases they missed him, and in both cases so widely that their intent seemed to be to frighten him, not harm him. It did succeed in frightening him, but it did not succeed in dissuading him. Hunger, if sufficiently intense, trumps fear. Soon Theodor became a kind of water mule for Herr Rittmann and two other sets of neighbours as well. In addition to bringing food and tobacco back he also carried messages back and forth as an informal courier service developed. For example, Mama wanted to let Tante Karoline know that we were okay, so Theodor passed the letter on to someone on the west side who passed it along to someone travelling roughly in the direction of Mellingen until, remarkably, a week or two later it arrived at its destination.

Curiously during this entire period nobody spoke about what had happened to Papa, not directly anyway. Mama would occasionally preface remarks along the lines of "Without Papa we will . . ." but his death and the manner of his death were not raised. I thought Theodor would want to talk about it, but given what he had gone through, and given that he always looked tired and sad, I waited for him to introduce the subject. By the end of June, he still had not, so one afternoon when the two of us had been sent to collect wood for the cooking fire, I decided that it was up to me.

"Theodor, do you really think Papa did that? Killed himself?"

Theodor did not stop walking and he did not look at me. For a minute I thought that he would ignore the question. Then he spoke. "Yes, I think he did. I've heard that hundreds, even thousands, of Party officials did the same thing."

"But why?"

"You read his letter — he just could not face Germany's defeat. But honestly I think that it might have been more that he did not want to endure the humiliation of capture at the hands of the enemy. Remember that some of his heroes in ancient times — Socrates, Cato, Seneca — ended their lives this way. There is a sense of romantic honour about it for someone like Papa. What a load of crap though. I think it's selfish. Do you see what it's done to Mama?"

"Yes, she is having a hard time. But even if he did not kill himself, he would be dead or he would be a prisoner, and our situation right now would be the same," I reasoned.

"I suppose."

"Do you miss him?"

"Miss him? Well, I haven't seen much of him the last three years or so, so I've had some time to get used to it. When I was little though he was actually a good father. He was very good in math and always helped me with my homework when I was having trouble. Other fathers totally ignored their kids or beat their kids. He never did that."

"No, it was Mama who would hit us when we were bad!"

"Ha, that's funny isn't it. The Nazi was soft, and the anti-Nazi was hard! Well, in child-rearing anyway. I think he enjoyed his self-image as the kindly and wise pater familias. He did have quite a temper though, just not a violent one."

"That is true. I remember him shouting at Mama. He did not shout at me, but I was more afraid of his stern voice and cold disapproval when he was angry than I was afraid of the back of Mama's hand. Papa would stay mad at me for days while Mama would hug me an hour after giving me a spanking."

Theodor nodded and changed the subject, indicating that we should take a different path today to find wood as the old area was surely picked through by now.

CHAPTER

THIRTY-TWO

JULY 1, 1945

Theodor did not have to swim the Mulde anymore. At the stroke of noon on July 1, Major Kozlov and a squad of smartly turned-out Red Army soldiers, two of them carrying large red Soviet flags, marched up the bridge where they met an American officer (not Colonel Armstrong) and a small group of GIs. Across the bridge a larger number of American soldiers were sitting in the backs of trucks. I could see them smoking and laughing. I thought I spotted the Black soldiers I had met in May, but I couldn't be sure. A brief conversation appeared to take place on the bridge, followed by a handshake and some saluting. This was a replay of exactly two months prior when Colditz had been handed over to the Russians.

I will confess to not having been especially attuned to the political situation, so this development surprised and confused me. It occurred to me that this might mean that I would finally have access to the forest again, but I knew enough to realize that the departure of the Americans from the west bank of the Mulde was probably not, on balance, a good development.

Theodor was beside me and read the bewilderment on my face. He paid much more attention to the news and rumours and was generally better at talking to people and listening to them. "The rest of Saxony plus Thuringia, Halle-Merseburg, Anhalt and Magdeburg are being handed over to the Russians. This is because of a deal between Roosevelt, Churchill and Stalin last winter. The Russian zone of occupation is increasing in size by at least a third today!"

"But why? Why would the Americans do that?"

"I hear that during the war the Allies were worried the Russians would push much further west than they ultimately did, and that they thought that they had actually got the better deal, that the Russians would have to give up some of their gains, rather than the other way around. But then Dönitz let the western front collapse. Clever man. There wasn't much fighting here, was there? The Americans more or less just walked in, right?"

"Yes."

"Well, I can tell you, it wasn't that way in the east. 'No surrender to the Bolshevik Hordes' was our motto!"

We jumped in alarm as the American trucks made loud backfiring noises. They were starting up and getting in gear. One of the Black soldiers waved in our direction, although possibly not at me specifically as there was a cluster of children with us on the east bank watching. The trucks backfired some more, belched dark grey smoke and then slowly rumbled off to the west. We could still hear them for a long while and we watched, straining our eyes, as their plumes of dust and smoke became smaller and smaller. The Russian squad in the meantime placed their flags on the far side of the bridge and then stood sentry as a column of their trucks, as well as a few tanks, drove across before splitting into two groups, one following the now vanished Americans and the other heading north, towards Schönbach, Grimma and presumably points beyond. Our little group watched this too, heads swivelling silently back and forth. Then all was quiet again, but for the murmur of the river below and the chirp of an unidentified bird in a nearby shrub.

"What will happen now, Theodor?"

"I don't know. I suppose I don't have to swim anymore, but now with the Russians over there it may not be any better there for food anyway."

"Yes, it will be. I know a place."

CHAPTER

THIRTY-THREE

SUMMER 1945

I expected more warnings from Mama about going into the forest, but in fact it was Theodor who cautioned me about the possibility of unexploded munitions or grisly remains. Mama was curiously flat in her emotions and said very little to us. I know that she cried a lot in the days after the letter from Papa, but it was as if those tears had drained all the feeling from her, emptying her and hollowing her. She had an unfocused way of looking and slowness of response that reminded me of the armless old soldier, one of the elderly Volkssturm recruits, I had seen in the market. Mama's pregnancy was also slowing her down and making her tired. She spent a lot of time in the bedroom. Theodor was good with Clara, Johann and Oskar, so this gave me the freedom to go out, more or less as I pleased.

My original intention was to search the forest to find food for the family, but as it happened the food situation unexpectedly became less dire. I did not hear a clear explanation, but it was logical to assume that the remaining farms were able to produce more now that it was properly summer, even though they were mostly back to nineteenth-century horsepower. It was also logical to assume that the transport of food had improved as travel restrictions within the Soviet occupation zone were loosened. The level of harassment and outright mortal danger from Russian soldiers was substantially less now, some important bridges had been at least provisionally repaired and most — not all but most — of the landmines had been cleared from the major roads. The other factor to consider was that with such a large proportion of the young to middle-aged male population dead or imprisoned, and with so many people having fled further west, there were fewer mouths to feed in this area than before the war.

As I approached the forest from the bridge it looked unchanged. I had not been sure what to expect, so I was cautiously pleased. The small road leading up to it was, however, heavily cratered by artillery fire from the American push on Colditz in April. There were also unidentifiable pieces of metal of varying sizes and shapes strewn about, so mindful of Theodor's warning, I avoided going near any. This meant that I had to slalom cautiously around the big holes and the metal shards. The 500 metres took twenty minutes rather than the usual ten. There was nobody else around other than a single bored Russian sentry squatting on the bridge, cleaning his gun, who did not so much as glance at me.

Once inside the forest the only immediate evidence of the war was some discarded equipment beside the path. There was nothing of value or interest, just a few German helmets, some empty ammunition clips and various decals and insignia ripped off uniforms. As was always the case, the minute I was deep enough into the forest that the trees closed behind me and sealed off the outside world I felt entirely different. Outside it was a hot July day, but in the forest it was cool. Outside there were various sorts of random, often unpleasant human noises, but in the forest, it was only birds and insects and the wind in the leaves. Outside I was unable to shake a pervasive sense of dread, but in the forest, I felt safe and confident. I realized that this was the opposite of what many people felt, which seemed to me like yet more evidence that people were generally strange.

But I had not come to the forest for selfish reasons. I had come to scout for food. Yes, for the moment we were no longer starving, but there was no doubt that this could change very quickly. Theodor was planning to explore the roads and identify accessible apple trees. In the eighteenth century King Frederick the Great ordered the roads to be lined with apple trees to feed and shade his armies on the march. Now this was primarily in Prussia, but the practice was followed in some parts of Saxony too. Also an ancient Saxon law required that a man plant six fruit trees before he could take a bride. These were typically also near roads and around farms. It was not apple season quite yet, but Theodor felt it wise to be prepared. For my part, the wild, or more or less wild, forest was my domain. I knew that red currants, gooseberries and blueberries should be ready. Blackberries and nuts would be easier to find and more numerous, but their season was not until later. I was also curious about mushrooms. I had seen them frequently when I had come to the forest last year, but I had not paid especially close attention.

I was walking along, collecting the few currants I could find in my canvas bag and listening to the birds — sparrows, robins, woodpeckers, warblers and, yes, the wren — when I heard a different noise. I ducked behind a bush and froze in place. It was not a bird or the wind. It was the rustling sound of branches being pushed aside. A larger animal perhaps? Like a deer? There were stories that wolves and bears had been pushed into Germany out of the Carpathians, fleeing the Red Army just like the people did. Then the rustling stopped, and I heard a quiet voice. I held my breath. The wolves and bears were replaced by Russian soldiers in my imagination. Or maybe German Werewolf partisans. Being in the forest usually made me feel more confident because I knew the rules, but that only applied when I was alone. When other people were involved, that confidence evaporated. The voice was clearer now. I still could not make out the words, but the rhythm was distinctly German. And it was a child's voice. A girl I guessed. I would still rather there be no people at all, but if there had to be, a German girl was the best possible scenario. I stepped out from where I had hidden, taking care to make a bit of noise first so as not to startle them. I was mostly right. It was a girl, but there was also a boy with her. They were quite young. The boy was close to my age, maybe a year younger, and the girl was likely a year younger than that. They were dressed in what can only be described as rags and they were barefoot. Their brown hair, hers in long pigtails and his very short, was quite neat though and their faces were clean. They each had a wicker basket and were obviously collecting berries as well. We stared at each other from across the small clearing.

The little girl spoke first. "What's your name?"

"Ludwig."

"I'm Anna and this is my brother Hans. Where are you from?"

"Leipzig. But I have been in Colditz for the last two years."

"We're from Waldenburg in Silesia," she said although the boy gave his sister a stern look. "It's okay, Hans, I can tell that we can trust him." She turned back to me and explained, "My mother told us not to tell people that we are refugees because we might be treated badly. We were near Chemnitz before and there it was a problem because the local people didn't have enough for themselves and there were so many of us from Silesia."

I did not really want to get into a conversation and was eager to go off deeper into the forest on my own, but it was clear that some sort of response was expected from me. "I heard it was bad in Silesia."

"It was not as bad in Waldenburg as in Breslau, but it was bad enough. Hans doesn't speak any more because of it and our father is dead. But then most people's fathers are dead. Is your father dead?"

"Yes."

She nodded. Neither of us offered condolences to the other. People had stopped doing that.

"Anyway," she continued, "all the German people had to leave. Polish people are going to live there now. And I hear that Russian people are going to live where the Polish people used to live, further east. Poland has just been slid over to the west like it had little wheels underneath it!" She laughed at her own joke. I smiled weakly and Hans did not change his facial expression.

I was about to make my excuses, wish them a good day and leave when Anna spoke again. "Watch out for the Rübezahl if you go deeper in the woods!"

"The Rübezahl?"

"Yes, the Rübezahl. Hans and I are quite sure that he came with the refugees from Silesia, and this is the kind of place he would like to be."

"I have never heard of him. Is he a man or a beast?"

"Neither!" The girl's eyes widened, and she gestured with her hands, enjoying the prospect of being able to tell this story to someone who had not heard it before. "He's a giant! But he's not just any giant — he is the guardian of the mountains and the forests. He can make weather with his storm harp, especially bad weather like thunderstorms in the summer and snowstorms in the winter. He will only do this if you don't respect him though. The most important thing is that if you meet him, you must not call him Rübezahl. You must call him 'Lord of the Mountains' or 'Prince of Gnomes.' This is tricky, because he might appear to you in disguise, as an old lady, for example, needing help. This is to test the purity of your heart. If you fail this test, he will take his real form and then your only chance not to get lost in a terrible storm is to beg for forgiveness using his real name. But if you are pure in your heart and pass his test, you will have good luck and you might even be lucky enough to be shown the path to treasures!"

"This sounds like a fairy story," I said.

"I know it does, but it's absolutely true. I know it for a fact. My great-grandfather saw the Rübezahl not just once but twice. Each time he passed the test. This is why our family was so fortunate right up until the war. We were wealthy and respected in Waldenburg."

I was still not entirely convinced. "Why would he come here? And why does he not want to be called Rübezahl, if that is what everyone calls him?"

"Silesia is gone now. The Rübezahl will move west until he finds a new home to protect. Here you have a perfect forest, although no mountains, so it is a fine place for him to rest until he finds the right kind of mountains again. And he is called Rübezahl because of the story that he fell in love with a lonely princess. To cheer her up he magically turned turnips into companions for her. She was afraid of him though, so she asked him to count all the turnips in the garden to distract him while she escaped! You see, Ruebe Zahl — Turnip Counter! This part might be a made-up fairy story though. His name might have a more ancient and mysterious origin. But the Rübezahl himself is as real as you and me and Hans, so you need to be careful and respectful." Anna beamed at me and gave the brisk nod that some people give when having told a definitive truth.

"I am always careful and respectful here," I said in a sharp tone.

"Of course you are," Anna said, still smiling. I noticed that she had dark eyes that reminded me of Clara's. I also noticed that her clothes, which had looked like rags, appeared to be carefully hand-sewn in a cheerful patchwork of bright colours.

It occurred to me then that I was actually relatively new to this place as well. Moreover, the story of the Rübezahl had an unsettling ring of at least partial authenticity to it. Perhaps it was best not to make enemies of these children, let alone the theoretical Rübezahl only for the sake of my pride.

"Thank you for telling me about the Rübezahl. It is an interesting story." I was careful to make my tone softer and friendlier. I hoped I succeeded. It was difficult to tell as Anna kept smiling regardless and Hans continued to look inscrutable regardless.

"You're welcome," she said. "Hans and I should go now. Just remember to help any old ladies you find, unless of course they're witches. Then you should be careful not to be tricked! Goodbye, Ludwig!" She took Hans's hand and they walked off down a side path.

"Goodbye," I replied.

Witches? I had not considered those before. They were likely real. On Walpurgis Night they gathered on the Brocken, a high mountain in the Harz, perhaps 200 kilometres to the northwest as the broomstick flies. Every German child knew this. Many people in the city dismissed these tales, but in the countryside, people still believed. They had more evidence for their belief because that is where the witches were. Witches did not go into the cities. The Colditzer Forst was safe though. I had seen absolutely no evidence of witches here. As this train of thought ran along it took a disturbing turn. I was still standing in the small clearing, with my canvas bag half full of red currants in my right hand. I decided to sit on a tree stump. I had seen no evidence of witches, but then it occurred to me that I really did not know what that evidence would be. A witch would not leave a broomstick lying about, or a cauldron, or live in a candy house like in Hansel and Gretel. That was a silly fairy story, but most of those had some dim and distant basis in fact. It was certainly possible that witches ate children. Probable even. I had never seen the bones of children or their clothing anywhere in the forest either. Was this evidence that there were no witches here? It was, I realized, very difficult to prove that something or some person, such a witch, was absent. One could always reason that one had missed the signs. Perhaps the witch was very good at hiding. Seeing a witch would definitively prove that she was present, but not seeing her was logically far less definitive.

This was as far as that train of thought would take me. Witches probably existed and I could not prove that one was not living in this forest. Nonetheless I felt safe in the forest and I reasoned that a witch always got her victims through trickery, and I was too smart to fall for that. The Rübezahl was a complication, however, as he could apparently also look like a feeble old woman in need of my assistance. But I was still not convinced that he was anything more than a Silesian folk tale conjured up to make people behave and to explain wild mountain weather. Moreover, there were plenty of mountainous areas in central Germany for him to go if he was real and on the move. There was no need to stop in the Colditzer Forst. And giants moved pretty quickly. Anna and Hans were younger than me and even a year or two difference at that age made a tremendous difference in wisdom.

CHAPTER

THIRTY-FOUR

OCTOBER 8, 1945

Mama suddenly said, "I need to go to Rochlitz. The baby is coming."

Rochlitz was ten kilometres to the south and had the only functioning hospital in the district. The Russians had dismantled the major rail lines going east but had left some of the smaller spur lines alone, so an antique coal-powered train with one passenger car had begun making the journey to Rochlitz again. The glass was missing from all of its windows, which was increasingly an issue as the weather turned cooler and damper. Cardboard had been provisionally nailed in place over parts of most of the windows to keep out the worst of the weather, but there was no power in the train car and some natural light was needed. The train was always absolutely crammed full too, with every available surface sat upon and stood upon. And it stank — the acrid stink of cheap brown-coal smoke and the reek of anxious people who did not have enough hot water to consistently do laundry or bathe themselves properly. Nonetheless there was no choice. Mama could not walk, so she would have to take the train.

Theodor went with her and I was left in charge of the little ones. It was not clear when they would return, although Theodor said that he would likely be back before Mama.

About two weeks prior we had had a stroke of good fortune. An old lawyer colleague of Papa's had been kept on by the Soviets in a low-level administrative position in the town of Colditz. He had done a good job of keeping his Nazi affiliation secret, but the Nazis kept thorough records. Many of these records had been hastily destroyed, but this gentleman's had not and the Russians were gradually working their way through the document archives until they came upon his file. I never met the gentleman and I do not recall his name, but I know that the details of his Nazi membership were enough to get him fired, although not enough to have him imprisoned. This all sounds like misfortune so far, but I am getting to the good fortune, for us anyway. This ex-Nazi, ex–town administrator subsequently left Colditz and because he knew about our bad situation and what had happened to Papa, he pulled whatever strings he was still able to pull to allow us to move into his old apartment. It was directly across the lane from the brewery, so the move was easy. It was still far below what we had been used to in Leipzig in terms of comfort, style and size, but it was much roomier than the back of the brewery where we had been. The biggest change was that we would now each have our own bed! The impact of this cannot be understated. Mama had been sharing her bed with Oskar, Johann and Clara, while Theodor and I had been sleeping on the floor in the other room. To go from one bed to six felt like the gates of heaven had been thrown open for us. They were small simple beds mind you, and soon there would be seven of us and some bed sharing would be happening again, but none of this diminished the delight we all felt.

This was the first time I was alone in charge of my younger siblings. While I was proud of the confidence placed in me by my mother, the three little ones seemed like somewhat alien creatures to me, so I will confess that I was a little nervous about how things would go. There would be no way to reach Mama or Theodor if I had questions. If a really serious concern arose, I was to go over to Frau Bergen's, but given what we had already survived in the last few years, the events of a few quiet post-war October days were not anticipated to be too much for me to handle. I was eleven and three-quarters years old after all. Cooking was simple as all we had were potatoes, apples, bread and a bit of bacon fat.

The only real issue was the old stove. It was larger than the one we had in the brewery flat, which was certainly nice as a cold winter was predicted by all the old crones in the marketplace, but there was something wrong with the chimney and with how it drew air, so large clouds of smoke frequently issued from every opening and crack in that black iron monster, forcing us to stumble outside, coughing and spluttering. I applied logic to the problem and reasoned that the chimney must be obstructed somehow. I allowed the stove to cool off and then got the longest, greenest stick I could find among the willows on the riverbank. It was slightly flexible, so I was able to feed it through the stove opening and up into the chimney. Clara, Johann and Oskar watched with fascination. I told them to be absolutely silent as I needed to concentrate. The stick was only long enough to go a short distance up the chimney. I knew this in advance of course. This was just a "proof of concept" exercise. Having thus proven the concept to be sound, I then put Clara and Johann to work tying a series of these branches together to make one long stick. I supervised their work carefully, correcting as necessary. Once I deemed it to be ready, I told them all to stand back in case a large amount of soot or some other nasty substance came cascading down. I did not want to be responsible for washing them. The places where the branches had been tied together were not flexible, but with a bit of maneuvering and forceful shoving I was able to get the stick up a long way. To my chagrin, I encountered no obstructions and then the stick broke.

My next strategy was to ask Herr Rittmann for help. As I have mentioned, normally I did not like approaching people to talk to them, but in my role as head of the household it was my responsibility to do so, and responsibility should trump shyness. Herr Rittmann came over, chuckling that he had smelled the smoke and heard the coughing from across the street. He examined the situation carefully and then said, "Well, Ludwig, I don't know what you're going to do about this. The stove and chimney are not drawing properly, possibly due to damage to the chimney, and possibly due to a creosote buildup in it. You need a proper chimney sweep, and they're all dead or far away in the big cities! I'm sorry that I can't help. Just build your fires slowly, don't use green or damp wood and keep your windows open whenever you can."

That was that. We had to adapt to the problem rather than fix it.

~

Theodor came back the next day already, reporting that we had a new baby brother named Paul, and that Mama would have to stay in the hospital three more days, but that she was doing well and was reasonably comfortable there. A new baby brother. I knew that pregnancy would result in a baby, but it had been abstract knowledge until now. I had gotten used to the new configuration of our family since Papa died and felt anxious about any changes. Much like the smoky stove though, I found that I quickly adapted. Theodor went to get Mama on the third day and when they returned, I made a point of welcoming the baby warmly in order to get our relationship off to a good start. I could not think of him as a proper person with a name, so for a long while Paul was simply "the baby" in my mind, but I did get used to him.

I was also pleased to see some of Mama's old personality return. She smiled more and talked more and even made a joke or two. It was still not the same as before, but it was a welcome improvement. She was especially animated when she told us about the Rochlitz hospital. Remarkably she had had a private room. It was tiny, but it was not the big open ward she expected. The problem with this arrangement though was that nobody saw or heard her go into labour. She had been labouring for three hours by herself when the door suddenly opened and a woman came in. She was not in a nurse's uniform and she spoke only very rudimentary German. It turned out that she was Croatian and that she was a midwife assigned to one of the Russian officer's wives who was giving birth in the next room. This Croatian midwife took one look at Mama's situation, declared, "You're ready," and proceeded to deliver the baby with a magician's ease. Later Mama learned that all the nurses had been Nazi Party members and had been dismissed! The Croatian was only officially there for the Russians. The other staff were local people with no formal training but were very kind to my mother and slipped her a little extra bread and milk as often as they could, since she was not getting any visitors. Normally visitors were responsible for supplying food.

Now we were seven.

CHAPTER

THIRTY-FIVE

DECEMBER 1945

We were all in the main room when there was a knock on the door. I remember seeing Mama being handed two letters. She opened them quickly with fumbling fingers and then after a long pause where I could see her eyes racing back and forth across the pages, she screamed and dropped them.

"What, Mama? What's happened?" Theodor asked as he ran over to her.

She sobbed, "Wilhelm's alive." She shook her head at all the inquiries that immediately followed and picked up the letters and wordlessly handed them to Theodor. They had been brought by one of the informal couriers who still operated throughout occupied Germany. She left the room, crying. Clara, Johann and Oskar were fortunately playing in one of the bedrooms while Paul was napping, so Theodor and I were able to read the letters in peace. Each was on a single page stamped with "Examined — No. 2 CIC" in English. A few sentences were blacked out with a heavy marker. Our father wrote in very small print and used all the margins in the much longer second letter. The dating of the first showed that it had been written two weeks prior to the second.

Dear Luise,

I hope this letter finds you and the children well. It has not been possible to write before now. I have been through some very difficult times and have suffered enormously, but I am better now. ████████████████████ ████████████████████████████ ████ There is so much to tell. For now, let it suffice to inform you that I am alive.

Your Wilhelm

Dear Luise,

I now have the time, the energy and the clarity of thought to explain how I came to be where I am. When last you saw me, I was preparing to assist in the defence of Leipzig. Our forces were divided into two groups. My group consisted of the armed city police, civil defence and Volkssturm under the command of Major Wilhelm von Grolman. The other group was regular army, SS and some Hitler Youth under Oberst Hans von Poncet. Grolman felt that the fight was futile and wished to negotiate with the Americans who were on the outskirts of Leipzig. I argued against this, especially as Poncet vowed we would fight to the last man and he was in overall command of the defence of the city. The street by street fighting was ferocious as the Americans cautiously moved into the city on April 19. Grolman and I were in the city hall. Poncet was five kilometres southwest at the Monument to the Battle of the Nations.

Finally, late in the day, the Americans penetrated to the centre of the city. Three times they attacked city hall with their Sherman tanks and three times we pushed them back. But the situation was not good. Bullets were constantly flying through the windows and the building shook badly every time a tank round hit it. The American commander was incredibly able to call Grolman on the telephone. He threatened that if we did not surrender, they would strike us with heavy artillery and then come in to mop up with their dreaded flamethrowers. In the next room deputy mayor Ernst Lisso killed himself as well as his wife and his daughter. Then the mayor, Alfred Freyberg, and his wife and daughter committed suicide too. As did Volkssturm commander Walter Dönicke. Fortunately he did not have his family with him. You cannot imagine the atmosphere there. At that point my aide Erich, do you remember Erich? He begged me to surrender along with Grolman. He said that Poncet was not there and was certainly dead anyway. He said that the enemy wanted us dead and that to be dead was to lose. It was over.

Then I was a prisoner. We spent three days and nights in an open field southwest of the city before being moved to the first camp. ████

████ On the march to the camp we were made to stop at a place where the Americans said our soldiers had burned 250 Polish and French slave labourers alive just a day before Leipzig fell. We were forced to look at their bodies and then dig graves for them. Luise, it was horrible to see this. The Americans told us of much worse things even. Things that I do not want to write about.

I don't know if my description of life in the prisoner-of-war camp for the first two months will pass the censor, so I will not waste space writing much, ████████████████████████

██

Before the handover of Saxony and Thuringia etc. to the Soviets on July 1 the Americans sorted us into two groups. Some like Erich were simply released and some like me were deemed worthy of continued incarceration and distributed to other camps in the west. I was turned over to the British, which was a stroke of great fortune. My English is very good, and as my grandmother Mary Charlie was British, I get along far better with these people than with the Americans. (And I cannot imagine if the Russians had captured me instead.) The other aspect of my good fortune is that this camp is close to where Auguste lives. I have been classified as Category II and will likely be in the denazification process for a while yet.

You should have access to the safes at our two banks in Leipzig. At least one bank was still standing at the time of surrender. You should go and see what you can retrieve.

I will write again when I have a chance.

Your Wilhelm

"What . . ." I began.

Theodor cut me off, holding his hand up. He was rereading the letters slowly.

Papa was alive. This was wonderful news of course, but my dominant first emotion was confusion. Through the spring and early summer I had held out hope that he had not killed himself, or been killed, and that he was a prisoner of war somewhere, but some sort of word should have gotten out, so the longer we did not hear anything, the more certain I was that he was dead. Mama had quizzed the few released prisoners who came through Colditz and asked any ex-colleagues of Papa's she encountered for news, but nobody knew anything.

Theodor finally looked up from the letters. He shook his head slowly and wiped his eyes.

"I don't believe it," he said. "And I wouldn't believe it if it weren't his writing. It's weird how much detail he writes about the battle in Leipzig compared to everything else. Maybe he's trying to justify why he didn't commit suicide without directly referring to it."

"I remember Erich," I said. "He met Mama and me that day the front wall of our Kaiser Wilhelm Strasse apartment was blown off. Do you think he saved Papa's life with what he said?"

"I don't know. Papa does seem to hint at that. And maybe seeing those other horrible suicides changed his mind too."

We both paused for a moment and looked at the letters again. We could hear Mama crying in the next room.

"Why are those sentences blacked out?" I asked.

"He must have written something that the British censored."

"Something secret?"

"I don't know. I suppose secret or just something he's not allowed to say."

"And what's denazification? And what is Category II?"

"I don't know any of that either. I'm guessing that it is some way to make him not be a Nazi anymore, and the category is how bad he was. I don't know whether a lower number is better or worse."

There was another pause as I tried to picture what that would entail. The only image that came to my mind was Papa writing lines on the blackboard. "I will not be a Nazi" thousands and thousands of times. This was silly of course.

"And what or who is 'Auguste'?"

Theodor laughed. "Your aunt, you dummy! She's Papa's sister. She married an artist in Worpswede. That's near Bremen in the north."

"Oh." If I was honest with myself, I really was not that interested in distant family and did not pay very much attention when they were discussed. I knew Papa had sisters, but who exactly they were did not register deeply enough to be memorable.

We wanted to discuss the letters with Mama, but she was still in her room and we felt it better not to disturb her. We also thought that the little ones should be told by her and only when the time was right and only when the story had been carefully prepared. But we did want to discuss it with someone, so we decided to go see if Herr Rittmann was home. He might know something about censorship and denazification. He was home and he was pleased to see us. He lived alone and seemed bored a lot of the time.

"Come in, boys," he said. "I can make tea? Would you like tea?"

"No, no thank you, Herr Rittmann," Theodor said. I had decided to let him do the talking, which he probably would have done anyway.

"Well then, please have a seat and tell me what brings you here." He smiled and indicated to a wooden bench on the far side of his dining table. He sat in a rickety wooden chair opposite us. It was very warm, especially near his stove. I noted that there was no smoke.

Theodor cleared his throat and then put the letters on the table, turning them towards Herr Rittmann and smoothing the creases. "Papa is alive," he said quietly.

Herr Rittmann looked up, astonished, and then fished in a vest pocket for his glasses. He read the letters quickly and then let out a low whistle. "Wilhelm, alive. Well, I don't know whether I'm surprised or not. I didn't know him that well, but it was always clear that he was a clever man. In any case, I'm very happy for you children and for your poor mother."

"Thank you," Theodor said. "We have some questions we thought you might be able to help us with."

"Yes, please ask."

"Do you know what they might have censored?"

"Naturally I can't be certain, but my nephew Matthias in Rochlitz was released by the Americans in June and he described horrible conditions in the prisoner-of-war camps. Men died of exposure and of starvation. Many men. There were also beatings and arbitrary shootings. I'm sure the Allies don't want to advertise any of that."

"Oh."

"But the Allied camps have improved a lot. Your papa will be fine now. You know what those first months were like. It was mass chaos everywhere, and there was hardly any food, for prisoners or civilians. Also the Allies were very angry at all Germans with what they saw in the concentration camps."

"Concentration camps?" I asked.

Herr Rittmann took off his glasses and rubbed his forehead. Then he put them back on and looked at us. "It's not for me to tell you what went on there. You'll find out more than you ever wanted to know soon enough. For now it's enough to just know that we Germans committed horrible crimes against millions of innocent people. Unspeakable crimes."

I stayed quiet, and I could see that Theodor was struggling to formulate his next question. Mama had warned us that Herr Rittmann was prone to exaggeration, but something in his manner told me that he was speaking from a basis of fact.

Herr Rittmann smiled warmly. "I know what you're thinking. I can't be sure, but I don't think your papa committed any of these crimes I speak of, at least not directly. I don't say this because I particularly liked him — I didn't know him well enough and in fact we certainly did not see eye to eye politically — but I say it because of the classification he lists."

"Class II?"

"Yes. They use a five-class scale with Class V meaning exonerated or found completely blameless. Class IV is for the simple Nazi followers, Class III for minor officials, Class II for the activists and militants and Class I for the major offenders such as war criminals. Class III, IV and V are dismissed, with III being on probation for a few years where they are restricted from some jobs and IV with some lighter restrictions. Class I goes to trial with the risk of the death penalty. For all their crimes and faults, the Nazis kept excellent records, so what is recorded about your papa's activities is likely accurate and if the Allies read that and classified him as II, that means he did not commit any crimes."

This was pretty abstract to me, but Theodor looked visibly relieved.

Herr Rittmann went on. "Your papa's class is one of the larger ones. They will be kept for a few years to be denazified. The truth is that the activists and militants of the Nazi Party represent the cream of the German crop with respect to the major professions required to run a country. Ten percent of all German adults were in the Nazi Party, with a much higher percentage in the educated classes! The Allies want people like your papa to help run Germany. They don't want to do it themselves forever."

"How will they denazify them?"

"Who knows?" Herr Rittmann chuckled.

"And here, in the Soviet zone?"

"Ah, yes, here it is different." He smiled broadly. "Here they do not need to denazify because here German socialists are at home and can help run this part of the country. People like me."

"You? You are a socialist?"

"Yes, I am. I have always been one. This is why I said your papa and I do not see eye to eye politically. But during the Nazi time I kept very quiet about politics."

"So, you did not join the Party?"

"The Nazi Party? No!" He laughed. "It was easier for ordinary workers to avoid joining. I suppose I'm a bit like your papa — clever enough to know what to say to whom and when to say it."

I'm sure Theodor and I both had questions about the implications of socialists helping the Soviets and ex-Nazis helping the Americans and British, but it was time to go back home and check on Mama and our siblings. Also any questions I had were vague and unfocused. And ultimately I did not care that much about politics, so long as it did not lead to war again. We thanked Herr Rittmann for his time and went back across the street to our place. Mama was waiting for us. She had wiped her face and fixed her hair. She gave us both a big hug.

CHAPTER THIRTY-SIX

WINTER 1945-46

We did not hear from Papa again for almost two months. And then when we did hear from him, it was a brief Christmas message that was delivered in late January. It consisted of three sentences. In the first he wrote that the English had allowed them to celebrate a proper German Christmas. The second stated that they were even permitted some special foods, and in the closing sentence he wished us a good Christmas. That we probably did not have access to special foods ourselves did not seem to occur to him, or possibly he knew this and thought we would want to know about his relative good fortune regardless, given how he had suffered. According to Herr Rittmann, it was likely that Papa had almost starved to death in the American camp. I cannot speak for the others, but my reaction was to shrug inwardly. Papa, who I had not seen since last spring, and especially his diet were abstractions to me at this point. The letter may as well have come from a distant acquaintance for all the emotional impact it had on me. His first letters naturally had had a much bigger impact because they contained so much information, much of it shocking, but even that quickly faded into the background for me. This may have been because we were starving, and starvation tends to focus the mind on the immediate and the tangible.

We were so lucky that it was a relatively mild winter. Had it not been, the combination of cold and poor nutrition would have killed many more people. As it was, elderly and ill people steadily, quietly disappeared from Colditz, as if simply deleted. Sometimes roughly one a week, sometimes in clusters of two or three or four. There was no fuss and there were no big funerals. Even though I hardly knew any of the individuals who died this way, there was a palpable sense of diminishment in the town, a sense of ebbing, with everyone still alive straining to swim against this tide.

We were also lucky that the Russians had begun to establish a ration system since the informal markets, which were at the best of times somewhat capricious and unreliable, had disappeared entirely by mid-winter. When the occupation began, we assumed that the Russians hated the Germans so much that they would simply allow us all to starve, perhaps to save on the cost of bullets. But after the immediate post-war chaos and revenge lust settled down, they appeared to come to the realization that, as Herr Rittmann said, they would need some Germans alive after all, just like the Western Allies had realized. Moreover, a political angle was starting to become evident. By February 1946, posters began to appear exhorting the advantages of communism and trumpeting how the "Soviet Big Brother" (only much later did I learn the irony inherent in this phrase) stood in solidarity with his "German Little Brother" and was generously helping him to rebuild and join the glorious family of socialist nations. It was better not to have a nation of half-dead starvation victims in your family, lest it make the family appear less glorious and reflect poorly on your family values. Incidentally Churchill made his famous Iron Curtain speech around this time, but we did not hear about it until much later.

The Soviet ration system was almost identical to the Nazi one we were familiar with from the war. There is no irony in this, as there really are not that many different ways to organize such a thing. The difference was that these ration cards were much more meagre than those handed out during even the worst days of the war. This stood to reason as the occupiers, powerful though they might be, could not just make food magically appear, especially as their own people back home were also struggling. At least it cut down somewhat on the hoarding and profiteering that had been occurring. They made a big deal of publicly executing a couple of the more notorious profiteers, but I am sure the black market for the controlled and rationed foodstuffs still flourished quietly somewhere. We just did not have the connections we had back in Leipzig to know much about it.

We had a separate little punch card for Paul's milk, which allowed exactly one-quarter litre of milk five days a week. The rest of us did not get milk. The family's main ration card permitted a varying amount of semolina wheat and, curiously, quite generous rations of sugar — usually a half kilo per person per month. There were various other notional items listed on our ration cards, such as the generic "fat" — it could be butter or pork fat or a kind of margarine — or bread or meat. But they were notional because they were rarely available and when available often only in laughably small quantities. One of my jobs was to keep an eye on the notices that were posted on the front door of city hall. These would update the citizenry on what they could actually claim from their ration card that week. For example, such a notice might read:

Week of February 10–16 Ration Distribution
Colditz District
Fat – 50 gm per household
Bread – one loaf per household
Meat – 0 gm per household
Eggs – 0

The official rations were supplemented by potatoes and apples we had stored from the fall. Vegetables and fruits were never part of the ration system, so each household continued to trade with farmers for these items or, as in our case, forage for them. Garden plots were very common too. Nobody grew flowers or anything pretty anymore. Every arable square metre in town was turned over to the cultivation of potatoes especially, but also turnips, cabbages and other vegetables that would keep through the winter. Our apartment, being in the centre of town, unfortunately did not have any garden associated with it. We did, however, have the advantage of being able to keep stored food items cool, as the stove only properly heated one room. This is, I suppose, what one might call a silver lining to a dark grey cloud.

Mama's spirits rose dramatically after learning that Papa was alive, but soon after began to quickly erode again like a sandcastle in the waves. The strain of caring for six children and making sure that they had enough to eat under these circumstances is unimaginable. It was literally unimaginable as I did not imagine it, at least not at the time. Theodor and I helped quite a bit, but we did not carry the burden of responsibility that she did. This only became clear to me later. At the time I found myself occasionally getting irritated at her black moods, reasoning that we were all in the same boat and the rest of us managed to keep our chins up, so why couldn't she? But the rest of us were merely passengers who helped at the oars. Mama had also lost a lot of weight and was visibly too thin now.

I tried to help by going into the forest. I do not know what I was hoping to find in the middle of winter. There would be no fruit or mushrooms. Any acorns not covered by snow would be frozen and likely even less edible than they already were. It's amusing now to think that I actually entertained the notion of hunting, like my heroes Winnetou and Shatterhand, but of course there were a number of barriers. First of all, for obvious reasons, guns were strictly prohibited for Germans on the pain of immediate summary execution. Also I was still pretty small to be lugging a hunting rifle into the forest, though I had some training with the Hitler Youth and it is worth noting that Peter in *Peter and the Wolf* was not any bigger than I was, but as stated a gun was out of the question. This then led me to imagine tying a knife to a sturdy stick to make a spear, which was in any case probably more in keeping with the spirit of Winnetou. Somehow I allowed myself to reason that I would be pretty good at stalking an animal such as a rabbit or deer and sneaking up on it, and that, moreover, I knew the forest very well, so I knew where these animals were likely to be. But inevitably this mental image led me to the most significant barrier: I did not want to kill anything. Killing had always repelled me, even in fun when we were playing toy soldiers as little boys — my soldiers would just "fall asleep" or "be stunned" when hit — and the war definitely served to embed this feeling. Logically this barrier should have been the first one in my mind and thus have prevented the train of thought getting even that far, but that train does not run its scheduled route when one is as hungry as I was.

Once in the forest I encountered a fourth barrier. There were no animals. No potentially edible mammals anyway.

It had snowed lightly overnight, so there should have been tracks, but there were none. The small birds still flitted about, including, when I got to the stand of oaks, the wren, but even he was quieter than normal and more furtive and nervous-looking. My knowledge of the language of birds failed me. It was not clear whether he was frightened or ill or just hungry like the rest of us.

The changes made no sense. Mind you, I had not been in the forest for two or three weeks, but at that time there had been more life about, much more. Then I saw it. Actually thinking back, I heard it first which caused me to walk over that way and look. I heard ravens cawing loudly. That had been the case the whole time I was in the forest, but now I began to tune in and wonder, because their noise was coming from one specific spot and was not the general swirling and swooping raven noise I was used to as they flew this way and that, alighting on branches to alert the others of my approach. Today they ignored me and were all clustered on a mound of something. As I approached, I could smell it too. It was entrails and deer heads. Dozens of them, maybe scores, in a grisly heap mixed with countless smaller bits, possibly from gutted rabbits. As I stepped through the new snow my boot prints became red because of the blood-soaked snow below. My mind immediately, irrationally flashed to the Rübezahl that the girl, Anna, had mentioned. But if he even existed, which I doubted, he caused deadly weather rather than the evisceration of deer. And then as quickly as that thought left, I thought of witches. But their diet was toadstools, strange herbs, slimy things and of course unwary children, not forest creatures. Besides this pile was much too large to be the handiwork of even a small group of old women, no matter how magical.

Then I saw the bullet casings. There were possibly hundreds of them. I do not know why I did not see them immediately. The larger ones I recognized as being from machine guns. Not the Rübezahl or witches then, but Russian soldiers. The Russians were hungry too, not as hungry as us perhaps, but hungry enough that it made sense for them to hunt in the winter when other meat was scarce and there was less cover for the wildlife. This seemed wildly excessive though. Did they really need to kill every animal? With machine guns? I became very angry, but then almost immediately, fear took over from anger. I suddenly felt deeply afraid and very alone and exposed and vulnerable. Just as I had done when I came across that encampment of deserters, I ran out of the forest faster than my skinny legs should have been able to move me.

CHAPTER
THIRTY-SEVEN

SPRING 1946

S pring is normally the season of hope. Since the start of the war, however, it was the season of death, as that was when major new military offences began. But after the war, that was when starvation intensified as the food stored through the winter ran out and no wild foods were available yet. The ration cards still provided enough semolina and sugar to keep us alive, but Mama and Paul in particular were becoming alarmingly emaciated. She was breastfeeding him but was worried that her milk was too nutrient poor because of her own condition. Theodor and I made sure that she took a generous share of the food, arguing that it was for the baby's sake, but even that was not nearly enough.

Spring brought rain and mud, so much mud. The condition of the roads deteriorated to the extent that it hampered our ability to reach farmers who were willing and able to trade, not that we had very much left to trade. Most of our valuables had been depleted, but two things gave us hope. First of all, Mama was preparing to travel to Leipzig to retrieve whatever was left there, as Papa had suggested. Secondly, we had lots of books. Astonishingly much of our library had made it from Leipzig to Colditz when Mama moved here in 1944. She had reasoned that the books were the most vulnerable to damage in the apartment and that they would be valuable for both entertainment in the dark days to come — which had proven itself true — and for knowledge as events could take unexpected turns, which was about to prove itself true. We had a number of excellent plant guides. The mild winter and the present rains were causing weeds to sprout quickly. With our books we knew which of these weeds were not truly weeds in the pejorative sense, but wild greens.

You did not need a book, however, to know about nettles. All but the most ignorant city dwellers know that once you get past the sting, nettles are an excellent source of vitamins and protein. The books were, however, helpful to identify *Sedum telephium* (Rote Fetthenne in German or, amusingly, "witch's moneybags" in English) and *Aegopodium podagraria* (Giersch or "gout weed"). These were also nutritious and plentiful but were generally overlooked by the other foragers. We were careful to pick these when other people were not looking so as not to give this secret away. I suppose that is yet another of starvation's effects — the evaporation of any sense of community spirit. The best place for this was just steps away on the banks of the Mulde. In previous times this was a spot where people let their dogs run to do their business, so gathering food there would have been unappetizing, but there were no dogs around at all anymore as nobody was able to feed them. This is another example of a dark grey cloud producing a silver lining. Mama, Theodor and I gathered as much of this weed bounty as we were able, and she combined it with the semolina to make a healthy stew. With this Paul began to look a little better as spring moved into summer, although Mama still worried me.

Letters from Papa continued to be highly sporadic and brief, although in the early spring one arrived that had a little more information.

Dear Luise,

The denazification camp continues to be a better experience than I had feared or dared to expect. The Americans must have been very angry with Germans to treat us the way they did after we were captured. I can understand that now. It is interesting to observe that the British have even more reason to be angry, yet they have been nothing but courteous and just.

Camp life is very structured. We rise early to the sound of a loud bugle. Then we wash and we muster for what they call parade, which is a head count of the prisoners. I don't think anyone has tried to escape though. Where would they go? Some days there is a short speech from the commander, Colonel Ross, and some days there is music. Sometimes bagpipes are even played. I will avoid tempting the censor and will not give my opinion of this aspect of British culture!

After morning parade, we have a short breakfast, usually of porridge, and then we go to class. We are taught history, politics, economics and moral philosophy, with of course an emphasis on the errors of the Third Reich. They do this very well.

Lunch is always a soup made from the scraps of last night's dinner and then we are off to work. By work I mean actual manual labour, which is not something I am used to, but I surprise myself with how quickly I have adapted to it and even become good at it. We are told that the work will become more useful and oriented towards skills soon. Many of us in Category II were professionals who will not be permitted to return to our professions after we are released, so there is an intent to teach us trades that we can earn a living with instead. Sometimes we are taken out of the camp under guard to clean up debris from the war. So much was destroyed. It is very hard work.

The evening meal varies but is always nutritious. Sometimes we even have what they call "pudding" by which they mean dessert. Before the children become very jealous though I must emphasize that this is rare. After that we are free to read or write or play cards. I am very tired by the end of the day and I sleep very well. Curiously, I never dream anymore.

Your Wilhelm

What stood out to me most in this letter was the reference to Papa performing manual labour. This produced a comical image of him in one of his fine grey suits, with his polished black dress shoe set tentatively on a pile of bricks while he gingerly holds a shovel, looking deeply displeased, as if he has been asked to clean up after the dog. I knew he would not be wearing his suit in denazification camp, but I also knew that he would definitely not be wearing his Nazi Party uniform either and I was unable to picture him wearing anything other than one of those two outfits. Consequently my inner picture-maker selected the slightly less improbable of the two.

~

I think that malnourishment has had an effect on the formation of memories from this period. The events of 1946 and 1947 come to me as free-floating vignettes, rather than as crisply defined sequences with probable dates (or at least months) associated as before and after. In any case, I am reasonably confident it was in the spring, or possibly early summer, of 1946 that we returned to Leipzig for the first time since the end of the war. We just went for the day to see what we could salvage that might be of value. Mama, Paul and I took the train while Theodor stayed home to watch the others. He was considered a better choice for this role than I was, although I think I handled things quite nicely that time that Mama and Theodor went to Rochlitz.

The train was as crowded and uncomfortable as any I had been on. In fact I do not recall having a truly pleasant train journey at any point in my childhood. I remembered seeing gleaming, well-lit and well-appointed trains, with every window intact, when I was a small boy and was taken to the grand Leipzig train station to meet a visitor or perhaps see Papa off on a business trip, so I had direct knowledge that they once existed. But the pre-war world felt wholly fictional, even fantastical, as if the small boy version of me was himself a character in a storybook. The train went slowly to save on coal and also stopped frequently because of the state of the track, so a journey that would have taken under an hour in normal times now took two hours. Knowing this we took the earliest train so as to have a full day in the city.

Leipzig was unrecognizable. There had been so many more bombing raids since I left the city in December of 1943, and then the final battle last spring caused a tremendous amount of destruction as well. At least half the buildings were not standing anymore. Entire city blocks had been transformed into small mountain ranges of scree and rubble. Very few cars were on the streets and all of those were Russian. The train slowed even more as it entered the city, so I was able to watch as groups of children clambered on these mountains and picked various treasures out — bits of metal, occasional intact household items. Women pushed wheelbarrows down the narrow streets that had been cleared as passes. They appeared to be moving some of the debris away, but the task seemed to be of an impossible scale, as if ants had been sent to clean up after a housefire.

Everything moved very slowly, absolutely everything. It occurred to me that the war had been so calamitous that it had warped time. Among our many books was a basic physics primer. Being a precocious reader and having an abundance of free time, I had carefully read it at least a half dozen times. In it I learned that Albert Einstein posited that time was a relative phenomenon. Here was proof. In fact, the entire post-war period was moving through time with thick jelly in its mechanism, but because everyone and everything moved this way, nobody noticed. I felt I had stepped out of time for a moment to see this properly.

We had to visit two banks and miraculously both were still standing. The first one, the Leipzig City Giro Bank, was pockmarked with bullet holes and missing several windows, but it was otherwise undamaged. Inside the main hall was a long table with Russian officers and soldiers sitting at it. Mama had to fill out a form and then hand the safe key over to one of the officers. He led the way down to the vaults and, motioning us to stand aside, unlocked the safe. With a quick smile he pocketed an antique watch while Mama kept a poker face. He then took out a teak box of fine silverware and in reasonably good German stated that this was being officially confiscated as part of the reparations owed Russia. The rest of the safe contents were documents such as birth certificates, Papa's diplomas and the like. Although these were very valuable to us, they were fortunately of no interest to the Russian, so he handed them over politely. Back in the main hall Mama signed for the documents and signed a statement declaring surrender of the silver. There was no mention of the watch. Everyone was calm and scrupulously courteous. The loss of the silverware and the watch aside, this had gone better than I had feared. On the train ride up Mama told me stories of bank vaults that had been completely looted and even urinated on and defecated in.

The Commerce Bank was a different story. No urination or defecation, but no courtesy either. In this vault we had stored Opa Hugo's paintings. Mama's father was a moderately renowned artist from Weimar. He died seventeen years before I was born, but I grew up hearing stories about him. I also felt connected to him through his widow, my favourite oma, and I can picture his face clearly from the self-portrait he painted. He looked very much the part of a turn-of-the-century gentleman painter with his small round glasses, bushy moustache and rakishly tilted Edwardian hat. At this bank the officer assigned to us did not speak German, so we were accompanied to the vault by a translator as well, a sparrow-like woman with a high chirpy voice. Upon viewing the paintings, the two of them exchanged a few words in Russian. The officer looked at us sternly while the translator declared that all of these paintings were quite obviously war booty stolen by the Nazis from Russia. The fact that Hugo Flintzer had signed each and every one of them and that Mama had documentation proving herself to be the daughter of Hugo Flintzer had as much impact on their bizarre assertion as a louse has on the plans of an elephant. They did not respond at all but simply ushered us out with a firm hand on Mama's shoulder. In the next vault we could see a man weeping loudly while two Russian soldiers dragged him out. Mama told me later that he was a well-known publisher and that she had heard through a mutual acquaintance that the Russians had torn apart and stomped on all of his most valuable documents and first editions. It was a bad day at the Leipzig Commerce Bank.

Mama's face was a mask and she managed to keep her composure until we got on the train. Once it pulled out of the station she broke down and began sobbing. She had loved her father so dearly and this was like losing him all over again. She was ten when he died and here before me was the ten-year-old girl again, overwhelmed by grief. Fortunately Paul was sleeping. An older gentleman was in our compartment and inquired what the matter was and whether he could help. I explained what had happened as he listened intently, nodding, brow furrowed.

"Well, I'm sorry to hear that. The methods of our liberators are sometimes a little boorish and indelicate, but their aims are pure. In time you will come to see that the loss of bourgeois goods is in fact a kind of liberation as well. We must leave such things behind if we are to build the just socialist future for Germany." His tone was so kind and gentle, and he was clearly concerned for our welfare, but I could see that Mama was struggling mightily to bite her tongue. To my surprise, diplomacy won out and she just dried her eyes and smiled and thanked him.

When we got to Colditz, Mama went directly to her room. I told Theodor everything that had happened, right up to and including the socialist supporter on the train. He asked me to describe the man and when I did, he chuckled and said that he knew who I was talking about. This man was well known in town as one of the local Nazi Ortsgruppe officials who managed to destroy his records

on time, even at the Gau level, and then ingratiate himself
with the occupiers by identifying other ex-Nazis for them.
He seemed so nice.

CHAPTER

THIRTY-EIGHT

SUMMER 1946

The food situation improved in the summer. The spring rain led to decent crops, which had a ripple effect through to the ration system. Also the berries and fruit were especially good that summer. I found some particularly productive raspberry patches in the forest that nobody else seemed to know about. We were still hungry most of the time, but at least we were no longer actually starving. Mama still looked terrible though.

Through the year to this point we had been receiving short letters from Papa at the rate of about one per month. These were mostly of the "I am fine, how are you?" nature with a note about the weather or possibly a brief anecdote he thought we would find interesting. These were all stamped "inspected" but none bore any censorship black marks, which stood to reason, as what could be controversial about "It has been pleasantly sunny all week," or "Heinz is teaching us some Italian, which he picked up while stationed near Florence"? We were happy to hear from him, but his life in denazification camp in the West (we were coming to refer to the British, U.S. and French zones of occupation collectively as "the West") was as remote and abstract to us as the life of a yak herder in Tibet. I did wonder about this "denazification" though. Then as if he had read my mind from hundreds of kilometres away, one summer day a longer letter arrived. As always it was addressed to Mama and did not mention us except in passing, and as always Mama let us read it immediately after she was done.

Dear Luise,

I hope you and the children are well. I understand that conditions in the East may be more difficult than here. I hope that the worst stories are exaggerations.

Life here in camp is not without its own difficulties as we have to work hard, but our camp commander is a fair man and we are not abused or mistreated. As I have written before, work is one of the major features of camp life. They understand that it is not in their interest to have idle prisoners. We are mostly doing woodwork now and are building furniture.

I am now at the point where I can write about the other two specific things the British are doing to allow us to be able to return to society.

The first is that they are making us understand and believe what actually happened during the Hitler era. We were lied to by the men I most admired. This was perhaps the hardest thing to swallow. Not so much that they would lie, but that I would be gullible enough to believe those lies. We were shown the film of Göring's trial in Nuremberg. He called us all simpletons for having followed him and Hitler and the rest of them into war. He said that we were easy to manipulate. They knew what they were doing. They knew how to persuade people like me by calling on our pride as Germans. I made such a terrible mistake and I feel very foolish now.

The other thing the British are doing shows how smart they are. They don't try to humiliate us further. Perhaps they learned from the mistakes of 1919. They actually also call on our pride — not pride in military power or "ethnic purity" of course, but rather pride in the deeper German strengths of culture and science. They remind us of Beethoven and Goethe and Humboldt and Gauss, and they remind us of the spirit of the 1848 democratic revolutions. True liberal democracy is not alien to the German people.

I feel I have been asleep for a very long time and am now waking up. This makes one groggy and weak, but at least one is finally in the real world again.

Your Wilhelm

Theodor snorted. "He doesn't accept any responsibility. He was just a dupe he says, an essentially innocent victim of smooth talk about pride."

"But he did not do anything bad that he needs to accept responsibility for," I said, feeling odd for defending my father, but Theodor's superior tone always made me want to say something contrary.

"Being such an active Party member was bad enough. A machine needs many parts and he was one of them. It's especially bad for a man who has the education and intelligence to know better."

"Then an awful lot of people did something bad."

"Yes, an awful lot of people did something bad."

CHAPTER

THIRTY-NINE

AUTUMN 1946

At some point in the autumn of 1946 school began again. It was a struggle for the authorities because of the damaged buildings, the lack of basic school supplies, and especially because of the shortage of teachers. Primary school was not as bad, but in high school, where Theodor and I were supposed to go, most of the teachers had been men. Many of them had of course died in the war or were still in Siberia, and many of the remaining ones had enough association with the Nazi Party that the Russians refused to rehire them. A lowest-rank Mitlaeufer (simple Nazi follower) could be a baker or a streetcleaner, but certainly could not be entrusted with molding young minds to build that socialist future the posters and both Herr Rittmann and the gentleman on the train had referred to. Consequently only enough suitable live teachers were scraped together to staff one high school in Rochlitz to serve the entire region, and only the most gifted students would be able to attend.

This meant waking at five in the morning in order to catch the train. We did not have a clock or a watch in the house. All of these had been bartered away for food. Fortunately, however, we were only a few doors down from the town hall and its clock tower. As surprising as it sounds, our subconscious was immediately trained to tune into the five chimes. Four chimes and we would still be fast asleep, but five and we would wake up. This worked each and every time. We did not sleep in once. The train was of course another one of those windowless rattlers, but the discomfort was trivial compared to the excitement of going back to school. I did not count the classes at the KLV-Lager as proper school, so it had been three years, which when you're twelve is an enormous portion of your life.

This excitement did not survive the first day of school. This time it was not the bullying, as we were a generally more intellectually oriented group, so even my sometimes overloud squeaky voice or overeager hand-raising did not attract any hard stares or covert slaps to the back of my head. No, this time the problem was the instruction. First of all, the teachers they had found were, with one or two exceptions, truly the dregs. I knew more than the math teacher and at least as much as the science teacher. Secondly, the curriculum had changed. Now history was being taught through the lens of a Marxist dialectic. Suddenly ancient Greece was no longer a groundbreaking civilization, but rather a prime example of the class struggle wherein a small slave-holding elite exercised violent control over the other classes. History was an evolution towards the ideal paradise of workers and farmers that we were creating right now, right before our very eyes. We were so lucky to be the generation to reach this apogee of human develop-ment! Looking out the window at relentlessly shabby and grey Rochlitz, this seemed as disconnected from reality as the Nazi teacher's assertions that we were winning the war when we had just been evacuated from a destroyed city. I suppose it was still early days for utopian socialist Rochlitz though. Perhaps paradise was still coming.

More interesting was the Russian class. I had always enjoyed languages and Russian seemed as good to learn as any, and for the time being obviously more practical than English or French. Once a week on Fridays there was an assembly for the students in the big hall where the school director would give a speech. Herr Schimmler was a small bald man who favoured bowties. He was often accompanied by a Russian officer who sat silently off to one side. The speeches alternated between rambling and hectoring. The contrast was quite stark. The rambling speeches were delivered in a genial and benevolent tone, but they were obscurely philosophical and difficult to follow, while the hectoring speeches were extreme in their accusations against us. We may not have been the most energetic of groups, which one could easily attribute to the rampant ongoing malnutrition, but to call us lazy filth and fascist sympathizers who were trying to undermine the working class's reconstruction of our country struck me, even at the time, as excessive.

Then one day in mid-autumn a film projector was set up in the big hall for our Friday assembly. Boys scrambled to volunteer to set up the large linen screen, excited that we would be seeing a movie for the first time in years. Herr Schimmler looked grim, however. There was a short struggle to thread the film properly and then the lights were dimmed, and the picture began to flicker on the screen ahead.

There was no sound, only the rhythmic rattle of the projector and then a few scattered muffled gasps as we realized what we were looking at. It was footage of pits full of corpses. These corpses were naked for the most part and emaciated to the point that every bone I knew the name of was visible on every corpse through thin, tightly drawn pale white skin. There were hundreds, maybe thousands as the camera pulled back and panned across a larger area. A few people beside the pits wandered about listlessly wearing what looked like striped pyjamas. I looked around quickly to see if I could catch Theodor's eye. He was staring straight ahead. Other boys were covering their eyes with their hands.

Herr Schimmler began stalking up and down the aisles, smacking the boys who were covering their eyes with a long thin stick. "You must look!" he barked at them. He looked really upset, not just angry but distraught. When he was satisfied that everyone was watching he returned to the front at the side of the screen, and with the film playing on half his face and the other half in the dark, he shouted, "You must watch this! All of you! This is fascism! Your fascist fathers, your fascist uncles and your fascist brothers did this! They murdered millions of innocent civilians! Women, the elderly, children, babies. Jews, communists, dissidents, Gypsies, the mentally ill. They sent them to camps and murdered them and disposed of their corpses like they were garbage. Fascism is the greatest evil the world has ever known. You need to be very grateful that you were liberated by the brave soldiers of the Union of Soviet Socialist Republics. The USSR is the only true and steadfast foe of fascism. It will help those of us who opposed the fascists rebuild this country. This can never happen again."

The room went silent again and the film ran on for another twenty minutes, showing a hell that I had never imagined possible. I mean this very literally. I have a tremendously powerful imagination and I have read some very dark stories, so I have conjured many fantastical scenes of horror while sitting by myself. But nothing like this. Not ever, not even close. The silence made it worse still.

CHAPTER

FORTY

WINTER 1946-47

This was the coldest and snowiest winter in recorded memory. Temperatures of -20° Celsius were common. Apparently this was the case all across Europe, although we had only the dimmest awareness of anything outside of a small circle around Colditz and Rochlitz. We did not have a functioning radio and the only newspaper was the *Neues Deutschland* published by the Socialist Unity Party in Berlin. Week-old copies would circulate Colditz and eventually reach our hands, but the *ND*, as we called it, mostly consisted of the driest possible political news. For me to call it dry, given that I enthusiastically read long-winded descriptions of the habits of snails or the esoteric musings of medieval monks, indicates how profoundly tedious this newspaper was. But much as my children now read the sides of cereal boxes, I read it anyway. With respect to the weather, one article blathered on about the failures of capitalism, using as an example the unequal distribution of coal in Britain during their very cold winter. Here was another sharp irony as just earlier that morning, in part because of a lack of coal, Theodor and I had gone out into the forest to collect pine roots, which were particularly good fuel for our stove (although not as good as coal would have been). Incidentally we greatly improved the efficiency of this chore when we found an old four-wheeled wagon abandoned in some bushes. Theodor recognized it as the kind that had transported Panzerfausts during the war.

In December we had been forced to move yet again. This time it was because Herr Peschel, the landlord, had returned from POW camp and wanted the front apartment back for himself. He had rented it to Papa's colleague during the war because he had another much nicer place to live, but this had been destroyed in the final days of the war when he was already a prisoner. Mama took note of the fact that he looked very well fed. Apparently he had been in an American camp where the conditions were much better than in Papa's first camp and, moreover, rumour had it that he had somehow bargained for extra rations. Herr Peschel was definitely, as we would call it today, a wheeler-dealer.

In any case it was to the back apartment for the Schott family. This had no sun and a stove that was even worse than the one before. Fortunately, though, Herr Peschel's astonishing abilities came to good use. He was able to secure a large new stove for us from a tavern that had mostly been destroyed, and he found some nice wooden flooring to cover the bare stone. We also watched in wonder as luxurious furnishings appeared in his place. Somehow in this grey, semi-apocalyptic wasteland of deprivation, this man was able to make material goods appear, as if conjured by a sorcerer's spell. Surely there was a price, if not for him, then for someone, but we never learned what it was, and for us it was very much a case of not wanting to look a gift horse in the mouth.

That old tavern stove is the centre of my most vivid visual memory from that desperate winter. It was made of black iron, but half of it was covered with bright green tiles, with an abstract pattern in smaller yellow tiles picked out on it. The tiled portion included a flat surface that was meant to keep food warm or to dry wet socks and the like on it. By this point we had some electrical power again, but it went out at five in the afternoon when, given that it was winter, it was pitch black outside. This struck me as silly. Would it not be better to have the power available in the evening instead of when it was still light? But Mama explained that the town's generator could only be staffed during the day. So we would light a single candle and one of us would read aloud to the others. I can so clearly picture how Paul would be sat on the flat tiled part of the stove to keep him warm, while the rest of us huddled close in a semicircle around the reader, candlelight flickering on our faces. We would read everything from fairy tales to history to poetry to the classics.

Sometimes afterwards I would step outside and walk the few steps to the dark and empty market square so I could see the expanse of the night sky. On one particular moonless night, the sky was so luminous with stars that in the absence of earthbound light, starshine cast a shadow of my outstretched arm onto the snow. I was able to recall every constellation Mama had taught us during those blackout times in Leipzig, and I was pleased to easily find two new ones, Taurus and Gemini, that I had learned from a book. I ran back to tell Mama this and to ask her to come out and see, but she declined without giving a reason. Clara, Johann and Oskar came, however, and I enjoyed pointing these things out to them.

On other nights when we were allowed individual candles, I embarked on a project to memorize our Langenscheidt English-German dictionary. Russian was immediately useful here and now, but I was growing a dream in my mind of life somewhere where the skies were always star-filled and the forests vast and empty. These places were usually English speaking. Yes, Russia, ironically enough, also fit the criteria, but nobody moved there of their own free will. Russia had war and starvation, and another criterion was life somewhere where there could never be war or starvation. I would still be a forest ranger, but being one in the Yukon might be even better than being one in Germany. My siblings sometimes made remarks or jokes as I quietly mouthed, "Accomplish, durchführen. Accord, gewähren. Accordion, Akkordeon. Accost, ansprechen . . ." but I barely noticed, and I did not care in the slightest.

~

In this time another slightly longer letter arrived from Papa.

Dear Luise,

Is it so cold in Colditz too? It must be. I hope Peschel has kept the stove in good condition.

This week in our civics class Major McWhirter asked us to write an essay on the fall of the Roman republic. I noted that although the republic was flawed in many ways, the empire that followed, which superficially seemed glorious, led to far more suffering and inhuman crimes against common people. He was so impressed by what I wrote that he asked me to his office for tea and biscuits. This was a great honour and I was pleased to discover that we had much in common.

I will ask Major McWhirter if it is possible to send a package to you. I earn a little bit from the woodworking and there is a camp canteen where I can buy food beyond what I need for

myself. Please write to me to let me know what
you might need and I will see what I can do.
      Your Wilhelm

This new version of my father was as strange and distant
seeming as the last, perhaps more so. I could no longer
connect what I read to the tense hard man in the uniform
I had last seen in the spring of 1945. My stomach tight-
ened when I read the reference to inhuman crimes against
common people. I thought unavoidably of the film we had
been shown in school. Belief and disbelief about Papa's
potential incarnations — scholar, student, leader, wizard,
criminal, prisoner, father — swam around each other like
different coloured fish, each distinct when viewed individually, but collectively forming a blur that I could only disperse
by taking Thomas Mann's 731-page *Buddenbrooks* off
the shelf and losing myself in it. That night I had a nightmare about witches whose faces were concealed under the
wide brims of their hats, cooking something in a large pot
suspended by chains over an unearthly green fire. I could
not see what was in the pot, but I felt that some part of me
knew what it was, just out of reach of conscious awareness, like a briefly forgotten name at the tip of my tongue. I
grasped for the word and the knowledge, but I was grasping
into smoke and vapour.
      The first package, and the only one for many months,
arrived surprisingly soon after. The postal system was
highly capricious, especially when crossing from one zone
of occupation to another. A few letters and parcels arrived
as quickly as they had before the war, but most arrived a
month or two after being sent and many did not arrive at
all. To my disappointment, this small parcel, festooned
with various inspection marks and stamps, was entirely
filled with tins of fish oil from Bremerhaven. This seemed

odd at first until Mama explained that this was an excellent way to get vitamins and it would serve very well to fry our remaining shrivelled potatoes in.

CHAPTER

FORTY-ONE

SPRING 1947

I have written of starvation before, but there had always at least been some food — a little semolina, some soft old apples, some equally soft old potatoes — so, in retrospect, when I referred to starvation, I was actually referring to being very hungry. But by the spring of 1947 we had entirely run out of food for the first time. The nettles and other wild foods were late due to the hard winter. Some weeks we would receive a single loaf of bread through the ration system and some weeks it supplied nothing. Under other circumstances it would have been comical to read the notice tacked to the town hall aloud: "Fat: zero grams per household. Bread: zero loaves per household. Meat: zero grams per household. Eggs: zero per household." But now even the gallows humour had fled.

Women who had illicit relationships with Russian soldiers and officers did better, people who had connections to farmers did better and people like Herr Peschel did better, but we starved, eating absolutely nothing for several days in a row. Those tins of fish oil seemed like a distant golden dream. Only the occasional loaf of strange gritty bread from our ration card, plus a few things given in pity to us by Herr Peschel and Herr Rittmann prevented us from actually dying of starvation. I am completely serious. People around us were dying. Theodor developed tuberculosis. We all coughed, but his cough was deeper and sounded much more threatening. He looked ghastly.

Despite having no money to pay for treatment, Mama took Theodor to the doctor, an elderly gentleman with a snow-white pompadour and a gentle manner that I did not mind seeing the one time I had to go. They were gone for several hours, and when they returned Theodor told me that the doctor had given him antibiotics at no cost. These were a relatively new wonder drug and were quite difficult to get a hold of, so this was an amazing stroke of luck. He said he was able to do this because he was leaving for the West next week. Antibiotics were not in short supply in the West, so he could afford to give them away here. He then told Theodor and Mama that they should leave as well, that the East was no place for a young family. Mama had apparently replied that this was her home and that there was nothing for her in the West since her husband was still in prison camp.

"What do you think, Theodor, should we leave?" I asked.

"I don't know. I think the doctor is probably right, and it can't possibly be worse there than it is here. But it is illegal to leave the zone and Mama is absolutely against it."

"Mama is so weak and so depressed. I am not sure she knows what she is talking about." It felt transgressive to say this about the mother I loved and respected so much, but it was the truth.

"Perhaps, but I'm not in condition to go anywhere myself anyway." This was punctuated by a horrendous bout of coughing. I saw blood-flecked phlegm in his hand. It is incredible in retrospect that the rest of us did not become ill.

The first grain to appear in spring was winter barley, sown back in the fall. The official rations were still scant at best, but the nettles had come back and the barley promised a new source of food. Mama, Theodor and I set off after dark, leaving Clara (now eleven years old) in charge. We took scissors and a baby carriage down a country road to the northeast where we knew of a barley field out of view of any farmhouses. We were just a family out for a stroll with a remarkably quiet baby. Then when nobody else was around and a fat cloud scudded over the moon, we quickly ducked off the road into the field and began frantically snipping barley heads off their stalks and tossing them under the baby blanket in the carriage. At one point when I heard the rustle of what I thought might be a bird, I carefully raised my head up to see, to my absolute horror, another face looking at me from just a few rows over! Shit, the farmer! But he looked equally terrified and turned out to be just another townsperson stealing barley.

When we got home, we threshed the barley heads with a wooden spoon and then ground the grains in a coffee mill. This was mixed with whey, which had recently begun to appear on the ration list, thus making a rough porridge. This was our sustenance for the better part of a month. It probably saved us from actual death by starvation as bread no longer appeared on the ration list and Herr Rittmann had suddenly disappeared to the West, leaving behind a note that he had a sister in Kassel and that sometimes political principles had to take a back seat to survival.

In the midst of all this an entirely surreal letter arrived from Papa, the first in a little while.

Dear Luise,

It is so lovely to see spring again after that winter, is it not?

Camp life has developed a certain dull sameness day after day, but I am making the best of it. The work is hard, but as my strengths are more in working with my head than my hands, they are assigning me more paperwork-related tasks, which is more satisfying for me.

The highlight of my week is tea on Tuesdays with Major McWhirter. We have made it our routine. I practise my English, although it is already very good, and he practises his German, which is also not really in need of practice. We discuss literature and philosophy and music and sometimes we play cards. He has taught me whist, for which he brings in a colleague and an aide to make a foursome. Sometimes we even have a small glass of sherry afterwards. This is a special privilege.

The war becomes evermore distant. I have learned so much since the darkest days and am very grateful for this second chance.

Did my parcel arrive?

Your Wilhelm

And then not too long afterwards we received another, possibly even more surreal, letter.

Dear Luise,

Do you know *The Clicking of Cuthbert*? It is a collection of comical short stories by the marvellous English writer P.G. Wodehouse. I cannot claim that it is truly literature in the way we normally understand the term and, furthermore, the stories all concern the game of golf, which, as you know, I have not the slightest interest in, but the humour and warmth in these stories is simply wonderful. I haven't smiled or chuckled like that since before the war. Major McWhirter lent the book to me, taking a guess that although it was not at all an obvious choice for me, I would still enjoy it very much, which I have. I know that you will not have access to *The Clicking of Cuthbert* in Colditz, and possibly not even in Leipzig, but I thought you would be happy to hear about this lovely little bit of sunshine in my day here.

Your Wilhelm

CHAPTER
FORTY-TWO

SUMMER 1947

Russula cyanoxantha, Amanita phalloides, Agaricus dulcidulus, Tricholoma equestre, Cortinarius orellanus and my favourite, Boletus luridiformis. This was the poetry of the summer of 1947. The poetry of mushrooms. I could recite verse after verse of this beautiful epic poem. Barley thieving season ended just as mushroom picking season got underway. I shifted my reading from Mann, May and Langenscheidt to Edmund Michael's classic Führer fuer Pilzfreunde ("Guide for Friends of Mushrooms"), which we also had in our impressive home library. The problem with relying on mushrooms for food was not that some are poisonous, but rather that mushroom picking was a beloved national pastime, so as soon as word got around that the season was underway it felt like every second person from Colditz was in my forest, crouching down with a basket over one arm.

No, the fact that some are poisonous was not a problem, it was a solution. I do not mean that Colditzers were being removed from mushroom hunting competition by being poisoned! They were far too careful and experienced for that. I mean that it was a solution because Colditzers were actually too careful and avoided mushrooms that looked similar to poisonous ones. For example I was always delighted when *Boletus luridifromis* began sprouting. In German we called it the Flockenstieliger Hexen-Röhrling ("spotted stem witch's little pipe" — quite a mouthful in either language!). As the witch part of the common name implies, people were generally very suspicious of this mushroom because it looked so much like *Suillelus satanas*. That hardly requires translation. See the "satan" embedded in the species name? That is not an accident! It is not usually fatal when consumed, but the days of projectile vomiting and uncontrolled bloody diarrhea are reputed to be highly unpleasant. *Boletus luridifromis* on the other hand is safe and delicious. Not that taste was an important consideration — we were delighted with edible, regardless of taste. So, I went into the forest with E. Michael's book tucked into my canvas shoulder bag, to be pulled out only when nobody was looking, lest our secret strategy be exposed. Clara wanted to come along, but I preferred to go by myself. It is easier to be secretive when one is alone, but it was also simply my preference. Sometimes it was fine to be around other people, especially people I knew well, but more often it was distracting and annoying.

It was easy for me to find a place in the forest where others were less likely to be because I knew the smaller, more hidden pathways. Moreover, I was no longer nervous to be there on my own. I had always felt very confident and in my element in the forest, but the deer slaughter and the talk of witches and the Rübezahl had unnerved me a little, if I am fully honest with myself. But now there was no wildlife left to hunt, so the chance of encountering hungry machine-gun-carrying Russians was much lower, and now that I was thirteen, I had decided to make a careful rational examination of my previous belief in witches. The conclusion of this examination was that the witch stories were probably based on real women who had an unusual knowledge of herbs and special plants and who were viewed as strange outsiders but who did not otherwise possess special powers. Moreover, they were no more likely to eat children than anyone else was, which was not very likely at all.

The boys at school had been trading rumours about cannibalism and they all involved people in the ruined cities driven mad by trauma, grief and starvation. In particular somebody in Dresden or possibly Hamburg or Duisburg — accounts varied — was scavenging flesh from dead bodies, processing it through a meat grinder and selling it as fresh ground pork. I was skeptical but took note that it was always in cities, never forests. I also took note that the perpetrators in these stories were always men, never women and certainly not elderly women. Consequently I was only briefly taken aback when I encountered a very old woman, stooped and using a cane, in a distant clearing in the forest. She had her white hair tucked into a red kerchief and her nose was long and hooked, so she looked very much like a fairy-tale witch. I did not notice a wart though. When she spoke to me her voice was soft and gentle, not at all like the screechy voice Mama used when she spoke the witch's parts in "Hansel und Gretel." She had been looking at a patch of chanterelles when we saw each other.

"Hello, how is your day?" she asked.

"It is good, thank you. And yours?"

"Good as well. It is beautiful and peaceful in here as always."

The strict rule among mushroom hunters was that while it was permissible to exchange pleasantries, one could never ask the other person how the mushroom hunting was going, let alone ask where they were finding their mushrooms.

That would be tantamount to asking them for the keys to their bank vault! Everyone wondered but nobody asked or tried to follow, not ever. The system worked well. She picked the chanterelles, wished me a good day and shuffled off into the woods to the east. This was the direction I had intended to go, but protocol and custom prohibited me from doing so. Instead I turned west. The old woman had come from there, but I reasoned that her vision was probably not very sharp and that she might have missed some smaller mushrooms.

The birds had been quite active and loud in the deciduous patch of woods behind me, although the wren was absent that day. Ahead to the west it was all pines with very little undergrowth and almost no birds, save a trio of chickadees who appeared to be following me, hopping from branch to branch, perhaps hoping that I would drop something tasty. This did not look like a promising area for mushrooms, but then one never really knew for sure. Mushrooms were mysterious organisms and the speculation around their ways was often distinctly irrational to my ears. Then I spotted a Fliegenpilz (fly agaric, *Amanita muscaria*). It was beautiful, and as if on stage, it was lit by a single brilliant sunbeam that penetrated the otherwise dark canopy. If you can picture a fairy-tale toadstool in your mind's eye, you are probably picturing a Fliegenpilz. They have white stems and brilliant red caps dotted with slightly raised white spots. I did not pick it because it is not something you would want to eat. They are not deadly, but they are not eaten because in addition to a very bitter taste they can cause nausea, sweating and in some cases very vivid and unwelcome hallucinations! Seeing the Fliegenpilz here confirmed that the old woman was not a witch, even in the non-magical sense. I had read that the tales of flying witches came from those old women who collected medicinal plants nibbling on Fliegenpilz to induce a euphoric sense of flight. No wonder these people were viewed with suspicion and outright fear! I do not know where the broomstick part of the stories comes from though. I looked at the Fliegenpilz for a few minutes, enjoying the brightly lit red against the dark green and brown all around. The chickadees had left, and the forest was silent.

~

The key, and I think unique, part of my mushroom hunting strategy took place back at the apartment. For this I must give credit to Mama. Apocalyptic world war, or no apocalyptic world war, education and knowledge were priorities for her. In addition to having our library sent from Leipzig to our very humble accommodations in Colditz, she also had our microscope sent. Yes, we had a microscope. It was a small student model mind you, but I am confident in stating that we possessed the only microscope in the Colditz district. This gave me a strong edge in the mushroom hunting competition because so many little brown mushrooms look essentially identical. The features described so confidently in the book as being distinctive sometimes blur alarmingly between edible and inedible species in real life. The *Boletus luridifromis* and *Suillelus satanas* mentioned before are an excellent example. Nobody should fully trust the very subtle differences in appearance, let alone their "instinct" (I always had to suppress a laugh when people spoke of this) to make the judgement. One could, however, trust a spore print. To make a spore print one need only cut off the mushroom's cap, set it on a white piece of paper with the gill side down and wait a few hours. The mushroom will obligingly drop its spores during this time, which you can then examine under the microscope. The dropped spores, incidentally, also make a lovely pattern on the paper, hence the term "spore print." But this aspect is irrelevant, although it does give you the spore colour, which can be important. Once viewed under the microscope, the spores tell their story with clarity and precision — eat me or do not eat me! It is that simple, but the large majority of people do not know this. Consequently, *Boletus luridifromis* and other mushrooms with worrisome doppelgangers became an important part of our diet in the summer of 1947.

Similar to the mushroom story is the story of the Traubenkirschen (very closely related to the chokecherries so abundant on the Canadian prairies), which were commonly believed to be poisonous. Here the majority of people were again mistaken. To be fair, when eaten alone they are exceedingly tart, even astringent, and thus not very inviting, but as I mentioned before, the ration system was at times peculiarly generous with sugar. Right through the summer very few other rations were available, but we continued to receive our half kilo per head per month allotment of sugar. Traubenkirschen made a marvellous juice when cooked with sugar. This juice was full of vitamins, so although it felt very much like a treat, it helped our health tremendously. This was Mama and Theodor's department. They collected large baskets full of these small black berries in July. Theodor also found a large cache of old beer bottles behind the brewery, so these were washed and stoppered with rags to store our bounty.

In this manner, with mushrooms and chokecherry juice on top of the other fruit beginning to ripen and the occasional pleasant surprise from the ration card, we managed to survive. None of us put on weight, but none of us lost weight either. Unspoken was the fear of winter as the first signs of autumn began to appear. By late August the birds were already changing their behaviour.

At some point in the late summer a startling letter arrived

from Papa. It was a change in tone, and it was also the first in a long while that had been censored at all.

Dear Luise,

I have been here two years now and it is not clear yet when I will be released. ███████████ ████████████████████████████████████ ████████████████████████████████████ ████████████████████████████ We do leave the camp at times, sometimes, as I mentioned, to clean up rubble but sometimes also for an educational purpose. I didn't mention it before, but I want to tell you now that in the early days our first such trip was to see the Bergen-Belsen concentration camp southeast of here. I'm sure that you know of this and similar camps now too, so I don't need to describe it. You can imagine my emotions given my position in the Party. Some of my fellow prisoners think the camps are fake, but I have come to understand that they are not, and I don't just write this because I know my letter will be read by the censor.

I see how terribly broken this country is. There is a painful irony in having believed one is doing the very best for one's country and then discovering that in fact one has been doing the opposite. I still think there was good in the beginning, but it all went too far, too extreme and we were swept along in a mass hysteria. I have learned to beware when everyone in a group starts to say the same thing and I have, thanks to the diligence and good sense of my captors, relearned the wisdom of aurea mediocritas.

Your Wilhelm

"Aurea mediocritas?" I asked Theodor.

"The golden mean. It's a Greek idea that it is best to be moderate in all things, not only politics but food and wine and so on, and to avoid extremes."

"That makes sense."

"But he still doesn't accept personal responsibility. Not really anyway. Not in an honest emotional sense. He mentions the concentration camp and the 'broken country' like abstract lessons he is learning to pass a test."

I did not reply to this. It occurred to me that perhaps pride had something to do with the way Papa wrote things, but I did not have the right words at the time to express this. Also Theodor did not look interested in discussing it further as he had put the letter down and was busying himself with sorting raspberries. I asked myself, If I had done something really wrong, would I fully bare my soul to other people about it? Or would I hold some of that back, especially if my self-image was that of a good person (which it was) and a smart person (which it also was)? I hoped I would not hold back. I hoped I would put reason and morality and contrition before pride. Beneath these hopes was a deeper quieter answer, like a small ripple on a dark pond, that I chose not to pay attention to.

Immediately after this and for the first time in over a year, the image of Frau Doctor Burkhard appeared in my mind's eye. Sometimes my subconscious was a mischievous card dealer. Where was the Frau Doctor? Was she even still alive? Did Papa write to her too? And if he did, did he write the same things, or was he more candid? Or perhaps less? This was an abstract and ultimately pointless line of thought and I was hungry. I went over to help Theodor with the raspberries.

CHAPTER

FORTY-THREE

AUTUMN 1947

When I think of the autumn of that famine year, I think of one thing only: potatoes. The apple harvest was poor, in part because so many people were roaming the country roads looking for free fruit, and there was no way to preserve the mushrooms or berries of summer, not that we had any surplus anyway. Some mushrooms like *Russula ochroleuca* and *Meripilus giganteus* (which is a very interesting-looking giant bracket fungus) have their season in the fall, but these were popular, not that common and not easily confused with poisonous mushrooms, so competition was intense for them. No, in the autumn of 1947 our attention turned to what was under the soil. Theodor and I walked out into the country every day and watched carefully as the potato harvest proceeded.

After a farmer finished with a potato field, we would race onto it and drop to our hands and knees to quickly sift through the muddy soil with our hands, looking for small potatoes the farmer had left behind or even little chunks of potato cut by the harvesting spade. The farmer did not care. He had taken everything that was worth his effort, so having starving townspeople come onto his fields after only helped him clean his field up nicely for the next season. We were not alone. In fact we were far from alone. One evening I counted one hundred people in the field, all of them crawling along, looking intently, working to beat the failing light. Some became adept at blindly finger-searching the fields in the dark and continued their hunt well into the night, but Mama wanted us home by sunset. Usually Theodor and I managed to get enough of what we called stubble nuts (these remnants were just the size of nuts) to allow Mama to make a reasonably nourishing soup. But there was never enough to save for the coming winter.

You would think that this monotonous diet of potatoes would put me off them, that I would only eat them for survival, not for pleasure, but I continued to love them. When I dreamed of my far-off future life as a forest ranger, the dream included a large clearing near my treehouse, or perhaps a field just past the forest edge, where I could plant potatoes. Maybe even an entire hectare of them. This is the only thing that Adolf Hitler and I agreed on. He had also been a big fan of the potato, although even in this he was an idiot. I smiled when I thought of his pronouncement in the latter days of the war that the encirclement of Germany and impossibility of food imports did not matter because we would happily live off the potato. "Like the ancient Germanic tribes did!" he declared. That potatoes were a New World crop that did not arrive in Germany until the seventeenth century was not a fact that had penetrated his delirium. In fact they were initially considered "the devil's apple" and widely assumed to be poisonous until only about 200 years ago.

The turnip harvest followed the potato harvest. It was later because turnips can tolerate some frost and, for those who still cared about such things, it was said that the taste improved after a nip of cold. It was a much smaller harvest though, so we did not make too many meals of turnips. Mama saved some of these as the fear of the coming season deepened. Theodor and I also did another round of the potato fields, reasoning that between rows and in odd corners something might have been missed in the frantic after-harvest harvest. We were right. There were not many and these stubble nuts were frozen, but they were starch and calories. We would have collected and eaten the actual soil if it had calories.

Papa's knack for oddly timed letters with surreal content continued with what I remember as the "Shakespeare letter." It was waiting for us one afternoon after we returned with a small sack full of tiny frozen potatoes.

Dear Luise,

I have wonderful news. Major McWhirter and I are going to put on a Shakespeare production for the camp. He has made a present to me of a beautiful 1922 Methuen's edition of *The Tempest*. This is one of my favourite Shakespeare plays and as it happens it is one of his favourites as well. We have recruited a few other British officers and men, as well as several of the prisoners who have a passable command of the King's English.

Life in camp can be very dull and many of us long for some sort of cultural diversion, so this will suit very nicely. I will be quite busy as we prepare for this. We hope to stage it in the week or two prior to Christmas. As you might expect, I will take the role of Prospero, although it will take some time to learn the lines and I am also involved in the general preparation and stage management. Prospero has the best lines. "Let us not burden our remembrances with a heaviness that's gone."

I hope your autumn has been better so far than your summer and certainly your spring. I'm sorry to hear that not all of my packages are making it to you. Did you receive the most recent, with the tinned beef?

Your Wilhelm

We had not received a package from him for several months. It seemed that the Russians were seizing them. It was also possible that hungry postal workers were making off with them. Fortunately this changed in late autumn when packages from the West began to arrive again. "Fortunately" is a significant understatement as we were once again teetering on the knife's edge of actual starvation. The packages had been opened and inspected, but pilfering appeared to have subsided — not disappeared entirely but subsided. In retrospect this was the first indication that the chaos of the last two and a half years was beginning to transform, little by little, into some sort of new order, like particles in turbulent water settling out and forming a discernible, semi-solid layer.

Around this time the Sowjetische Militäradministration in Deutschland — universally known by its acronym, SMAD — made more pronouncements about the shape that this new order was going to take. In addition to the weekly ration notices, which were gradually becoming less laughable and occasionally even contained happy surprises of meat or eggs or bread that did not threaten to shatter your teeth, new information from SMAD began to appear as well. It was my job to check the notices as soon as they were posted early on Sunday mornings. Sunday had lost all meaning as a "day of rest" as the struggle for survival does not permit such things and our occupiers were vigorously atheistic. I was an early riser and often in the square waiting when the young Russian officer walked up to post the week's notices. He and I became familiar with each other and although we never spoke, he would smile and nod to me as I sat on a bench beside the town hall's door. I would smile and nod in return and waited until he left before reading what had been posted. In addition to the ration list (100 gm of fat! Six eggs!), there was the following notice:

A meeting of landless people is called!
The final expropriations of exploitative
bourgeois holdings of greater than
60 ha has been completed and
5 ha parcels are ready for
distribution to members of our
Agricultural Production Cooperatives!
SMAD–Colditz District

I asked Mama what this meant, but she just shrugged. As the autumn deepened, a dark period gradually settled on her again, like a heavy grey cloak. I often tried to engage her in conversation, but she usually resorted to the shortest possible answers, or no answers at all. Theodor was out collecting pine roots for firewood, so I asked him about the notice when he came home.

"They haven't told you about this in school yet? Maybe collectivization is only part of the senior curriculum."

I shrugged. We had missed quite a few days of school scattered through the autumn as the search for food sometimes took priority and also sometimes the train did not run. It was possible that I missed the class where this had been discussed.

"Well, the communist idea is that all the farmers should

have equal access to land, that this is fairer and will lead to more food production than a system where a smaller number of wealthy farmers control most of the land."

"That does sound better."

"I suppose it sounds better as a theory, but when I was still going to school in Leipzig, we learned that this system was put in place in Russia twenty years before and led to famine because it was less efficient. Not every farmer is a good farmer, and the bigger farmers can afford to have better equipment."

"Maybe that was Nazi propaganda?"

"Maybe, but you know Herr Dietmann, the potato farmer three kilometres south? He's the one who was kindest and left some slightly larger potatoes on the field. His land has been expropriated and will be worked by people who fled East Prussia and who had been farmhands on pig farms there, not actual soil farmers. And all the equipment will have to be borrowed from a central cooperative. The so-called farmers themselves can't own the equipment under this system. It won't go well."

"I suppose we will see."

"I don't know whether I want to see, Ludwig. I'm graduating in the spring and I'm thinking about going to the West. Many of my friends have the same idea."

Coincidentally, not long after, this notice appeared on the town hall door:

Residents are reminded that travel between the
Zones of Occupation is restricted solely to those persons
bearing an officially issued Certificate of Travel.
All other inter-zone travel is illegal.
Offenders will be caught and will, without exception,
be punished with imprisonment and hard labour.
SMAD–Colditz District

CHAPTER

FORTY-FOUR

WINTER 1947-48

The dreaded winter came, not with heavy snow and deadly frost this year, but with low ashen clouds and icy rain that fell unrelentingly for days and then weeks and then possibly months, I do not remember. I only remember it was a very long time to live in a world leached of all colour. But none of this mattered, not really, because this winter we did not starve. Better to have a full stomach in a miasma of chill damp than to be hungry under a cheery blue sky. The famine had staggered to an end through a combination of, as I mentioned before, more reliable parcels from the West and improved rations as well as through the reopening of a few shops and a regular weekly market.

Money, which had been useless before, began to circulate again. Our bank accounts had been frozen since the end of the war, but Mama had stashed old Reichsmark coins that we could use. Unfortunately the value of these was very low and the ones minted during the war that had swastikas on them were banned from circulation. Mama had also begun receiving a small support payment from the SMAD. In any case, the opening of the shops and markets was encouraging and Mama's Reichsmark coins plus the SMAD money did permit a few small but useful food purchases.

I had not been inside any sort of shop since we lived in Leipzig, so I was curious to have a look at the first two that opened. I was realistic enough not to expect something really exciting like books to be sold in them, but I was still disappointed to see that both the shops contained nothing remotely of interest beyond a few items for small children and an odd assortment of foodstuffs. One shop had a large stock of cheap children's sandals even though it was winter, jars of preserved plums, jars of pickled onions, jars with indecipherable Russian labels that contained some unknown brown liquid and an array of mostly dented tins of fish. These were also labelled in Russian. By this point I had learned some Russian in Rochlitz, but none of the basic vocabulary we had been taught so far was helpful here. Fortunately, however, the label also featured a smiling green cartoon fish, so although I did not know what sort of fish, I at least knew it was fish. Before the famine I had not been fond of fish. Now it was impossible to imagine a time when I turned my nose up at anything edible. As this appeared to be the best bet, I bought the least battered of these with the coins Mama had given me. The other shop was mostly empty except one shelf that had a colourful tin toy elephant with two sad-looking girl dolls carefully set beside it and another shelf that also had a selection of dented tins with the same smiling green cartoon fish.

This was my introduction to the primitive beginnings of state-owned retail in the communist system. It did improve over the next few months, but it never came close to what comparable shops offered in Leipzig before the war. The weekly market was not under direct state control, but in the winter its selection was just as sad, and its prices were significantly higher than in the government shops. So, we survived on the now almost adequate ration offerings, supplemented by Papa's parcels.

School continued through the winter and although the weather was not as cold as the previous winter, our classrooms were ironically even colder now because of an obscure bureaucratic issue affecting coal allocations to the schools. We all wore scarves and gloves as we struggled to write during our lessons. I was supplementing what I was being taught in Rochlitz with reading at home as the quality of the teaching continued to decline. Whereas immediately after the war the teacher shortage was due to men being dead or in Siberia, now there was the additional factor that teachers would simply vanish, presumably having fled to the West.

This got Herr Schimmler especially exercised. Speeches were given regarding the cowardice inherent in abandoning the glorious project to build the workers' paradise, and we were given even more instruction on the righteousness of the Marxist-Leninist worldview and the manifold benefits generated by that system. Some of what they said had a purity of logic behind it that I found attractive in an intellectually bracing sort of way, like a cold clean wind sweeping the horrible chaotic detritus of the last decade away. From time to time I listened with something even approaching excitement. However, this never lasted very long, because in the creation of all that foregoing horrible chaotic detritus I had observed that human weaknesses and emotions always seemed to triumph over logic. The natural world, in contrast, operated on sets of logic-based rules. This was foremost evident in mathematics, physics and chemistry, but it was also true in wild nature, such as in the workings of the forests I was so familiar with. To be sure, these rules were complex and functioned like nesting gears in an inconceivably vast mechanism, but they were ultimately subject to comprehension. Human society had escaped that mechanism and was in contrast not subject to comprehension. I certainly wished it would not be so, but at the age of fourteen I was already a cynic.

I have never been good at reading people and trying to guess what they might be thinking or feeling, but even I could sense that these lectures on communism were having the opposite of the intended effect on most of the other students as well. It certainly had the opposite effect on Theodor.

Early in the new year another letter arrived from Papa.

Dear Luise,

I am very glad to hear that the packages are now getting through to you. I hope they have been helpful. I will continue to send as many as I can. I am starting to become hopeful regarding the possibility of release this year, at which point I should be able to send far more. I hear that the economy in the western zones is gradually improving, so it should not be difficult for me to find work. I may soon have even more good news regarding these matters, but I don't want to say anything now.

On the subject of good news, our production of *The Tempest* was a triumph! You will recall that Major McWhirter, myself and a few other doughty volunteers planned to put on a performance of that great Shakespeare play before Christmas. Despite the lack of proper costumes and sets, we were very pleased with the outcome, and the audience, both British and German, was delighted. We provided a translation for the latter.

Major McWhirter is a good man and a wise one too. In studying *The Tempest* so closely I began to see themes in it that are applicable to our situation — both the situation of we Germans as a people, and of me personally with respect to what I once believed. In this play Shakespeare writes very cleverly about the difficulties in defining justice and fairness, and about obedience and disobedience and how the latter is sometimes proper. He also manages to movingly blur the distinction between monsters and men. None of this involves direct explicit lessons, but this subtle and crabwise incursion into one's psyche is often more powerful.

I apologize if discussion of Shakespeare makes me seem obtuse and narcissistic given your struggle to put food on the table for our children, but this is ultimately part of the path to more food, and then better and better things.

Your Wilhelm

CHAPTER
FORTY-FIVE

JUNE 1948

Theodor graduated from high school in Rochlitz with excellent marks. I was happy for him, but equally unhappy for myself as I enjoyed having my big brother there as a familiar and occasionally even friendly face. The timing of his graduation was fortuitous though as the SMAD had just pushed through significant currency and economic reforms. The most noticeable aspect was that the old Reichsmarks were replaced by new Deutschmarks. The same happened in the western zones a few days prior, but the western Deutschmarks were not legal tender in the Soviet zone. Here our new Deutschmarks were simply old Reichsmarks with new stickers applied. Everyone called them Ostmarks to keep the confusion to a minimum. The way this related to Theodor's graduation was because the accompanying economic reforms resulted in the cessation of Mama's support payments from the SMAD. It had been a small amount and Mama's pride was injured every time she accepted this payment (although how that differed from accepting ration cards was unclear to me), but every penny was needed. The fortuitous part was that with Theodor done school, he could begin to work and make up for the lost income. Given how he excelled at school, in another time and another place he would have gone directly to university after graduation, but the thought of a young man in the Soviet zone of occupation attending university was roughly equivalent to a young man having thoughts of climbing the Himalayas or sailing the South Seas. We all just considered it the height of good fortune that he quickly found work. The octopus-like Peschel was able to call in a favour with the owner of a small local electrical repair shop who was willing to take Theodor on as an apprentice.

Happily right from the start Theodor's wage at the electrical shop fully replaced the SMAD support, so we were able to continue to tread water financially, with the reasonable hope that he would eventually advance and be paid even a little more. Mostly his job consisted of rewiring broken lamps and turning old Volksempfängers into useful radios. I take credit for the latter as I had already done so to our own Volksempfänger and I showed Theodor a shortcut that he was able to impress his boss with.

These modified radios were able to receive BBC, Voice of America, AFN (the U.S. armed forces network, which was excellent for jazz music), Hilversum (in the Netherlands, also good for music) and Radio Luxembourg, among many others. I even tuned into Radio Moscow from time to time in order to try to have a better understanding of what was happening in our occupation zone. I was frustrated, however, that I was not always able to cleanly separate the wheat of truth from the chaff of propaganda. I assumed that the BBC and Voice of America also had some chaff, but their announcers were less bombastic and grandiose than Radio Moscow. I had learned through the Göbbels years to distrust bombast and grandiosity. To be fair, Radio Moscow had some nice classical music, but when Mama was out I often twirled the dial until I could find jazz. One evening I was absolutely transported when for the first time I heard Sidney Bechet play his jazz clarinet. I could not form any sort of mental image of him playing or where he lived; instead the music created a kind of synesthesia for me with the high notes being bright yellows and the deeper ones inky purples, all in a living flowing abstract collage, a swirling river of vivid colour. The contrast to the grey of our lives in Colditz could not be starker.

But I exaggerate a little there. It may have been grey in the town of Colditz itself, but in June it was green in the fields and in the forest. The wildflowers were especially brilliant that spring, perhaps because of all the rain. The ditches were filled with yellow daffodils and bluebells bloomed in such numbers in the forest that some meadows turned entirely purplish blue, with barely a flicker of green showing from underneath. I sat an entire afternoon beside one of these meadows and watched the light change and the birds fly about — robins, sparrows, warblers, chickadees and, yes, the wren.

CHAPTER
FORTY-SIX

JULY 1948

One evening at the beginning of July when I was playing with the radio a news broadcast from the BBC caught my attention:

Today aircraft from the RAF, the U.S. Air Force and various Commonwealth air forces have taken an important step towards being able to supply the needs of the people of Berlin who are otherwise cut off from the world by the Soviet blockade. Aircraft are now landing at Gatow and Tempelhof every four minutes. The goal is to every single day fly in 646 tons of flour, 125 tons of cereal, 64 tons of fat, 109 tons of meat and fish, 180 tons of dehydrated potatoes, 180 tons of sugar, 11 tons of coffee, 19 tons of powdered milk, 5 tons of whole milk, 3 tons of fresh yeast, 144 tons of dehydrated vegetables, 38 tons of salt and 10 tons of cheese. In all, 1,534 tons of food are required each day to sustain the over two million people of Berlin. Additionally for heat and power, 3,475 tons of coal, diesel and petrol are also required daily. The scale of this undertaking is historic. Nothing like it has ever been attempted before. An RAF spokesman confirmed for the BBC that they expect to have enough aircraft and logistical support in place to achieve this herculean goal by the end of the summer. In the meantime the people of Berlin look to the air with hope and gratitude.

I knew that Berlin had been divided into four sectors, mirroring in miniature the division of Germany. The Soviets had reached Berlin first in 1945 and it lay deep within their zone of occupation, but when the Americans pulled out of Saxony and Thuringia, they and the British and French were given pieces of Berlin to occupy in exchange. These three Western sectors formed an island in the East. I recalled hearing a snippet on the Voice of America a week prior saying that the Soviets had stopped supplying power to the Western sectors in Berlin due to a claimed coal shortage and that at the same time the one functioning railroad between Berlin and the West was being closed for "technical reasons." I did not think too much of it at the time and continued my hunt for good jazz, but now I realized that that was the start of the blockade the BBC referred to.

Later I would learn that it was in retaliation for the currency reforms in the West that made the Soviets fear that the economies would begin to diverge quickly between the zones. They assumed that the Allies would have no stomach for supporting their so recently hated German foes in Berlin. All of Berlin would become part of the East and would strengthen it. The Soviets were wrong of course. In retrospect, this was the real start of the Cold War, but to me at the time it was just another example of people being irrational and unpredictable, and another example of why life in the East was becoming more worrisome.

It was not all bad news that summer though. Another letter arrived from Papa. Mama handed it to me with a blank facial expression and without comment. Theodor was at work and the other children were playing outside. I assumed the letter was another literary analysis of Shakespeare or a description of teatime with the English officers.

Dear Luise,

I am delighted to finally be able to write to you from freedom! I was told a few weeks ago that my release was pending, but I didn't write to you then because it was always possible that the paperwork would not be processed properly or that a problem with my file would be found, but none of that happened and yesterday, almost exactly three years after I arrived here, I walked out of denazification camp, fully discharged and free to live as I choose with only a few limitations. Chief among these is that I cannot yet work as a lawyer. Many men in my classification are barred from influential professions for life, but I am optimistic that my case will go better. I have a very strong letter of recommendation from Major McWhirter. This will certainly help.

In the meantime, I am confident that I will find some sort of administrative work in a small business. I am living with Auguste right now and although I am grateful to her, I am eager to obtain a place of my own as soon as possible.

Your Wilhelm

Mama's muted reaction confused me. She had generally been in better spirits since our food situation stabilized, although when I say "better spirits" I do not mean laughing or even smiling much, but at least she was not withdrawn in her room for hours at a time anymore.

"Mama, this is wonderful!"

"Yes, it is good news for Wilhelm."

"And it is good news for us as well!"

"You are right, it is. He will be able to send us more food and possibly even money now that he is out of the camp and will probably be able to get a job."

"I mean that it is good news for us because now we can go to the West and join him, right?"

"No, Ludwig. To begin with it is illegal to leave the zone. It is one thing for an individual adult who is fit and strong to slip unnoticed across the border, but quite another for an old woman and her six children."

"Mama, you are not an old woman!"

This at least prompted the flicker of a smile.

"You're right in the sense that at forty-one years of age I am not old compared to, say, Frau Klempner or Frau Schneider," she said, naming the two most bent and gnarled old crones we knew. "But everything that has happened in the last ten years makes me feel like I am sixty-one or seventy-one. I truly do. I feel this age in my bones and in my heart. And that is not the only problem. Papa is living with Tante Auguste right now and there is simply no space for us there, nor will there be enough space in whatever new flat he moves to as he will not be able to afford more than just a room at first."

These all seemed like excuses rather than reasons.

"Mama, please. I do not want to stay here. It is becoming clear that life is better in the West and with this currency reform it is also becoming clear that the zones are pulling further apart, rather than closer together."

She ran her fingers through her hair and looked at her lap. When she looked back up at me, her eyes were moist and she said very softly, "Ludwig, we have not been a real family since the early days of the war. We have all changed so much. We have passed through a long series of doors and many of those doors have closed behind us. Have you not noticed that Papa never mentions us all living together again? That he never writes that we should come?"

I had noticed and I had not noticed, some internal mechanism having checked my full awareness. Papa had never shown me affection, but to the best of my knowledge that was simply the way of fathers, and it did not mean that he did not love me or want me to be with him, did it? He was proud of me when I was invited to skip a grade in school, I remembered that. I struggled to summon other positive father and son memories — Papa leading Sunday family walks like a satisfied gander showing off his flock, Papa sharing wisdom in Latin or Greek, Papa helping with math homework before I became better at math than him. In all of these memories he appeared like a storybook character, two dimensional and peripheral. While these thoughts flashed quickly through my mind Mama gave me a brief hug and said, "We'll be fine, Ludwig, we'll be fine."

I nodded, handed the letter back to her and excused myself to go outside. I ignored my sister and brothers and began to run, running through the market square, over the bridge and into the forest.

CHAPTER

FORTY-SEVEN

OCTOBER 1948

In many ways, despite the disquieting political situation, life continued to become appreciably better. Starvation was no longer a threat, and for the first time we had enough money to buy a few things beyond the most basic necessities. Papa had gotten work as a manager in a small furniture factory in Osterholz, a larger town near Worpswede. There he got to know a welder who helped him seal coins into cans labelled as fish oil. These were the old fifty pfennig Reichsmark coins that were no longer legal tender in the West but were still in use in the East where they were accepted at 10 percent of their face value. Sealing them into cans would not fool a thief who picked the can up, as they were much heavier than fish oil and of course rattled in a way that even the nastiest fish oil did not, but the ruse was effective as none were ever stolen. Other people we knew routinely had cash and valuables pilfered from the packages sent to them by relatives in the West.

In addition to this help from Papa, we received a windfall from the bank. Before the end of the war Papa had transferred 16,000 Reichsmarks (or about 5,000 U.S. dollars, which adjusted for inflation would be the equivalent of $60,000 today) to bank accounts in Colditz in the children's names. He evidently thought that this was a clever way to minimize the risk of losing all his money if the war did not go well. At first it seemed that his plan had failed as the Soviets simply froze all bank accounts, but now three years later Mama received notification that every individual who could demonstrate that they had not been a member of the Nazi Party was entitled to receive 300 of the new Ostmark from their frozen accounts. The remainder would be officially confiscated as part of the ongoing war reparations. Mama had not joined the Party (inconceivable!) and this ruling applied to children as well. Obviously we were not Nazis either and our Hitler Youth time was not held against Theodor and me. Consequently seven of us lined up at the bank and each received our 300 Ostmark, so we had 2,100 in total. We were rich! Or if not rich, at least in a position where we would not have to worry about paying the rent through the winter. Mama did not permit us to spend one pfennig of it, making it plain that she felt bad times could be right around the corner again.

Indeed some of what was being said in school was beginning to alarm me. One particular speech by the school director sticks in my mind. The gist of it was that as young men and women of the new socialist Germany we needed to prepare for the possibility of confrontation with our erstwhile countrymen in the West. Those fourteen years of age and younger should join the Young Pioneers and the older students should join the Free German Youth. He seemed oblivious to the effect of that pronouncement on those of us who had been in the Hitler Youth. I looked around me and saw many stony faces as well as a few wry ironic smiles. The echoes of the past were tragicomic. He then went on to say that Joseph Stalin had done everything humanly possible to reach across the zone frontier and offer the hand of friendship and cooperation to the Americans, British and French, but they had again and again spurned this offer because they were so intent on rebuilding a fascist Germany. Yes, fascism was back, and its successor state was in the West where the Allies coddled ex-Nazis and groomed them to return to power. Such was their fear of the Worldwide Socialist Revolution! Such was their hatred of rights and freedom for workers and peasants! And on it went.

As I listened to this I naturally thought of Papa. He was an ex-Nazi. He was in the West. Had he been coddled? Is that what his friendship with that English major was about? I was so accustomed to the word "Nazi" as it was omnipresent when I was growing up and thus no more shocking to hear than "squirrel" or "lamppost." It was, I suppose, a little like a curse word that is used so much that it becomes drained of all of its power, and "Nazi" was not even a curse word until 1945, at least not in our house. But "fascist" was another thing. That word had bite to it. It sounded evil in a way that no other political label did. Had Papa really been a fascist? Was he possibly still a fascist in some small way that would infect the new Germany in the West? I was going to have to process these thoughts slowly, although I was fairly certain that I would conclude that yes, he had been a fascist and that I just was not yet used to thinking that way, but that no, he had been persuaded over the course of three years that being a fascist was not the correct thing to be. After all, as I learned new things I continued to change some of my views, such as my belief in witches for example, so why would that process not also be available to adults? This was a rational thought and that pleased me. Also, much as with Radio Moscow, Herr Schimmler spoke with that bombast and grandiosity I associated with questionable factual content.

I recounted the speech to Theodor when I got home from Rochlitz that evening. He listened, nodding, and then quietly asked me to step outside so that he could tell me something in private.

"Ludwig, I'm going to escape to the West. What you heard today is exactly why I need to go. The Russians and their friends here are starting to do the same kind of shit Hitler and his gang did. Different words but the same nonsense. I can't go through that again. I'll check the route and the situation in Worpswede and then you and the others can follow."

I was shocked. I should not have been, as Theodor had dropped strong hints before, but I did not believe that he would follow through and leave us. "We need you here, Theodor! And how do you know Papa wants you to go? Maybe you will be on your own in the West, on the street!"

"You don't need me. The money Papa sends more than replaces my wage, and the economy here is not good, so my job is not secure in any case. Herr Grün has been grumbling that he can't afford me unless people start buying more electrical goods that need repair. And I have written to Papa. He wrote back to say that I could come. It would be tight quarters, but I was welcome. I'm sure Mama suspects. She hasn't said anything though, and I am worried about her. It's the only thing that holds me back."

I wrestled with the contradiction between knowing that Theodor was right but not wanting him to go. With respect to Mama, despite her likely distress at seeing Theodor go, this could end up being the nudge she needed to allow us to make the same move. It takes a minute to write this but less than a second to think it, so after the briefest of pauses I replied, "You are right. What you say makes sense, especially if you can live with Papa. How are you going to do it? Escape, I mean?"

"I have been quietly asking around. Peschel has lots of contacts, but I'm not sure I trust him. Do you remember Gerhard in my class? Well, he left last month, so I asked his sister how he did it and she put me in touch with someone in Grimma who organizes escapes through the Harz. This fellow is willing, and he says that I am lucky with the timing, as winter is best. The patrols are less and there is more fog. I'm leaving in a month, in the first week of December."

The Harz were the mountains I mentioned before in reference to the witch legends on their highest peak, the Brocken. They straddled the zone boundary and were famed for their dark forests. "That sounds dangerous," was all I could think of to say.

"Maybe." Theodor shrugged. "But after being sent with a Panzerfaust against Russian tanks, danger seems very much to be a relative concept. And this border runner has a good reputation. He has obviously not been caught or killed yet, otherwise he would not be in business!"

"How will you pay him? Mama has all the money."

"She'll agree. Don't worry about that."

CHAPTER

FORTY-EIGHT

DECEMBER 1948

A nd she did. Mama gave Theodor the money to pay the border runner. She said that she could not hold him back. Theodor was an adult (he had turned eighteen in September) and he had been earning money. Maybe he was right about life in the West, maybe not. We would see.

We all got up at four o'clock on one icy cold early December morning when Theodor got ready to walk to Grimma as the first part of his journey. Mama was to tell Herr Grün that he was sick and could not come to work; we were not sure whether he could be trusted with the truth or not. She hugged Theodor fiercely and wished him good luck. I called after him that he should write immediately when he got to the other side. He turned his head, mouthed "of course," and then marched off into the dark.

True to his word, two weeks later a letter arrived.

Dear Mama, Ludwig, Clara, Johann, Oskar and Paul,

I am here in Worpswede with Papa! What an adventure! We took the train from Grimma to Leipzig and then to Quedlinburg via Halle. Wernigerode would have been much closer to the border, but my guide (I won't use his name in case this letter is read by others) said that the border security people watched those trains much more closely. It was better to get off further from the border and walk the extra distance. It was only fifty kilometres in any case. Normally that would take me no more than two days at the very most, but in winter and in the mountains, it is a different story! There had been a large snowstorm the day before, which made the going slow, especially as we stayed off the main trails, but it also meant that the patrols were less frequent than normal. My guide knew a spot (I won't say where in this letter and in any case it would be too rough for you when you come) where the patrols did not often go when the snow was heavy. I should mention that these are Russian Red Army border troops, and they have dogs and trucks. In some places they are starting to use VoPos instead, but only at towns and roads — not places you want to try to sneak across! But despite the weather and the carefully selected spot we almost got caught! We came to the border in the middle of the night. In these remote areas it's still only marked with a few posts, there are no fences there yet, but the Russians must have known that these parts of the Harz were becoming popular for people like the guide and me because they seemed to be waiting for us. Fortunately they can't cover every metre, especially in the dark, especially in the deep snow, so we were able to run across, followed by shouts and a few bullets, but only the trees were injured! I was so cold and so hungry, but so elated too.

Papa was pleased to see me and although we only have an eight square metre rented room in an attic, we are comfortable. He has found work for me at the Bergolin paint factory.

I just wanted you to know that I am safely here and how the journey went. I will write more soon.

With love,
Theodor

Mama began to cry, and Clara and Johann shouted "Hurrah!" I knew enough not to then ask Mama if we could follow, and in any case Theodor's route was not going to be practical for us. We should probably take our chances with the VoPos in a less remote area. I should explain that these were the Volk's Polizei, or "people's police," German recruits trusted by the Soviet authorities.

As it happened I did not have to ask Mama because she raised the subject with me after the younger ones had gone to bed. Electricity was still often off in the evenings, so we were sitting at the dining table by candlelight, the cheap candle guttering and casting weird shadows behind Mama's head.

"I'm glad of course that Theodor made it across, and that Papa has welcomed him, but I need you to know that we cannot follow." She said this quietly but firmly.

"But why? The fact that it is illegal has not stopped thousands. Probably tens of thousands now. If we learned anything through the Hitler years it was that obeying laws is not always the same as doing the right thing. And of course we will find a safer route. So many have gone with small children now too." Mama did not say anything in reply and was looking off to the side towards the dark window, so I forged ahead with my arguments. "Also with both Papa and Theodor working, we can afford a large enough place. I can work too! I can finish school later."

"There's something else, Ludwig." Mama was still looking away as she said this.

"What? What else?"

"Papa has a woman there."

I did not know how to reply to this, so we sat in silence, the candle flickering and the faint sound of wind in the lane outside.

"How do you know that?" I finally asked, trying to hold my voice even.

"I know because she wrote me and told me not to come. She wrote that Wilhelm was hers and that I did not deserve him. That's how I know that." This was stated as a plain fact, but bitterness painted the edges of her words.

"Are you sure?" I regretted this the moment I said it. It was a stupid question.

"What do you mean, am I sure? Nobody would write a random woman in Colditz to lie about having an affair with her husband half a country away!" Mama snorted and then fixed me with a hard stare. "Do not tell anyone else. I could not bear the shame. Despite everything, despite absolutely everything, I have my pride. My father was a great man and my mother was a great woman. I come from great people. I can lead what is left of this family here. I do not need to follow Wilhelm to the West like a whipped dog only to stand by and smile politely while he makes a fool of me with another woman. And that is the end of this discussion."

It really was the end of the discussion. I had no way to respond to this. And I wondered, Was it Frau Doctor Burkhard or a different woman? I never did see the letter. I wanted to write Theodor to ask him what he knew about this woman and what he thought about the situation, but my courage failed me for fear Papa would intercept it and for the pubescent embarrassment I felt in acknowledging or addressing this.

CHAPTER FORTY-NINE

JANUARY 1949

The further we move away from the famine time, the clearer my memory is for dates, although unless there is a specific associated historical event, I can often just narrow things down to the month, rather than the specific day.

Sometime in mid to late January there was a sharp rap on the door. It must have been a weekend as I was not in school. I opened the door to see Squish Eye and two VoPos standing there. Squish Eye was the head of the local Volk's Polizei. I do not remember his real name, but his nickname is unforgettable. Everyone called him Squish Eye because his right eye had been damaged in the war by a piece of shrapnel, leaving something that looked like a shrivelled date sitting in the socket. Anyone else would have worn a patch over that small horror, but the fact that he did not tells you something significant about the man. The first police the Russians put in place were mostly half-wit ex-cons, as again manpower was a significant problem, but Squish Eye was serious. I do not know what he did before the war, but whether he had been a police officer then or not, he was perfectly suited to the role, at least in a totalitarian system. His other qualification was that he was ideologically pure. While many mouthed the communist tropes to get along, I had the feeling that he was a true believer. And now he was at my front door.

"Good afternoon, young man. May I please speak to your mother?" He was certainly polite. I did not have to get Mama because she had heard and came forward to the door.

"Yes, good afternoon to you. How can I help you?" she said, wiping her hands on her apron.

"You are required to come with us to the town hall, madam."

"Oh, why is that?"

"It is only for some routine questions. It will not take very long."

"Can't you ask me these questions here?"

"No, I'm afraid not, madam. It is protocol." He stepped slightly to the side and beckoned her to come out. Mama sighed heavily, undid her apron and handed it to me.

"All right then. If it is *protocol*." She put a heavy emphasis on this last word, enunciating every syllable.

After the four of them left, Johann came up to me, looking very upset. "Where are they taking Mama?"

"Just to the town hall for questions. There is no need to worry! She will be back right away!" I forced cheeriness into my voice, but the forced aspect was obvious. Johann still looked worried.

"What are they asking her about?"

"I do not know. Maybe it is about Theodor leaving."

Johann nodded and looked grave. "Will they try to bring him back? And why would they be worried about him leaving?"

"Ha! No, they cannot bring him back. It is a different government over there in the West and the government here does not get along with that government. That is also why they do not want people to leave. They do not want the world to think that this is a bad place that people want to leave and that the government in the West is doing a better job of making people happy."

"Oh." Johann nodded again and went off to play.

My guess was correct. Squish Eye questioned Mama for half an hour about Theodor's absence. He had intelligence that her son had fled illegally. She was to order him to return. She laughed at this, saying she could not, and she would not. Was that all? Could she go now? Squish Eye told her no, stay seated, there is more. He then detailed how he and his men were going to keep a careful watch on our family lest anyone else get the idea to flee. He reminded her of the strict penalties for even preparing to leave and then he reached into a drawer and pulled out a piece of paper. This was a document, signed by the district supervisor and decorated with a fancy seal, that proclaimed that Luise Schott, Ludwig Schott, Clara Schott, Johann Schott, Oskar Schott and even three-year-old Paul Schott were under Official Police Supervision. He smiled as he brandished this document, smiling a smile that according to Mama was one of idiotic triumph, as if that piece of paper had settled the matter definitively.

We both had a chuckle about this. Mama then busied herself with preparing dinner and I went for a walk to the forest to think. The oaks had long since been cut for firewood, but the special spot was still there. The sun had already gone down, but it was a clear sky with a full moon and there was fresh snow to absorb and reflect the pearly light. The birds were all in their beds, but I did not need them. I only needed to listen to my own thoughts, coming in sequence, one after the other, clean and crisp, like the snow.

CHAPTER

FIFTY

FEBRUARY 1949

The answer was obvious. If I applied logic to my understanding of human frailty, I could make it happen. I was sure of it. The ten-year-old me or even the thirteen-year-old me would have struck immediately, but not the fifteen-year-old me. The fifteen-year-old me was more mature, much more mature, and knew that a little time would help the cause. Let her think about this a little more herself. Let her begin to approach the idea herself. She had too much pride to be pushed. Squish Eye had done me a favour.

I waited for the right moment. Mama frequently still had black moods, but from time to time, seemingly at random, she was almost cheerful. I picked one of those days. It also happened to be a day when school had been particularly odious. The science teacher had been absent for several days, presumably gone to the West, and his replacement was an idiot. I cannot put it any plainer than that. I loved science, but this idiot was going to make me hate it. The value of my education in Rochlitz had dropped several more points. It was almost a negative value now. I could feel myself in danger of becoming dumber by the day.

Mama was agreeable when I suggested a walk after dinner. It was a warm evening for February, and I did not want to upset the others if the conversation did not go well.

I launched right into it. "I think you know why I want to talk to you."

"Yes, I do. The answer is still no." Her tone was soft though, not confident.

"School is terrible, really terrible. I am learning nothing. They are also starting to talk about us needing to join the Young Pioneers and the Free German Youth. You know why I cannot do that. And the economy is worse every day here. Did you see that Herr Grün's shop closed?"

"Yes, I did."

We shuffled along through the market square and stopped to look up at the castle, which had quite a few lights on that evening for some reason.

"But even more importantly I have been thinking about what Squish Eye said to you. Do you remember that story you told us about the wren and the bear? Squish Eye is just another bear or wolf or fox. No different than Reinhard or Felix or Kohl or Kozlov or Schimmler. Do you really want someone like that telling you how to live your life? Or" — I paused for a moment and gathered my courage — "some ridiculous and probably quite stupid husband stealer telling you how to live your life?" Mama did not say anything and kept looking up at the castle. "You said that you have your pride. Does your pride not dictate that you stand up for your family and laugh in the face of pompous fools like Squish Eye and shrill jezebels like this woman?" I wanted to say more, and again my ten-year-old and thirteen-year-old self would have, but my fifteen-year-old self knew better. He knew not to dilute the power of his argument with too many extraneous words.

Mama pulled her eyes away from the castle, looked down at her feet, drew in a deep breath and then looked at me. "Yes, Ludwig. We will leave."

CHAPTER

FIFTY-ONE

MARCH 1949

Mama and I began preparations at once. We decided not to tell the other children until it was absolutely necessary so as to reduce the risk of accidental disclosure. We set the target at April 1. One month to plan the route and sell as much as possible as discretely as possible. Mama knew someone who could change Ostmark for western Deutschmark. The rate was ridiculous, but we knew that Ostmark were worthless anywhere outside the Soviet zone. Mama felt strongly that we needed to have as much cash with us as possible in case things did not go well with Papa. I was less concerned about this but conceded her point.

First to go was a lot of the beautiful old oak furniture. Some of it was old enough to be considered properly antique and some of it had been designed by my grandfather, Hugo Flintzer, in Weimar. For this we had to make use of Herr Peschel's connections to an auctioneer in Leipzig who could be relied upon to obscure the provenance of his merchandise. This was a difficult decision because neither of us trusted Herr Peschel completely. I am not convinced that anyone in Colditz did. It was impossible to tell where his loyalties truly lay, and it seemed odd that an enterprising man like him continued to stay in the East, but we reasoned that he was doing well here and that this was in large measure because his loyalties were only to himself. As soon as it was no longer profitable to stay, he would go. Moreover, as our landlord and occasional visitor to our apartment, he was the one person we could not conceal our plans from for very long, so we had little choice but to trust him. He also had an unusually close relationship with the police, one that I assume involved well-chosen and well-timed gifts. This was obviously a double-edged sword and we were careful not to give him any reason to be upset with us and turn us in to his VoPo friends. In fact we took a leaf from his own book and offered him a very generous commission on the sales he facilitated. We considered this commission to be a well-chosen and well-timed gift.

Next was the cooking stove. Whereas at the brewery we had cooked and kept warm and heated water all with one stove, in this place we had that large heating stove that Herr Peschel had acquired from the tavern, as well as a smaller modern electric cooking stove, which was wonderful when there was electricity. The heating stove belonged to the landlord of course, but the cooking stove was ours and Mama was determined to sell it as she thought it would fetch a good price. To sell it quietly, she decided that the best plan was to place a small advertisement in the Leipzig newspaper. It was a valuable enough item (consumer appliances such as this were in short supply in the East) that she reasoned a big city buyer would be interested in even if they had to come out here to get it. All the better if they came from somewhere other than Colditz.

On the Saturday morning that the advertisement appeared there was a knock on the door, too early for anyone to have made it from Leipzig yet. Mama opened the door and I could see that a VoPo officer was standing there. He was tall and young and only vaguely familiar-looking.

"Good morning, madam. Are you Luise Schott?" He was reading from a small piece of paper that he had unfolded just then.

"Yes," she responded cautiously.

"And you are selling a Heiliger electric enamel cooking stove, 'used but well cared for and functions like new'?"

The blood drained from my face. The VoPo was reading from the newspaper advertisement. He had clipped it out. Oh no. Of course the police got all the regional newspapers. Selling an appliance was the number one sign that someone was preparing to move. Even if we claimed to be moving to a different part of the East, we did not have any of the necessary permits and paperwork for that. I sat there, paralyzed with fear. I should do something, but there was nothing I could do. Fortunately Mama remained icy calm.

"Yes, I am, officer. We don't need the stove, but we do need the money." She smiled at the officer and then added, "Are you interested in buying it?" She told me later that she meant this as a joke to try to lighten the mood and engender sympathy.

"Yes, yes I am, if the price is agreeable." The VoPo smiled what looked like a nervous smile.

Oh, thank God. I almost slumped right over from the sudden release of tension. After the deal was concluded and the VoPo had gotten a friend to help him carry his stove, Mama sat down beside me and shook her head. "That was too close. He didn't seem suspicious, but I hope he doesn't tell Squish Eye. There are probably some rules about police officers buying things on what amounts to the grey market, especially while in uniform. These people have rules for everything. He probably will keep mum," she said.

The third major category to deal with was in many ways the hardest: the books. As I have mentioned a few times, we had a marvellous collection, really the equivalent of a well-curated small-town library. While I knew that these would ultimately be replaceable when we had money again, it still hurt to see them go. Many of our volumes were particular and individual, with evidence of heavy use despite how carefully we looked after them. Some seemed to have personalities. We could no more truly replace them with other copies than we could replace Paul with another tousle haired three-and-a-half-year-old boy. Similar but not identical. But we had to be practical. As a concession I did not have to go to Leipzig to watch Mama haggle over the value of these "family members." This would be too sad and now that I no longer lived in a big city, I decided that I did not like them, even to visit. Too many people. Too much noise. My job was to organize the books in advance as Mama would be taking only the valuable ones to Leipzig. The more ordinary ones were sold in box lots through Herr Peschel again. Organizing is one of my strengths, so I enjoyed this, despite the loss it was contributing to.

There were enough in the valuable category that Mama had to make two trips. She had an amusing story when she returned from the first one. The streetcars were running again, so she took one from the train station to the antiquarian bookseller. A Russian officer was sitting across from her on this streetcar. She did not know what rank he was, but he had a magnificent uniform, festooned with all manner of gold braids and impressive shiny medals. He smiled pleasantly at Mama, who had put on lipstick and her best dress for the first time in years. She wanted to make a good impression when negotiating with the book dealer and not look like a desperate refugee who could be taken advantage of. When the streetcar got to her stop at Augustusplatz she struggled a little with the large bags bulging with heavy books, so the Russian officer leapt to his feet, took the bags and accompanied her to the bookshop, where he held the door for her and bowed crisply as she entered. Mama laughed about this when she told us because she found it so funny that this Russian officer had inadvertently helped us get ready to escape!

And then finally there were the clothing and the linens. Mama decided that we had raised enough money from the furniture, stove and books that we would not have to sell any clothing or linens, which would not bring us much money anyway. Instead she decided to try to have them smuggled to the West. This was really interesting. Again the redoubtable Herr Peschel knew the trick. The first step was to sew everything into cloth parcels, each no more than seven kilograms. So, Mama used old blankets and sheets to act as the parcel wrap, filled them with our tablecloths, pillows, bedding, towels, clothing and such and then sewed them shut. Unfortunately thread was one of those everyday items that simply was not available in the East. Mama was consequently forced with a heavy heart to obtain thread by undoing the fine needlework on many of the pillows done by her mother, my beloved Oma Flintzer. Ultimately we ended up with forty of these seven-kilogram parcels. This seems like an astonishing number, but with eight of us (if you counted Papa, as we still had a lot of his things) it can add up to quite a lot.

This is not the interesting part yet. The interesting part is that Herr Peschel then put us in touch with an unnamed gentleman who operated out of a small yard off a back lane in the Leipzig suburb of Moeckern. We were instructed to destroy the written directions to this place once we had been there. This gentleman arranged for the transport of the parcels to East Berlin, where a large number of couriers were employed by this secret network. These couriers took advantage of the curious fact that the pre-war subway system was still in operation in Berlin and that several lines crossed back and forth between East and West. Residents of East Berlin, such as the couriers, could pass through West Berlin subway stations and thus be able to deliver the parcels to the West! In theory East Berliners could illegally stay in West Berlin, but as they had to cross East German territory to reach the rest of the West, they were trapped. This freedom of movement within Berlin ended with the building of the Berlin Wall in 1961, although even then the subways rattled through heavily guarded ghost stations in the East on their way from one part of West Berlin to another. Every one of our forty parcels arrived intact in Worpswede after the Berlin blockade was lifted in September 1949.

Once the books and linens started going, Mama had to tell Clara and my brothers what was planned, but we decided not to write Papa or Theodor as we feared the VoPos were monitoring our mail. Theodor had gotten away with writing Papa, but we had not been under Official Police Supervision then.

On March 31, Mama picked up our seven ration cards for April and handed them to Herr Peschel as a final gift. They would be worth something on the black market. That night she sewed the 4,000 Deutschmark she had traded all our Ostmark for into the lining of Paul's baby bag. He was not a baby anymore, but he was exceptionally small for his age, so a baby bag would not attract interest or suspicion. We each packed one backpack. My siblings used their school bags and Mama sewed a larger one for me from a blanket. The next day we were leaving Colditz for good. Every bridge had been burned.

CHAPTER
FIFTY-TWO

MARCH 31 & APRIL 1, 1949

To reduce suspicion we decided to leave Colditz in two separate groups. I went ahead with Clara and Johann. As the train left the station, I was so nervous and excited that I forgot to take one last look at the town and at the castle, but once we were into the country I saw the spiky dark green fringe of the Colditzer Forst off to the south. I felt a pang from an unexpected feeling of loss and even grief, which was strange as I was headed somewhere that should be far better. I watched the forest for as long as it was in view, straining my eyes and ignoring Clara and Johann, who were making excitable noises beside me. Goodbye, Fence King!

At the Leipzig station we were met by old family friends, Herr and Frau Buheitel, whom we spent the night with. The next morning they took us back to the station to meet Mama, Oskar and Paul, who had taken the early train out of Colditz after spending the night on the two remaining bare beds and a beat-up old chaise longue that we had not tried to sell. We greeted each other with nervous smiles and looked for the train to Halberstadt. The adventure was now truly underway.

We were going to Halberstadt because, after some debate and consultations with various people who knew something about illegal border crossing, we had decided to cross through Osterwieck, which is the last town west of Halberstadt before the border, just immediately north of the Harz Mountains. This was the solution I had pushed for. The mountains themselves would have been too tough for the little ones and I was even a little worried about Mama. Despite the improvement in our nutrition, we were still short of protein and vitamins and she did not look good, presumably also because she worked harder and worried more than any of us. The country lanes and fields west of Osterwieck would be easier to walk across, although they would also be more heavily patrolled. I thought it was a reasonable trade-off, especially as we planned to cross in the night and were used to walking through fields, unlike many of the big-city people who were trying to escape.

From Halberstadt we took a smaller train to Osterwieck. This was the end of the line as no tracks crossed the zone frontier anywhere other than the one line to West Berlin (when the Soviets allowed that to operate). This train had a few young men with empty backpacks on it. This struck me as odd, but as I was not one to engage strangers in conversation, I just tried to puzzle it out for myself. One of them noticed me staring and smiled.

"You're wondering about our empty bags, aren't you?"

"Yes, I apologize." I was embarrassed that he noticed my interest.

He laughed. "We are herring traders! There is almost no fresh fish to be had here in the East, but they have plenty in the West, so we sneak over one way with empty bags and sneak back the other way with our bags full of herring, fresh caught from the North Sea and brought by the morning train from Bremerhaven to Vienenburg."

"Is that not dangerous?"

The young man smiled. "Yes, it is dangerous, but we know the best way over, and regardless it is definitely worth it. The price of herring is so low in the West and so high in the East!"

I nodded and then settled into thinking about how the train must smell on the way back from Osterwieck. This was yet another reason to be happy that we were going west one-way. I considered asking him about this "best way over," but my instinct told me that they would not welcome a gaggle of noisy little children tramping down their secret route.

It seemed that very few people came to Osterwieck for any reason other than to try to sneak over the border. That should not have been a surprise to us, but somehow the implications of this particular aspect of our plan were not something we discussed. Part of it might have been that Osterwieck was smaller than we expected. Mama and I both assumed that we could just get off the train, leave the station quietly, do our best to avoid attracting suspicion and then keep a careful eye out for the VoPos and for the more fearsome paramilitary DGP (Deutsche Grenzpolizei, the border patrol). "Just a family out for a hike in the beautiful countryside." Hence the relatively small backpacks, just like hikers, and the lack of other baggage. I did not think we looked like refugees, certainly not like the people I had seen fleeing Silesia at the end of the war.

But it was not to be. The train was met by a large contingent of VoPos armed with rifles that dated from the 1870 Franco-Prussian War, similar to the ones I remembered from the KLV-Lager. All the passengers were herded into a fenced-off area beside the station. Those of us who could not prove we were from Osterwieck or who could not provide another plausible and verifiable reason for being here were then herded down the road a short distance to an abandoned farm. We were ordered into the barn where presumably it would be easier to keep an eye on us as there was just the one door to guard. The rifles may have looked almost comically old, but there was nothing in the slightest bit comical about the attitude of the VoPos. There was no doubt that they would use their weapons if they felt the need. I knew that bullets fired from old rifles would kill you just as effectively as those fired from new ones.

It was about five p.m. when we arrived at the barn. There were perhaps fifty of us in there. We all stood around for a moment, taking in the dirt- and manure-covered floor and the handful of short benches that could accommodate only a fraction of us. However, before we had a chance to deal with this, a DGP officer came into the barn with several men. He pulled one of the benches up to a crude table and began the process of registering us. Everyone in occupied Germany had to carry identity papers with them at all times. The penalties for not doing so were quite severe. The officer carefully examined all of our documents and entered the particulars in a ledger. It was becoming chaotic in the barn as people were increasingly anxious. Some were even arguing with the DGP men, which struck me as pointless and ill-advised. A thick jostling crowd developed around the table. It was difficult for Mama and me to deal with the registration process as well as keep an eye on the children and our belongings. After the officer was done with us, Mama noticed that her leather satchel had disappeared. This contained our food (bread and hard-boiled eggs) and the bit of jewellery she had left. Mama thought one of the police had taken it, but I reasoned that it could just as easily have been one of our fellow aspiring refugees. Either way it was going to be a difficult night.

CHAPTER

FIFTY-THREE

APRIL 2, 1949

It was a very long sleepless night of mostly standing, leaning against the barn wall, but occasionally sitting when Mama decided to stand. We could only go to the outhouse in the farmyard accompanied by one of the guards. Even Clara, though very small for a twelve-year-old, was escorted by a guard. She said he kept his finger on the trigger of his rifle the entire time. When morning finally came, we could see through the small broken windows that it was going to be a glorious spring day. Fingers of dusty sunlight stabbed through the barn, illuminating clusters of exhausted people, many slumped against the walls, some sitting on the benches and a few braving the filthy floor. It had been thirty-six hours since I last had anything to eat. I should have breakfasted in Leipzig, but I had been too nervous then to think about food. I had the faint hope that we would be given something to eat, but all that was provided was a cup of Muckefuck for each of us, even for little three-and-a-half-year-old Paul, who wisely refused it.

At around eight the DGP officer strode back in and shouted at us to form three roughly equal length lines. We were then taken outside and each line of about fifteen to twenty was told to climb into the back of one of the three waiting trucks. There was only enough room to stand, and barely even that. Mama held Paul in her arms, and we all squeezed tightly together, which while uncomfortable prevented us from falling over as the truck bumped along a deeply rutted country road. Fortunately we did not have far to go. The trucks stopped at another abandoned farm. We were taken into the farmhouse and told to wait in a large empty room. Farmers often had large rooms like this that served as dining rooms, living rooms and even kitchens all in one. Here there were only two small benches, so there was again a lot of standing as we waited to be processed again, this time by the Russians. I do not know why this processing could not have all been done by the DGP, but my dark suspicion is that each of them — VoPos, DGP and Russians — wanted the opportunity to scare us and shake us down.

It was late afternoon by the time it was our turn to be called into the small adjoining room where a Russian officer sat at a desk with a translator behind him and two soldiers standing off to the side. I remember fixating for some reason on the small bright red desktop flag of the USSR that was on the desk in front of him. The soldiers began rifling through our backpacks while the officer fingered our identity papers, looking bored. The soldiers had emptied our spare clothes and sundry bits and pieces into a heap in the corner of the room. They looked angry and said something to the officer. He apparently asked them to hand the bags over. They passed them to him, one at a time, and he carefully inspected the linings and kneaded the cloth wherever there was a double layer. It was obvious that he was looking for money or jewellery. I am glad that he did not notice that we all had become very still as he went through Paul's baby bag, again squeezing the sides. The padding was thankfully thick enough to prevent him from detecting the Deutschmarks. When he was done and had not found anything, he shrugged and tossed the bags back to the soldiers. Then he turned to face Mama. His expression changed from boredom to anger.

He spat something out in Russian, which was translated as "You will go back to Colditz first thing in the morning!" He then loudly stamped each of our papers. "You are lucky. I should send you to labour camp now and put the children in state care, but I am a family man myself. Consider this a warning. These stamps mean that if you are found trying to cross the border again you will be imprisoned for sure. I swear this to you."

We were then permitted to leave the building and go out into the farmyard. It was a gorgeous sun-drenched late afternoon, the saturated greens of grass and blues of sky vivid in my memory. Russian soldiers were playing soccer while most of our fellow travellers were milling about. I noticed that the young herring smugglers were nowhere to be seen. Mama sighed and ran her fingers through her hair. We did not speak for fear of being overheard by the wrong ears, but I am sure that we were both thinking the same thing: we had come this far and there was nothing for us in Colditz anymore. Somehow, some way, we would try to escape tonight. First we would wait for darkness and then we could see what opportunity might present itself. In the meantime we sat down on a patch of grass and tried to enjoy the sun.

A middle-aged man dressed like a hiker with knee socks and a dark green wool coat with carved deer antler buttons came up to us. He smiled and sat down beside Mama.

"May I?" he asked.

Mama nodded.

"You are headed west. I can help. For a reasonable price I know a guaranteed way." He spoke very quietly and very calmly.

Mama looked at him with that steely look I knew so well. "Thank you, kind sir, but I am afraid that you are mistaken. We have no money and we are, in any case, returning home at the earliest opportunity, as ordered."

The man raised his eyebrows a fraction and then gave a "have it your way" shrug and moved on to the next group of people.

The sun was starting to drop towards the western horizon. It was less than an hour until sunset. The Russians were still playing soccer, but they had become louder and were laughing a lot more. I watched carefully and then spotted the source of this merriment. They were passing a large, almost empty, clear glass bottle between them.

Mama whispered to me, "That border runner in the hiking clothes? I saw him give that bottle to the soldiers. It's vodka."

Sometimes the best decisions are made spontaneously without long discussion, or really any discussion. I stood up and looked at Mama, inclining my head slightly towards the sun. She understood and whispered to each of the children. None of the Russian soldiers were looking our way and the officer had not even once come out of the farmhouse. To my quiet astonishment we were able to simply walk out of the yard, as if casually wandering over to look at something in the next field, and then we ducked out of sight behind a fence.

We did not know where we were as it had been impossible to keep track of directions while in the back of the truck, but the orientation was simple — the sun set in the west and west was where we wanted to be. So, we walked directly into the sun, crossing fields and trying to keep out of sight by staying behind hedges and clumps of trees. The Brocken was clearly silhouetted on the horizon on our left, to the south. The land here was gently rolling, so soon a series of low hills lay between us and the Russians. The countryside was empty, almost eerily so. There were no people or animals about, not even any birds. After an hour, just as the light was beginning to fade, we came upon two elderly farmers who were planting potato seedlings. They seemed trustworthy, so Mama asked them whether we were headed the right way. They said yes, just keep going the same way, it was not too far to the border anymore, maybe three or four kilometres.

It is one thing to walk west when you have the setting sun to aim for, but now it was gone and the glow on the western horizon quickly disappeared as well. The hills and small woodlots also made it difficult to walk in a straight line. We had been walking a couple of hours at this point and we were all very hungry, so fatigue had definitely set in. My siblings were remarkably quiet and brave though. They understood the importance of soldiering on without complaint, even seven-year-old Oskar. Paul was asleep on Mama's shoulder. I could only imagine how exhausted she was carrying him, but she led the way.

After a while I was sure that I recognized a particular tree, even in the dark.

"Mama, I think we have walked in a circle."

"Oh?" She was too tired to say anything else.

I stopped walking and looked up at the inky sky. The moon was just a thin waxing crescent and gave no appreciable light.

"Look there, Mama. There, below the Big Dipper. That is Polaris, the North Star. If we keep him to our right, we will be walking west. You taught me this in Leipzig during the blackouts."

Mama and all the little ones, except Paul, looked up. "Yes, Ludwig, you're right. Thank you." Her voice was quiet and weak.

We adjusted our course and began to walk again. We were all in a kind of trance. I was so thankful that the weather was not foul and that there were no patrols about. In our state, even a small problem would have been insurmountable. I do not know how long we walked like this as time lost all form, like Dali's melting clocks. It was possibly hours.

We eventually found ourselves on a dirt farm track, which then became a small gravel road. I was very conscious of the loud crunching sound our five pairs of feet made on the gravel as I was sure we must be near the border by now. I was right. In the starlit dark I could make out a rise immediately to our left. There was a small structure on top of it. It was too small to be a farmhouse. I whispered that we should all stop for a moment. In that instant the door of the building swung open and yellow light flooded out. Silhouetted in this light I could see the shape of a soldier holding a rifle. He had a flashlight in his other hand. He swept the beam up and down the road, but miraculously not quite back to where we were. I held my breath for a long minute. Then the soldier turned around and went back into his hut. I could hear everyone around me exhale simultaneously.

Oskar whispered urgently, "I'm sorry, I have to!"

I whirled around to see what he was talking about. He had dropped his pants and was squatting. He was pooping right on the road, presumably out of sheer fright.

I hissed at him, "Be quick!" I was furious, he was seven years old after all, and I would have screamed at him had the circumstances permitted it.

Ahead of us on the road was a high gravel berm surmounted by a few strands of barbed wire. We scrambled over this as quickly and quietly as we could. I knew that in some areas there were barriers well before the actual border, so I was not confident that we were in the West yet. We walked a little further and then I saw it. We had come upon train tracks just as a train approached at high speed. As it zoomed by we could see that the cars had glass windows and bright lights on inside. My brothers stared, mouths gaping. They were too young to remember a time when trains looked like this. We were there. We were in the West.

CHAPTER

FIFTY-FOUR

APRIL 3 & 4, 1949

I t was then a simple matter to follow the train tracks and in a short while we were in the Vienenburg train station. There we spent a cold night in the waiting room with a number of other refugees who had trickled in by various routes at various times. A West German police officer came by in the early morning and asked for our papers and our destination. There was no fear that we would be sent back, but there was the strong possibility of being forced to stay in a refugee camp if we could not name a specific address that we were going to. The West did not want thousands of refugees roaming the country-side. Mama gave him Papa's address in Worpswede. The officer was satisfied with this but said that we would still have to go to the Red Cross refugee processing centre in Uelzen, three hours north by train, and prove to them that this address was legitimate. We were given a temporary travel permit for this. Before getting on the train, Mama arranged to have a telegram sent to Papa to tell him that we had decided to leave Colditz, had made it successfully across the border and were going to be in the Uelzen Red

Cross camp tonight. Mama and I exchanged glances as this telegraph was prepared, but neither of us said anything.

In Uelzen we were welcomed with a big bowl of beet soup. We had had a little bit of bread in the Vienenburg train station, but this was the first real hot food I had seen in days. I swear that I will remember that soup until I die. The camp was enormous with more barracks than I could count and about thirty families per barrack. It was noisy during the night and mice or rats scurried about beneath our beds, but none of us cared. I would have slept through an aerial bombardment. Before I drifted off I thought of all the other families bedded down around me. I saw that one child was missing an arm. I heard another child speak of his dead parents. My childhood often felt extraordinary to me, but I reflected that it was, for the times, an ordinary German childhood. Not the best, but not the worst. Somewhere in the middle.

~

The next morning a British officer sought us out, carrying a clipboard that had our barrack and bunk numbers recorded on it.

"Luise Schott?"

"Yes."

"And five children, Ludwig, Clara, Johann, Oskar and Paul?"

"Yes."

"From Colditz, Saxony?"

"Yes."

The officer smiled warmly. "A Wilhelm Schott is here for you. He says he is here to take you home."

I looked around at the faces of my family. Clara and Johann looked excited, while Oskar and Paul looked confused.

Mama's expression was unreadable but then she caught my eye and smiled at me. It was a small thin smile that somehow conveyed both relief and resolve. I knew what she meant.

EPILOGUE

I Philipp, will take over the narrative now, as in the
end it was me who listened to all of their stories and
then picked up the separate threads and wove them
together to write this book.

Ludwig did not become a forest ranger, although he
still dreamed of it while living in very cramped and difficult circumstances in Worpswede. It did not feel like home.
He ultimately received the highest high school graduation
marks in his state but had to work in the Bergolin paint
factory and complete a commercial apprenticeship at AEG
(a big electrical equipment manufacturer) before being able
to go to university. He went to the University of Kiel to study
plasma physics, which, while not his dream, fascinated him
with its esoteric worldview and abstract mathematics. There
he met a young woman named Ilse Jahnke who worked as
a technician in his lab. She was from a small town north of
Bremen. They married in 1963. I was born two years later,
and the year after that we sailed from Bremerhaven on the
Arkadia, bound for Canada. A big adventure for a young
family. My father had been offered a faculty position at

the University of Saskatchewan in Saskatoon. The stated plan was to stay for two years, but I know that in his heart he had no intention of ever living in Germany again. He never felt truly at home in West Germany. He said that he always felt like a refugee, like an outsider. And above all he wanted to own land somewhere where there was space and safety and solitude. Within a few years they bought an acreage outside of Saskatoon and he began planting trees, ultimately hundreds or even thousands of them, and sowing what seemed to me like acres of potatoes. He also built birdhouses by the score, mostly for bluebirds but also for owls and wrens.

Before we moved permanently to the acreage from the city my parents built a little one-room cabin in an aspen grove on a hill. My father loved to spend hours there by himself, enjoying being alone with the birds and the trees, proud of being self-sufficient, proud of living simply. The generation of Germans who grew up reading *Winnetou* was the same generation who had seen their country commit heinous crimes and then be destroyed in an apocalyptic war. There is a reason why you can fly directly to the Yukon from Frankfurt or Dusseldorf but not from Winnipeg or Toronto. My father was one of the lucky few who made his escape permanent, not just a fleeting holiday fantasy.

He wrote to his mother regularly but did not stay in close contact with the rest of the family. One of the few times he went back to Germany was for Luise's funeral in 1992. This was also his last visit. Two years later he developed an aggressive brain cancer and was dead in six months. He continued to tell stories about his early years right up to the end. Despite the tenuous nature of their contact over the years, Theodor, Clara, Johann and Oskar all came from Germany to visit him while he was dying. (Paul had an intense fear of flying.) Oskar had never left Europe before but said that he felt duty bound to come because he owed my father such a debt of gratitude.

~

To backtrack a little, Luise, my grandmother, settled into life in Worpswede after 1949 and stayed there with Wilhelm until she died. Many wondered why she didn't divorce him because he continued to be unfaithful to her, sometimes quite flagrantly, for many more years. In fact, in 1950 Wilhelm took a job in Luedenscheid, 300 kilometres south of Worpswede, that had him away from home for three weeks at a time. It was an open secret that he lived there with yet another woman, more or less as husband and wife. Also well into his sixties he continued to go to the discos in Bremen, until the pretty young things he was chatting up laughed at him and called him grandpa. I think there is more than one answer to the question of why she stayed. The obvious answer was that Wilhelm provided financial security. For all his failings he was very attentive to a specific notion of duty. My grandmother may have been a proud woman, but that pride was brittle, and beneath it lay deep pools of self-doubt. The more subtle answer is that by staying with him she could exact her revenge in a hundred little ways over the course of decades, which was more satisfying than a single dramatic move. Theirs was an odd relationship that underlined Tolstoy's dictum regarding the dissimilarity of unhappy families.

The last of the three principal players in the story to pass away was my grandfather. I saw him for the final time in the late summer of 1995 as my wife, Lorraine, and I passed through Germany on our way to our honeymoon in Italy. Perhaps my father's death had emboldened me, or perhaps it was the fact that I was then thirty years old and no longer so easily impressed by my grandfather's wisdom, charm and worldly ways, but I resolved to raise the subject of his past with him for the first time. It had been the proverbial elephant in the room for as long as I could remember, and I knew that there would not likely be another chance. He represented so many confusing contradictions. I was not, however, going to address the cognitive dissonance of him being a serial philanderer at the same time as presenting himself as the grand pater familias of the Schott clan. That was too private and well beyond the pale for grandfather-grandson chats. But the contrast between his warmth, humour and generosity as my beloved grandfather and his hard-core Nazi past was something I wanted to try to understand. If handled carefully and respectfully, I felt it could make for a positive conversation, for both of us. Perhaps he was ready to talk about it and just hadn't been asked.

Was he really an entirely different person at different times in his life, or were the two sides of him interwoven all along? How does a sophisticated, cultured and intelligent man not only join the Nazi Party but also join the SA Brownshirts, become an Ortsgruppenleiter and plan to kill himself because he cannot bear the collapse of the Third Reich?

It was a quiet and sunny afternoon. The only sound was the ticking of an antique clock in my grandfather's living room. Lorraine was napping and we were leaving that evening, so it was now or never. I planned to open the conversation gently with some softball questions about political and economic conditions in the 1920s. Opa had always been energetic and youthful for his age, but that day I could see every one of his ninety-two years on him. He was still a snappy dresser, but he was skeletally thin, his skin was almost translucent and his blue eyes had become very pale. First we made light chit-chat about my travel plans and we shared some family news. Then there was a lull in the conversation. He lit a cigarette and blew a perfect smoke ring that caught the sunlight and hung in the air for a very long moment. Opa looked down at his lap and then looked straight ahead, towards some unseen spot in the shadows on the far side of the room. The moment seemed right. I swallowed hard and was just about to start asking my questions when he began to speak.

"Philipp," he said slowly, "I have seen so much in my long life, but now I think it has been too long. Of everything that has happened to me, the very worst has been to have my own son die before me." He turned to look at me. His eyes were red rimmed and moist.

My courage failed me.

He died the next year at the age of ninety-three. He was still living at home. He had a small heart attack and the house-call doctor recommended that he be taken to the hospital. He refused. He asked the doctor to call the three of his children who lived nearby and tell them to come. When they had gathered at his bedside Opa asked for a cigarette and a glass of champagne. This was provided and a couple hours later he slipped away in his sleep.

Several months later I received a small package from Germany. The will had been read and I was one of the few people Opa had selected a specific object for. It was his 1922 Methuen edition of Shakespeare's *The Tempest*.

ACKNOWLEDGEMENTS

&

AUTHOR'S NOTE

This book is born from a memory of memories. My memory of my father recounting his memories. A meta-memory if you will. Ludwig was a marvellous storyteller, and unlike many of his generation who did not want to talk about it, he often told detailed stories from the war and the difficult years after. He told them often enough that I will confess to my share of teenage eye-rolling and tuning out at their repetition. This book would not have been possible, however, without my grandmother's Erinnerungen — her memoirs that her children privately published for her eightieth birthday in 1987. It provided me with a detailed timeline and factual framework to embed my father's stories into. Her anecdotes from life under Soviet occupation were useful as well. My grandfather also wrote memoirs. While they are fascinating and well written, his children did not elect to publish them. These memoirs, perhaps tellingly, conclude before he joined the Nazi Party. Consequently they were not useful for this book.

I am also grateful for my cousin Sonya Steiner's assistance. She is a journalist in Germany and interviewed Uncle

Theodor before he died. The account of his time with the Volkssturm relies almost entirely on this interview. In addition I am indebted to my aunt and my younger uncles for their contributions. They don't remember much, but the fragments they do remember were valuable. Uncle Johann in particular joined my cousins, my brother and me at the start of our attempt to recreate the fifteen-kilometre escape hike from Osterwieck to Vienenburg in the spring of 2019, marking the seventieth anniversary. "Recreate" I say — well fed, relaxed and without any threat from Russian soldiers or border police.

My father's stories, my grandmother's memoirs and a few memories from my aunt and uncles constitute the factual bones of this book, but a good portion of the flesh of it is from my imagination. The conversations, the minor characters, many minor incidents and the descriptions are all conjecture. Plausible conjecture, but conjecture nonetheless. I have subtracted nothing from what is known, but I have added much.

As aids to this conjecture, I would like to specifically make mention of Ian Kershaw's excellent *The End: The Defiance and Destruction of Hitler's Germany, 1944–1945* and *The Colditz Story* by Major Pat Reid.

Except for my father's name and the known historical figures, all other names in this book have been changed. His story is the only one I feel entitled to lay claim to. An exception regarding name changes, though: Squish Eye's nickname really was Squish Eye.

Purchase the print edition and receive the eBook free!
Just send an email to ebook@ecwpress.com and include:

- the book title
- the name of the store where you purchased it
- your receipt number
- your preference of file type: PDF or ePub

A real person will respond to your email with your eBook attached.
And thanks for supporting an independently owned Canadian
publisher with your purchase!